The Unseen Leopard
Bridget Pitt

The Unseen Leopard

Bridget Pitt

Human & Rousseau
Cape Town Pretoria

For Michael, Joanna and Lara

By the same author:
Unbroken Wing, Kwela (1998)

Copyright © 2010 by Bridget Ann Pitt
First published in 2010 by Human & Rousseau,
an imprint of NB Publishers,
40 Heerengracht, Cape Town, 8001
Cover image provided by Gallo Images
Cover design by Mike and Stefni Cruywagen
Set in 10.5 on 13 pt New Baskerville ITC by Etienne van Duyker
Printed and bound by Interpak Books, Pietermaritzburg

ISBN 978-0-7981-5223-5

All rights reserved
No part of this book may be reproduced or transmitted
in any form or by any electronic or mechanical means,
including photocopying and recording, or by any other
information storage or retrieval system, without
written permission from the publisher.

Chapter 1

ON the eve of her fortieth birthday, she has the dream. Again, she is standing outside the wrecked car on the mountainside, banging on the window, trying to break in. And inside, Melissa dies, as she always does, her hair fanned across her face like a shroud.

She beats against the window in a futile tattoo, as the car fills with water, and Khaya floats up through its darkness until he is pressed against the glass, his mouth gaping red beneath dead white eyes. *Wake up*, she screams to herself, *wake up before she dies, wake up wake up wake up*, until the scream becomes a real scream, more of a groan, in the dark room. And she is awake.

And Melissa is dead.

* * *

She sits up, shivering, the salty sting of tears drying on her cheek. Such an immoderate dream, she thinks irritably . . . so *Gothic*, so hysterical. As if some crazed messenger in her brain is still shrieking out its news: *She's dead . . . she's dead.*

I *know* she's dead, she tells herself. Okay? Three years, already. Shall we count our dead? Mum and Dad, sixteen years gone, Melissa three. Can we be done now?

But it seems as if she'll never be done. And even if she musters a convincing show of life-goes-on (and actually, let's be honest, her efforts are not that convincing), the lamenting Greek chorus is always waiting in the wings, ready to rush in whenever she is caught off guard.

Sam falls back on the pillow and tries to induce sleep, grimly ploughing through her repertoire of well-worn methods. *Breathe in . . . 2 . . . 3 . . . breathe out . . . 2 . . . 3 . . . 4 . . . You are floating in a blue pond . . . Play the alphabet game . . . birds . . . albatross . . . yes, bloody albatross around your neck. Christ, I'll be dragging it forever, hmm, b . . . b . . . blackbird, crow – no, crane, enough harbingers of death, drongo . . .* Her body is a forest of needles; each breath rattles mockingly in her ears. The light beats against her eyelids, but when she turns it off, her dream floats out of the darkness, as the child had floated to the window of the car.

Forget it. She climbs out of bed, pulls on her father's ancient navy-blue dressing gown with the braid piping and pads barefoot down the wooden floorboards, pausing to stick her head around Khaya's door. He lies like a starfish in the dim light, limbs outflung to the four corners of the world, a plastic dinosaur clutched in each hand. She carries on down the passage to the kitchen at the far end of the house. As she flicks the light switch, a squat yellow dog rises off a lumpy cushion and waddles amiably towards her.

"Frankly, my dear Mimsy, I blame it all on Dylan," Sam tells the dog, as she fills the kettle and switches it on.

Mimsy wags her tail – actually it is more like the tail wagging Mimsy, such is her delight at this unexpected midnight tea party. Richard the cat eyes them from his lair next to the fridge. He was named after a vagrant who'd traded him for some old clothes, a chicken pie and twenty rand. The animal developed rapidly from a cute hyperactive kitten to a brutish tom, until Sam and Melissa neutered him in self-defence. Whereupon he instantly became an oversized, attention-seeking glutton.

Melissa had doted on him, despite his lack of charm, and Sam often wonders whether Richard blames her for Melissa's departure. He certainly never curls up purring on her lap, or rubs against her legs.

Richard begins licking his personal effects with ostentatious contempt.

"It wasn't my fault, you know. I miss her too," she tells him now. He flicks her a disgusted glance and carries on washing.

She rummages in the red tin for a rusk, picks up the blue-striped china mug of tea, and walks out of the kitchen. She crosses the dining room to reach the wooden deck that circles her house, pausing to grab an orange from the fruit bowl on the table, which she drops into her dressing-gown pocket. She opens the sliding door and walks onto the deck, the rough wooden boards cool against her feet, and folds herself into the hanging string chair that Melissa gave her for her birthday four years ago. The last birthday, in fact, that had felt like something worth celebrating.

"It's for you to take on your travels," Melissa had said. "You can hang it up anywhere, so you'll always have a place to sit. And whenever you sit in it, you can think of me."

"Why would I want to do that?"

"'Cos I'm the most gorgeous thing you know, you old witch."

"No, you're not; you're a snotty little brat."

"Ooh, you desiccated shrew."

"Nappy face."

"Termagant."

"Milksop!"

It was a favourite game. When had it started? When Melissa was about five . . . standing in the Cedar Hills garden, squealing about the carpet of caterpillars crawling up the trunk of the stinkwood tree.

"Don't be such a milksop," Sam had said.

"Milksop!" shrieked Melissa. "If I'm a milksop, you're caterpillar poo!"

"Dog's breath!"

And so on.

Later, lying in bed, Melissa said, "Sammy, what's a milksop?"

"I haven't the faintest idea," said Sam.

For some reason, this struck them as hilarious. "Milksop, milksop, milksop!" they shouted, jumping up and down on their beds.

The one who got to say milksop always won. But you could only say it after the right number of insults – if you timed it wrong, you lost the game. They played it (she supposes now) to reassure themselves that the bonds of sisterhood were impervious to any amount of insult. They played it more often, she reflects, when those very same bonds had been eroded by the weaselly teeth of envy, resentment and betrayal.

* * *

As she sips her tea, relishing its warmth in the pre-dawn chill, she is struck by a sudden realisation: It's her birthday today. No wonder she had the bloody dream. Dylan *and* a birthday. Birthdays were always bad. And anniversaries, and Christmas, and New Year, and most days in between.

Forty years old. Christ.

She stares out at the lights of Hout Bay sprawled beneath her feet. The lights render it harmless, turn it into some twinkling village – the old fishing harbour, the shanty town clinging to the slopes on the far side of the valley, the wealthy mansions, the gated communities, the cluster developments spreading like acne on every available inch of land, the few remaining smallholdings with their ponies and cows, the pottery studios and historic wine cellars and overpriced gift shops are all swallowed by the deep well of a summer's night. Like the petty antagonisms, desires and bigotries of its diverse residents. You could write any story you wished about this place in such forgiving darkness.

An owl swoops past on silent wings. From below the deck comes a squeak and scuffle, heralding the end of some small, unassuming life. Her back tingles in anticipation of things that creep up on you – perhaps the darkness is not so forgiving after all.

"In a dark, dark wood," she whispers, remembering something that Khaya picked up at school, the way he'd recite it in a voice hoarse with terror. *In a dark, dark wood was a dark, dark house, and in the dark, dark house was a dark, dark room, and in the dark, dark room was a dark, dark cupboard, and in the dark, dark cupboard was a dark, dark box and in the dark, dark box was a* . . . GHOST!

The chant haunts her. It describes so eloquently the lengths to which people go to hide their secrets from themselves. The house it inevitably brings to mind is Cedar Hills on a moonless night, the doors rattling in the wind, the claws of the wild pear scratching her window. Where as a young child she'd lain in darkness as thick as tar, waiting for it to suck the last breath out of her body.

She doesn't want to think about it. She doesn't want to go there . . . she wants a thorny thicket to grow up around the whole place so that Melissa can sleep there for a hundred years and be woken by a magic prince. Why did Dylan have to come here last night, and start bleating on about the Koekemoers and the Stuurmans and that whole sorry heap of history?

And launching into it with that silly sentence – what was it? *So, things are all coming together down at Elandskloof*, or something equally inane. Why can't the boy just speak English?

She should've just gone to bed before he could say anything else . . . he'd been antsy the whole evening, so she'd known something was up. She was warned. But she'd let her curiosity get the better of her.

"What's all coming together, Dylan?"

And he was off, rambling on about the Stuurman land restitution and turning the whole valley into some mega-biosphere reserve. And in the middle of this, he had dropped his bombshell: "The Department of Environment is interested in buying Cedar Hills. They're hoping to buy all the farms in the kloof."

Well really! Buy Cedar Hills? It was monstrous.

Of course, she's glad that the Stuurmans are getting Rooikrantz back. But does she want to hear about it? It just stirs up stuff, doesn't it? Bringing a parade of images – the tyre swinging in the coral tree . . . the sun flashing on Chrissie's brown legs as she skips, chanting *My naam is Galiema, hoe! My naam is Galiema, ha!* . . . the blood seeping out of two dead donkeys in the Koekemoers' lucerne field.

Worst of all was that crap he'd spouted about how Sam could make this Elandskloof dream come true; how it was a way to lay Melissa's soul to rest and to heal the land. Honestly. How dare he use Melissa's death to give him some kind of glory?

"Dylan, please, spare me the New Age twaddle," she'd snapped. "You don't know what Elandskloof means to me. You have no fucking idea what Melissa would have wanted, and in fact she doesn't want anything any more because she's dead. If the Stuurmans are getting their land back, that's great, but it is nothing to do with me. Elandskloof fucked up my family, it fucked up the Stuurmans, and it killed my sister.

"I don't want to talk about it. I don't want to attend stakeholder workshops. I don't want to dig up dead old Dad and wave him around like a banner at community meetings. If they want to buy the damn place, they can make me an offer, and I'll think about it. You can toddle off and build your New South African dream. But leave me out of it."

Not that he was crushed by her outburst. Not Dylan. He'd just told her – what was it? Something about grief turning to poison if you keep it in a bottle. What a wanker.

Sam dunks her rusk, cursing when a piece breaks off in her tea. She fishes out the soggy morsel and gives it to Mimsy, who has laid her head on Sam's lap and is gazing at her with adoring, treacle eyes. Sam strokes her head absently, trying to block out this conversation by taking in her surroundings. The night is paling now, its diminishing shadow already being celebrated by a cacophony of birds, and the shreds of mist that hang over the river are clearly visible. A faint glow over Constantia Nek gives the promise of dawn.

Sam drains her tea, and sets the mug on the floor. She reaches into her pocket for the orange, digs her thumb into the peel, tears off a strip, and holds it to her nose. *The smell of oranges . . .* She closes her eyes, breathing it deeply. She is back thirty years, driving from boarding school to Cedar Hills in her father's car. On the last journey she had made there while still believing that good would always triumph and nothing would ever change . . .

* * *

She sits on the back seat of her father's Mercedes, breathing air thick with the smells of oranges and paraffin, both of which are piled in the boot along with other supplies. She is still wearing her yellow school dress, but she has kicked off her shoes and socks, which lie discarded at her feet. She amuses herself by trying to pick up a grubby sock between her toes and lift it onto the seat.

Her parents sit in front. Daphne smokes a cigarette in a long filter, her eyes inscrutable behind reflective green sunglasses. Her chestnut hair is tied back with a blue-and-white silk scarf. Occasionally she glances at Fergus, presenting Sam with her classical jaw line, curved mouth and elegant little nose. Each time she sees this, Sam unconsciously touches her own imperfect proboscis.

Fergus is moulded from a more robust clay than Daphne's delicate porcelain. His hair is a red-wire pot scraper; his brown eyes are set deep under bristling reddish brows. His nose, like Sam's, is generous, but (as Sam will hear throughout her childhood) a "strong nose looks good on a man". Clearly, it has no business being on a woman. Sam will also be told many times over that she is a "throwback" to grumpy great-great-grandmother Isabella, with her suspect Spanish blood, as evidenced by Sam's big nose, black hair, black eyes, black eyebrows and black moods. For years, Sam believes a throwback is something you throw back because you don't want it, like an undersized fish.

The drive takes them through small towns, past yellow-brick shops selling big white church hats and crimplene dresses and chicken feed. The towns feel sleepy to her, but with an underlying dis-ease, peering out warily at passing strangers from beneath the corrugated-iron overhangs that line the streets. Young farm workers lounge beside the "non-white" entrances to the bottle stores, whistling at the coloured girls going past in curlers. But never at white girls – Kobus Koekemoer is fond of telling her that if their farm workers even *look* at a white girl his father will hang them from a beam in the barn. He showed her one which he said was especially strong, and described in graphic detail the bulging eyes and black tongue that would afflict anyone who suffered this fate. She was steadfastly unimpressed – Kobus Koekemoer, in her eyes, is the King of Stupid.

As the road leaves the last town, something falls away from

her, as if she's just shrugged off her heavy school satchel. The road pulls them high above the rolling blue hills, layered like cardboard cutouts in dusty blues and purples, then plunges back down through a deep valley. Stone walls tower above them, embedded with smooth round pebbles and mashed-up rocks left by the vast glaciers that carved out this craggy kloof. "Enon conglomerate," her father calls it.

Enon Conglomerate, Enon Conglomerate, she sings inside her head. She wishes it were her name. It sounds much more impressive than Samantha Campbell.

They pass Queen Victoria's face, carved out by the wind in the rocks, and other gargoyle-like profiles, which seem to hector her as she passes . . . *Sit up straight* . . . *Brush your hair.* They pass through gates with boards reminding drivers in three languages to close them. She used to like opening the gates, but now she is content to leave this to the small brown children playing nearby.

The children look as though they were blown there by the wind. They stare at the ground when her father talks to them, as though afraid he might steal their souls if they let him see into their eyes. They sometimes smile, but their smiles seem to dangle on the end of a thread of fear. Sometimes Sam smiles back, and sometimes, if Fergus is not looking, she sticks out her tongue – if he saw her do that, his large-boned hand, hard as a shovel, would shoot over the back seat and smack whichever part of her it could reach. "Don't be rude," he'd say.

After the gates they follow the riverbed, rattling over the loose stones – every inch of the old Mercedes' German engineering is sorely tested, but Daphne refuses to go to Port Elizabeth in the farm bakkie. Then the car grinds and groans its way up and out of the valley and over the second pass – the Grasnek.

* * *

Grasnek. The shock of the name jolts Sam out of her reverie. Grasnek used to be the most beautiful place on earth, despite its humble name. Now it is the grave of her sister.

She closes her eyes, and forces herself back into the Mercedes, trying to conjure up the Grasnek that was, before Melissa died on its slopes.

*   *   *

On this Grasnek, Sam feels as if she can breathe properly for the first time since leaving the farm for school. The sweet mountain air makes her body sing with its lightness, and she opens the window wide and sticks her head out, closing her eyes against the warm rush of wind.

"For heaven's sake, close the window," her mother says, clutching the hairdo she's just had reconstructed in Port Elizabeth, and Sam reluctantly complies. They pass a herd of rooihartebees, crowned with hearts of sky framed by their inward-curving horns. When they leap away they take a piece of Sam with them, so that she can feel their hearts pounding and smell the grassy scent of their brown flanks.

From Grasnek the prickly grey-green bushes on the surrounding hills look no spikier than tufts of lamb's wool. The slopes are crowded with aloes – '*Allo*, '*allo*, they cry happily to her, waving their long, spindly arms. Chrissie Stuurman calls her *Aalwynkop* – Aloehead – because of her wild bush of hair, but Sam doesn't mind because she likes aloes. She waves back to them, pretending to be a queen, but secretly. Once Daphne had seen her and said, *Who are you waving to, honey?* in that voice that meant she would tell her friends about it later and laugh.

Daphne spends long hours on the phone to her Johannesburg friends, telling them how she longs for Glamour and City Lights. Fergus says City Lights kill the stars. Fergus and Sam sit on the stoep at night, and discuss the stars. He tells her the names of all the constellations, and boggles her mind with star demographics. "A million light years," she whispers to herself, unable to imagine either a million or a light year. She looks at Orion, with his three-star sword tucked into his three-star belt, and wonders if he feels lonely up there.

Sam is well acquainted with loneliness. It doesn't stalk her, strangely, in the big empty sky at Cedar Hills, but it follows her every step through her child-crammed boarding school. It hunches, grinning, on the shoulders of girls like Lottie and Rosalind as they march around arm in arm shouting WE-WALK-STRAIGHT-SO-YOU'D-BETTER-GET-OUT-THE-WAY, kicking her sandwiches as they pass. Loneliness crouches beneath her bed at night, amplifying the sound of the girls' breathing around her, until it roars like a tidal wave through her ears.

The road winds down from Grasnek, crosses the Elands River again over a permanently flooded causeway and skirts the gate to Rooikrantz before finally reaching the big white boulders that mark the entrance to Cedar Hills. They bump over the cattle grid and begin the ascent up the driveway.

* * *

Cedar Hills. Captured and tamed by swashbuckling Douglas Campbell in the mid-nineteenth century; home to five generations of Campbells since. The hills have long been denuded of cedars by Douglas and his kin, who chopped them down to make floorboards and furniture. But they are still rich with fynbos, aloes, euphorbia and spekboom. Fergus told Sam that the spekboom had been the favourite food of the elephants that once roamed the kloof. There is something elephantine about this plant, with its stubby, wrinkled grey stems . . . as if some elephants, reluctant to leave, had taken root and turned into plants. She used to leave inviting little piles of spekboom by the gate, but no elephants ever came to eat it.

A koppie rears up behind the house, a jumble of massive rocks, tossed aside by the long-gone glaciers that forged the valley. Its crevices are wooded with sweet thorn and stinkwood. The house, built with thick walls of honey-coloured stone, nestles sleepily at its feet, gazing out at the northwestern hills and mountains from beneath a green corrugated roof over the wide-front veranda. Beside the house are two weeping Brazilian peppers, humming with bees. Former generations of Campbells have done battle with heat and frost, wild pigs and badgers, droughts and floods to create some semblance of an English Country Garden – spindly rose bushes, honeysuckle, a magenta bougainvillea climbing the pillars of the stoep, rampant candytufts sprawling over all the beds, some grimly determined dahlias. But Daphne is a poor gardener and much of this is now overgrown with weeds.

It's not really a farm, because they don't grow anything on it – all the arable bits of what was once a sizable estate were sold off to the Koekemoers by great-grandfather Ian Campbell, to enable him to indulge in his fondness for brandy. But the farm boasts a sprinkling of livestock: chickens and ducks, five cats, two bull mastiffs called Bessie and Ivan and two Jersey cows called Mulberry and Mrs Moodle. Fergus calls it a piece of paradise; Daphne calls it a millstone. For Sam, it is simply the only place in the world where she can imagine living.

* * *

There is an air of suppressed excitement in the car, as they pull up under the pepper tree.

"Wait there," Fergus calls as Sam runs to the house, fending off the slobbery attentions of Bessie and Ivan, "and close your eyes. We've got a surprise."

She sits on the steps of the stoep with her eyes tightly shut and the afternoon sun on her knees. *A puppy . . . or a baby calf with a wet nose that I can bottle-feed.* After what seems like ten years, she hears the clatter of hooves on the driveway. *A pony.* She doesn't dare lift her head in case she's wrong.

"You can look now," Fergus says, and she forces herself to look up.

A pony. A rich chestnut brown, with a black mane and tail, and a white star on his forehead, and two white socks. Being led by a man with a red brick for a face and a stomach that an army could quite comfortably march on.

Sam feels a dull thud of disappointment. "Hallo Oom Hennie," she says politely. "Why have you brought Kobus's pony?"

A big grin splits the brick in half. "But it's your pony now, *meisiekind*. It's too small for Kobus, see?"

She stares, disbelieving. She thinks guiltily of all the anti-Kobus Koekemoer plots she and Chrissie have devised.

The Koekemoers named him Oneway because he only really goes in one direction – home. In the coming weeks she'll cajole him into going out as far as she can, with him stopping every three seconds to graze, but sooner or later he'll turn around and gallop home, with her clinging on grimly. Frequently, he will dislodge her on a passing gatepost or tree.

She'll fall off several times this summer. But when she goes clattering down the road to Rooikrantz on her reluctant steed, she will feel as resplendent as any triumphant king in history. And although Chrissie will toss her head and mutter, "Huh. It's just a *horse*," Sam will be convinced she sees a rare flash of admiration in her eyes.

Sam stands in the sun that summer morning, feeding Oneway carrots, feeling his velvet nose nuzzling her hand, breathing his sweet smell. The sun is shining; her mother's eyes are stars. She believes she will never be sad again.

* * *

"There you are! I found you! You weren't in your bed." Khaya stumbles out the dining-room door, clutching a bundle wrapped in his favourite flannel blanket. "Why are you here?" he demands, indignant, ever the lord who expects his castle to follow his rules.

"I wanted to say hallo to the sun. Come and sit with me – we'll wait for it to come."

He crawls onto her lap. "I brought them 'cos they woke up too," he announces, opening the blanket to reveal some carefully chosen members of his plastic dinosaur collection. Their wrinkled faces stare out with enraged yellow eyes; their red mouths bristle with improbable teeth. "Shush, shush, dinies," croons Khaya. "Shush, shush, little diny-dinies."

Sam bends to kiss the back of his neck, breathing in his

smells of biscuit and sleep and clean cotton. He squirms. "TICK-LES!" he squeals, wriggling his bony backside against her thigh.

"Look!" says Sam, pointing to the gap between Constantia Nek and Vlakkenberg, where the bruised red rim of the rising sun is just visible.

"Here comes the sun! Wow! Here comes the sun, li'l darling!" shouts Khaya, who is an avid Beatles fan. He holds up his dinosaurs. "Look, dinies," he cries, "here it comes." The reptiles snarl soundlessly at the dawn.

The sun moves higher, and suddenly the whole valley is flooded with a soft golden light. Despite the thin warmth, Sam shivers as a sudden lurch of fear makes her tighten her grip on Khaya.

He pulls away, and climbs off her lap. "Brekkie time," he says, wandering back inside, the mystery of the sunrise already forgotten. Sam watches him go, trailing the flannel blanket behind him. The dinosaurs lie discarded at her feet.

It has taken her so long to build some kind of solid place for Khaya and herself – a ragged, splintery thing perhaps, but firm enough. And now Dylan has dumped all these horrible decisions in her lap. And nothing seems solid any more.

Chapter 2
Confession of a Killer

DEAR Samantha

Is this how to begin a confession? It seems inappropriate, now that I see it written here. You can hardly be dear to me, since I've never met you, and I'm quite certain that I'd not be dear to *you*. I killed your sister, which is hardly endearing.

But if not dear, you are at least *significant* to me. You were her sister – the only other person on this planet, I imagine, who can take the full measure of her loss. Dylan . . . had he loved her as she deserved to be loved, I'd not be writing this. Khaya will grieve for the mother he never knew. But you and I – you and I will grieve for her as Melissa. And grieve.

And grieve.

It is your name that I have carried with me these past few years as the one who is owed an explanation. For the lack of a better word, a "confession". Perhaps I offer it simply as an account of a tragedy, a story of your sister's death. An attempt to explain what may, in the end, prove inexplicable. And I offer you a name to curse, which you may find more rewarding than lambasting whatever agency you hold liable for our misfortunes.

Of course, you may never see this. It is easy to address this to you now, when you are no more than a name, a half-remembered photograph, an unknown item in the dramatis personae. When I moved here, I'd half hoped, half dreaded that I'd bump into you – God knows where. In the tinned-goods aisle of Willowdale Cash & Carry perhaps, or behind a stash of watermelon-jam jars at some dispirited farmers' fest. I can't imagine why I thought that – I seldom shop in Willowdale and never attend social events. But I've had some dealings with your current tenant, and have gathered from him that you never visit here at all. Perhaps you fear your sister's ghost? You shouldn't, you know. I believe it to be benign – even towards me. Heart-breakingly benign, under the circumstances.

If I ever meet you in the flesh, I suspect I shall realise the foolishness of the whole enterprise, hold my tongue, engage in some restrained, polite interaction, and let this not quite sleeping dog lie. But I shall write it in the meantime, if only to fill these long evenings, when the moths fly hopelessly into the reading lamp on the table where I sit, and the wind carries the echo of Melissa's voice, either sobbing or laughing – I can never quite tell which.

You'll remember the wind. The way it bludgeons Cedar Hills on winter nights, rattling the windows with its bestial breath, whimpering or howling with the voices of the dead. Enough of those, I imagine, in an old family homestead. I wouldn't know about such things. I grew up in a four-roomed apartment in West Berkeley, no ancestral heirlooms, no traces of lives gone by unless you count the cigarette burns in the carpet. No wind either – just the inchoate roars that marked my father's eruptions of rage or lust, and the solipsistic whine of my mother's disappointment.

"Does it frighten you?" I would ask Melissa, holding her tight against the buffeting gales, breathing in the mysteries of her smell. I think I feared, even then, that she'd be carried away by some seasonal intemperance. But she just laughed, and once, as if to taunt my fears, ran out into the garden to shout it down, naked as the moon, her hair whipping her face like the snakes of Medusa. I ran after her, but she eluded me, her cool flesh slipping through my fingers, looking mockingly over her shoulder, her eyes violet slits of contempt. She had a wildness in her, your sister. She could turn vicious, when cornered. Let us not allow mawkish sentimentality to cloud our memories. A confession, after all, is in the business of truth.

Although I'd be the first to concede that truth is a slippery beast, which few of us grasp as firmly as we would like to believe. And I have no difficulty with lying. Lying has served me well; it serves most of us better than we like to admit.

But I shall endeavour not to lie in this, although sometimes you may wish I had. In order to explain precisely what happened and why, I need to tell you truths about Melissa that you don't know and that she didn't want you to know. Melissa's account of you suggested someone who values truth above kindness, but in my experience, people seldom do. Melissa claimed that she did, but when it came down to it, she was as brittle in its face as the rest of us. And I'll never know whether she ended up hating me because I lied to her – or because I did not lie to her enough.

Enough preamble. Let us begin.

Chapter 3

IN the weeks after her fortieth birthday, Sam finds herself examining her reflection more than usual, perhaps to find evidence of – what? What are you supposed to find in your forty-year-old self? Decay? Womanly wisdom? Resignation? Defeat?

She doesn't really know what she is looking for, only that the face staring back at her shows no sign of delivering it. It is as unimpressive as ever – wary black eyes, the vigorous eyebrows, that nose . . . and there on her head a lone white hair, caught *in flagrante*, shameless against its youthful black companions. She reaches up to pull it out, then hesitates. It is a milestone, of sorts. Like your first tooth. *You don't grow grey hairs, my dear,* her father used to tell her. *You earn them.*

What did I do to earn this one, Dad?

Otherwise, all present and correct. A bit saggier round the edges, maybe, except the nose which is looking bonier. They keep growing, she'd heard. Noses and ears. That's why they often look so large on old people. Who knows what glorious proportions her own might reach in years to come – it might eclipse her face altogether.

Daniel once told her that she had beautiful bone structure . . . she turns her head, considering. The boniness is evident. Beauty? That word seems incongruous. Or too simple, perhaps. Her face strikes her as a complex thing – not quite ugly, or hateful, really, but not easily categorised. Perhaps pitiful in some way. Particularly the mouth. That sad, sad mouth. So different from Melissa's, which had always seemed poised on the brink of a smile. And those discontented frown lines, looming over the jutting beak of her nose, like an umlaut. She makes a futile effort to rub them away.

Umlaut . . . she considers the word.

Plum coloured, Melissa interjects. *And smelling of old cupboards.*

Aalwynkop . . . The name rolls against her, all the way from Elandskloof, bringing with it a fleeting silhouette of the koppie behind their house; a scrape of aloe thorns across her hand. Grasnek.

Bugger you, Dylan. Putting it in my head like that. How am I supposed to get it out now?

* * *

Dylan misses his next visit. Sam indulges herself in tart mutterings about his being "too busy with his new mission in life". But in fact she is relieved, as she confides to Maddie over coffee at their favourite haunt, La Cuccina delicatessen in Hout Bay.

"It's so exhausting having him in the house," she explains while eating her cappuccino foam with a teaspoon. "Trips hither and thither. Crafty projects involving glue and glitter in every corner of the house, including the cat – Richard is still twinkling like Tinkerbell. Meringues, fudge, burnt-out pots . . . And he completely relies on me to bring any kind of order. He makes me feel like some old nanny goat, bleating away on the edge of the field while the young bucks get on with the real business of living."

"Poor you. Mind you, whatever he does will piss you off. Your relationship was doomed from the beginning," announces Maddie over her generous slice of chocolate-mousse cake. "For a start, you're jealous."

"Oh, don't be ridiculous." Sam watches her post the gooey parcels into her mouth with a little fork. How does Maddie eat such things? She feels sick just looking at them.

"Why on earth should I be jealous?"

"It's obvious. Jealous because Melissa loved him. Jealous because Melissa had him and Khaya, and sisters always covet each other's stuff. Furious that he stole Melissa. Pissed off that after dumping you with Khaya, he's now stealing Khaya's heart. Jesus, no wonder you can hardly talk to him." She denotes each point with a wave of her fork, which she then lays down, and smugly dabs her mouth with a paper napkin.

"What a load of crap! He's just a pain in the arse, that's all, with all his waffle about vibes and karma and energies. My response is perfectly rational. Melissa chose him, I didn't. I can't help how I feel about him."

"Well, you have to help how you feel about him, because you can't lay it on poor old Khaya. God, Samantha, this is elementary human psychology here. You have to give the kid permission to love you both, however much you want to keep him to yourself."

"Well, really. Keep him to myself? As if I didn't do everything I could to give Khaya back to Dylan in the first place. Besides, Khaya loves me just as much. Dylan's Mr Novelty Man, but I'm the one who really counts . . . I'm the one who's there when Khaya goes to sleep at night and wakes up in the morning. *Every* morning. Not just when the fancy takes me . . .

"And Dylan's so bloody irresponsible. Like the other night, when I had to go to that stupid publishers' dinner . . . I came back at about eleven o'clock. Khaya's still up drinking Coke and watching *Batman*, for Christ's sake. It's totally unsuitable for a five year old . . ."

"I don't know, Sam. I can see your point. But sometimes I wonder . . ."

"What?"

"Never mind . . ."

"Come on. I'm a big girl, I can take it."

"Well, it's just that you complain about Dylan being so dysfunctional as a father. But what would happen if he wasn't?"

"What do you mean?"

Maddie hesitates. But her meaning blares out like a blast from a trumpet. *If Dylan was a functional father, what place would there be for her?* The back of Sam's head prickles in outrage.

"What are you implying? That I push Dylan into being dysfunctional to give myself a place in Khaya's life? That's pretty fucking raw, Maddie."

"No, I'm not saying that. Look, the bottom line is, Khaya

needs a father. It's just not helpful to undermine Dylan all the time. You have to find a way of forging a more supportive relationship with each other."

Sam glares at her and stands up. "I have to go. I'll pay on my way out. You have chocolate on your nose, by the way."

"Come on, Sam, let's talk about this. Don't just stalk out. That doesn't help anybody . . ."

But Sam is stalking, not talking, and Maddie's entreaties fall on deaf ears.

* * *

She is determined to block out Maddie's unwanted insights. It makes her ill just to *begin* thinking about them. But Khaya's behaviour over the next few weeks forces her to concede that something is awry.

On his first day of school, a few days after this discussion, he appears for breakfast in his Batman suit. Batman suits are about the only thing he'll wear, ever since Dylan gave him one when he came back into his life. He has three new ones now. Sam can understand it, of course. A suit to endow you with superpowers – she'd wear one herself, if she could get away with it. But superheroes, outside of comic books and Disney films, are far too anarchic to be socially desirable, and Khaya is about to encounter his first painful lesson in society's relentless drive to clip the wings of its more wayward members.

"Khaya, love, you can't wear that. I explained to you," says Sam, brightly. "Look, here's your lovely uniform. There's your school name on your shirt!"

"'Snot a lovely uniform. It's stupid. Stupid lellow shirt and stupid yukky shorts."

And so follows a protracted and miserable battle, finally won when Sam agrees that he can wear his cloak. The teacher, a perky young woman called Ms Wilson, purses her lips, but mercifully does not tear it off him.

"I am sure," she says firmly, when Sam fetches him, "that Khaya will be happy to leave his cloak at home tomorrow."

But the next day, Khaya is not happy to leave his cloak at home, nor any day after that. Each morning, he and Sam enter a grim battle of wills. Khaya offers a range of reasons as to why he simply cannot force himself into the uniform: the socks have knobbles; the pants are too skwinky; the shoes stuffiate his feet and a range of other sartorial insults too ghastly for him to name. Sam tries brisk firmness, begging, pleading, bribing and, if all else fails, resorts to shamefully forcing his limbs into the offending items while he kicks her shins.

This operation leaves them both feeling appalled and humiliated, as Sam wraps up sandwiches which she knows he will not eat, and Khaya sits at the breakfast table with bowed shoulders and tears dripping into his corn flakes. She drives him to school in silence and leaves him at the gate, dismally reproached by the way his stalk-like neck emerges from the solace of his curly hair then scuttles for cover under the yellow collar of his offending shirt; by the air of defeat that hangs over his shoulders as he plods into class, with his big blue rucksack banging his knobbly-sock-tortured ankles. The whole thing made so much more poignant by the way his bowed head evokes Melissa's childhood self.

Oh, the treachery of it. How can she collude in this battle to strip him of his secret powers? She slinks away, crushed by guilt and self-hatred, neither of which is relieved by her daily stint as an educational publisher with Springbok Press in a megalithic slab of offices on Cape Town's Foreshore.

Khaya usually goes to aftercare in a school microbus. But whenever possible, Sam sneaks off work early on the pretext of an ex-office meeting, and fetches him herself. The other boys tumble out of the school in a mass of tangled arms and legs that ebbs and flows around a ball or some other object of interest. But Khaya is usually alone, staring at a beetle in the gutter, or hunched beside his bag, his face a stone wall of despair. And when they get home he becomes a limpet, clamped at her heels. He follows her all around the house, even into the lavatory, in case some invisible toilet monster swallows her up.

**

It is hardly a surprise then that she finds herself one day squatting awkwardly on a Grade 0 chair like a marabou stork on a perch intended for a canary, listening to Ms Call-me-Claire Wilson recount Khaya's lamentable record of ill-adjustment: inattentive for most of the term . . . reluctant to listen to instructions . . . unwilling to interact with the other children. That morning, he pushed a boy down a concrete slope, causing him to fall and gash his knees.

"Is there trouble at home?" Claire Wilson asks, her face knitted into the prescribed expression of Sincere Concern. She suggests that Sam seek professional help. She wonders if Khaya suffers from ADD.

Her hair falls in a smooth wave to her shoulders, her eyes are concerned, yes, but brisk. Her classroom is lined with neat charts of words and pictures. Sam sits meekly agreeing with her, wondering how mortal tragedy can ever be accommodated in this bright room. No, orphans and their motherless progeny are clearly misplaced here. They belong in the woods with the hunchbacks, dragons and witches, not in the gleaming, sterile halls of Well-adjusted Humanity.

She leaves the classroom feeling defeated by the notion that all human suffering can be swept away with the right battalion of acronyms, trauma counsellors, tranquillisers, anti-depressants.

Khaya and she are branded by loss, she tells herself grimly. "Branded," she repeats aloud, hearing the sizzle of the iron. Why pretend it can all be blown away by some wide-eyed girl with a psychology degree and a clipboard? They should have lived in an age when people responded to tragedy by holing themselves up in rambling houses and wailing in the corridors at night, or mutilating themselves in a gruesome attempt to manifest the suffering within.

* * *

That evening, when reading him his bedtime story – his current favourite is a book on anacondas – she asks Khaya why he pushed Rory down the slope. Khaya denies it entirely, explaining that he was five million kilometres away up in Giant Land with Hanky (his invisible brother) when Rory fell down the slope.

"Khaya," says Sam, in a girl-with-clipboard voice, "I know you may be feeling sad and hurt inside because your dad's away from you, but . . ."

"I'm *not* feeling sad. I don't care. Dylan's childish and stupid."

"He's not stupid."

"He is. You said so. You said, 'Why do you have to be so childish?' He's stupid, I'm stupid, Rory's stupid, Miss Wilson's stupid. Everything's stupid and I wish I was never born."

What can she say? It's true. There are days when everything is stupid. She is well acquainted with them herself.

She returns to the book. "Green anacondas can grow to more than nine metres and weigh more than two hundred and fifty kilograms."

"Wow," says Khaya, "nine metres! . . . How long is that?"

"Um . . . from your room to the end of the lounge."

"Wow . . . Can I have an anaconda?"

"No."

"Why not?"

"'Cos it would eat Mimsy. And probably us."

"Would it eat Rory?"

"Do you want it to eat Rory?"

Khaya hesitates, and then nods vigorously. His lip trembles, and tears pool in the corners of his eyes.

"Why?"

"'Cos he says I'm a NORFIN, 'cos I told them my mommy's died."

"Well, you're not, are you, because you've got your dad. But you know, Khaya, there's nothing wrong with being an orphan. Your mommy was an orphan, and so am I. But if that old Rory gets to you, just turn him into a worm."

Khaya's eyes grow round with delight. "A worm!" he cries. "Oh, that's brilliant. But how?"

"With your eyes. He may not look like a worm, but he'll feel like a worm. You've got really powerful magic in your eyes. All orphans do, and half-orphans, because when your mom or dad dies they give you all their power, and it shines through your eyes. You just need to practise."

Khaya runs to the bathroom and begins practising immediately in the mirror. Sam wonders if she has overdone it when she gets a note the next day urging her to have his eyes checked because he "seems to have developed an odd sort of squint".

* * *

Still. His weapon of choice has become the squint, rather than the shove, which she supposes is an improvement. But she is haunted by his comment that she considers Dylan childish and stupid – regrettably true, of course, but hardly what he needs to hear. Mind you, what Maddie said about her casting Dylan as a crap father to secure her own role is *complete* hogwash. Dylan *is* a crap father, she insists. He could no more take care of Khaya by himself than get a job on the stock exchange. In fact, all these problems with Khaya started when Dylan went off and abandoned him again.

But it's all going haywire. She can't pretend otherwise. This is her sister's boy, the closest thing alive to Melissa. She can't run the risk of damaging him any further. She needs advice. And Maddie, being pretty much her only friend, is the only one she can ask.

* * *

She raises it a few days later, as they sit after supper sipping wine on Sam's deck. Khaya and Mia, Maddie's two year old, are watching *The Sound of Music* in the lounge, and the nuns can be heard melodically pondering the problem of Maria (*A flibbertigibbet! A will-o'-the-wisp! A clown!*). She and Maddie usually meet at Sam's house, or at La Cuccina, or, rarely, at Luigi's in Hout Bay for supper. It is one of Maddie's gripes about Sam that she seldom goes to Maddie's house, or anywhere, in fact, other than work.

"You're like a princess in a bloody tower," she complains.

"I like being in a tower," Sam says stiffly. "No one can creep up on me. And if I don't like the look of my visitors, I can dash them to death on the rocks below."

"Yeah right, sister. Just make sure you're locking other people out, and not locking yourself in."

She tells Sam she is agoraphobic, and concocts annoying little challenges to entice her out of her extremely limited comfort zone. These are seldom a success.

"So what do you think I should do?" asks Sam after recounting the saga of Rory.

"Maybe you should try therapy again?"

Sam winces. "God, please no. That woman was a witch!"

Maddie laughs. "Oh really. She was perfectly nice, with a good reputation for post-traumatic counselling."

"But I couldn't stand the way she'd peer at me with her head on one side, like a robin eyeing a worm, and she always got this beady little gleam in her eyes when she managed to make me cry. She refused to confine her therapising to Khaya – she kept insisting that I needed it more."

"I wonder why . . ."

"Khaya didn't like her, anyway. No, we have to think of something else."

"Sam, the bottom line is you have to learn to like Dylan more."

"You like declaring bottom lines don't you, Maddie? Anyway, I can't. It's bloody impossible. It's all his fault – Khaya was doing all right last year. I don't know why the hell he had to up and off again to bloody Port Elizabeth."

"Come on, Sam, he was stuck in a dead-end job here. It was a great opportunity to work for Land Doctors."

"Yeah, right," says Sam darkly. "I bet he was planning to get in on this Elandskloof project all along. That's why he was so keen to go."

"Well, what of it? Why shouldn't he work on it?"

Sam closes her eyes, and leans her head back against the side of the house. The wood is still warm from the sun, although it is half an hour after sunset. She is exhausted by the conversation, by having to explain, to think, to remember.

"So?" Maddie prompts.

"Maddie, I just can't . . ." Sam bursts out. She pauses for a gulp of wine. "I just can't forgive him. I can't. I can't forgive him for abandoning Khaya. I can't forgive him for taking Melissa away from me. I can't forgive him for whatever horrible role he played in her death. I can't, I can't . . ." She falters, and puts her head down onto her arms, which are folded on her upraised knees. "I wish I could, but I can't."

"You *have* to. You've got no choice here, Sam. You know that. For Khaya's sake, you have to."

"I know," wails Sam. "But I don't know *how*. I've tried so hard. And now he's there, in Elandskloof, he's *there*, and I'm here, and I'm just so bloody angry with him . . ."

"You used to like him, didn't you? When he and Melissa were first together?"

"Yes . . . Well, he was quite sweet, although a bit annoying. So . . . *exclamatory*. So relentlessly enthusiastic. But Melissa adored him. I mean, Melissa was translucent even at the worst of times – do you remember? And when she was first with Dylan, she glowed, really – I know it's a cliché, but she did. And I was pleased, you know, because it was as if she didn't need Mom and Dad so badly anymore, now that she had him."

"And maybe you were also just a teeny bit pissed off because she didn't need *you* any more?"

Sam gives her a friendly shove. Well, quite friendly.

"You couldn't resist that, could you, Dr Spock? Okay, maybe that did come into it. But not that much, Maddie. I'm not *such* an embittered old cow. I was happy for her, honestly. It was only later . . . I mean I wasn't exactly over the moon when she fell pregnant, I must admit . . ."

Maddie snorts. "Not exactly over the moon? You came rampaging into my house like a demented buffalo. Dylan can't even pick up his dirty laundry, you said, and she wants him to be a *father*!"

"Okay, so I was less than over the moon. But it *was* insane – she was in sixth year medical school, he was two years younger than her, a varsity drop-out, running 'Earth Dreamers' landscape and gardening service . . . not exactly far up the shining ladder to success. Still, I said many things to her that I shouldn't have, and believe me I have tortured myself with every single nasty word a thousand times since . . ." Sam trails off, and stares bleakly into the distance.

Somewhere across the valley a peacock wails in alarm, as if it has suddenly realised it is wandering about long after bedtime. There are a number of feral peacocks roaming the valley, refugees from the stately gardens that have been sold to developers and carved into "country living" townhouses. Mimsy barks in outrage. She has hated peacocks ever since one chased her halfway down Valley Road.

"Mind you," adds Sam, with some asperity, "I wasn't wrong, was I?"

"Whatever . . . listen, I have an idea."

"Oh shit," Sam groans, knowing that she is about to be subjected to one of Maddie's Life-improving Experiences – which are rarely as improving as Maddie hopes they'll be.

"No, really, this is a good one. I think you guys need to meet on Neutral Ground, you know?"

"What, like dogs?"

"Exactly. As soon as Dylan sets foot in your place he's on the back foot. He's defensive, and you're neurotic about him further disrupting whatever faint semblance of order you've managed to create."

"Piss off. I know I'm untidy. But I'm not slovenly – he's slovenly."

"Hush now. No more Dylan-bashing allowed. No, what I suggest is that we all go on a lovely weekend together. I've got this place near Arniston for the Easter weekend. What do you say? You and Khaya, me, Hamish, Mia and Dylan."

Sam gives a snort of disbelieving laughter. "You're insane."

"I'm not. It's perfect. Hamish will get on like a house on fire with Dylan – they can talk about rocks and things. Khaya can hunt for Easter eggs with Mia. We can go for long beach walks – come on, Sam."

"Maddie, I don't even *do* holidays."

"Well, it's about time you started. That's it. No more arguments. What's Dylan's number? I'll phone him myself."

Sam sighs. This can only end in tears. But Maddie, once she is set on something, is as tenacious as a mongoose with a cobra. She will get her on that bloody weekend if she has to truss her up and drag her there.

And the way Sam is feeling, that is pretty much the only way she'll go.

Chapter 4
Confession of a Killer

WELL, then. Where to begin? I suppose with the day I fell in love with your sister. It was, of course, the first time I laid eyes on her. Which is extremely out of character, by the way – I am neither impulsive nor sentimental, and usually keep a tight rein on my emotions. But this was Melissa, after all.

It was February the thirteenth. An unlucky day for her, as things turned out, and for me in a way, although I could never wish that I'd gone through life without meeting her. Just an ordinary Thursday – one of those gritty, gusty February days, when the shacklands around the clinic seemed the very embodiment of squalor and desolation.

I'd driven down to Willowdale from Port Elizabeth, curious to see the social context for the research I would be conducting. The journey was longer than I'd anticipated, and I must confess to a sudden, uncharacteristic moment of self-doubt as I negotiated the forlorn streets of the township. By the time I reached the prefab building that served as the local clinic this had blossomed into a peculiar sense of dread – almost despair. I pulled my car over, climbed out and picked my way across the drift of hardened mud that passed for a road, under the watchful gaze of a knot of small children.

A yellow dog tied up outside a shack barked at me with hopeless outrage, a group of young mothers leaving the clinic glanced my way with lavish indifference. As I offered them what I imagined was a winning smile, a gust of wind wrapped a filthy scrap of newspaper around my ankle, forcing me to engage in an undignified struggle to remove it. The children snickered. I laughed to show that I shared the joke (Oh God, who did I believe myself to be?) and entered the clinic's open door.

A stuffy, intimate wall of heat enveloped me. The small

room was crammed with women and babies who were crying, or coughing, or gazing around with wide eyes, innocent of the perils that life was sure to throw at them. Illustrated posters on the wall exhorted the mothers to use condoms, refrain from defecating in the open, wash their hands, boil their water, plan their families, take their TB medication. The air was thick with the reek of unchanged nappies. On one side was a table on which babies were being weighed; opposite was an area where they were getting their shots, each piercing of a skinny arm marked by an indignant wail.

I stood in the doorway surveying all this, oddly unnerved by the realisation that many of these babies would be receiving my formula. The anxiety was not, you understand, from the possibility that I was subjecting them to anything harmful. That thought never crossed my mind. It was more – I don't know, it is hard to explain, and I doubt that you are interested – but more of a sudden, disconcerting appreciation of the fact that the organisms whose vital signs would make up my graphs were not lab rats or dogs, but babies in nappies, with names, with hopes invested. With all the complex paraphernalia that humans bear with them in the world. Even very small, very impoverished ones.

There was something quite dizzying about this insight. I suppose it was the first time I was conducting research with actual human subjects. My view of reality seemed abruptly to lurch and metamorphose before my eyes, as if the boundaries and walls of scientific endeavour which I had so diligently learnt to construct had been blown flat by unexpected wind.

I relate this to convey my state of mind when I saw your sister for the first time. Suffice it to say, I was not my usual imperturbable, well-managed self. As I stood there, scrabbling to regain my equilibrium and uncomfortably aware of the eyes that stared back at me, the door at the far end of the room opened, and Melissa came out.

She stood in the doorway for some minutes, chatting to the mother who had been in the surgery with her. A baby rested lightly on her hip and played with her stethoscope, while gazing up at her with drifting eyes. Melissa held it with an abstracted tenderness, brushed the back of its brown cheek lightly with one hand, and laughed with the mother when the baby grasped her finger and tried to suck it. She gently disengaged her finger and handed the child back, gave the mother a reassuring pat on her arm, and then glanced around the room.

I'd been watching her with what I can only describe as relief. There was no logic to this. She was terribly young, after all, and looked it, in her white coat, with tendrils of chestnut hair escaping from their restraints and curling around her ears. But she had an extraordinary air of self-containment – a stillness, and a kind of luminosity that was particularly striking in those shabby surroundings. I felt as if she would somehow make sense of what I was doing; bring these two disparate entities – the babies and my research – together in some integrated and meaningful way.

That was my first feeling. My second was more simple – a deep hunger, and longing to touch her and possess her in some way. I knew instantly that I had to find a way of capturing her and keeping her, and would not be able to rest until I had.

I was a little thrown, therefore, when her gaze met mine, and her eyes narrowed slightly. The smile cooled on her lips as she made her way across the room towards me.

I offered a hand.

"I'm Mel . . . uh . . . Dr Campbell," she said, giving my hand a brief, firm shake that was clearly designed to let me know that despite her youthful beauty, she was no pushover.

My hand tingled.

"The nurse told me you were coming. You should have checked with me first – it's not really a good time. We're very busy, as you can see."

"It's fine," I said. "I wanted to get a sense of the conditions you are working in, as well as to meet you. I can wait."

"It'll take a couple of hours. Perhaps you could drive back into Willowdale? I believe the Wagon Wheel offers a drinkable cup of coffee."

"I'm fine, Dr Campbell," I said. "I am perfectly happy to wait."

She shrugged, called her next patient, and retreated back into the surgery.

I sat down, feeling a little foolish. The eyes of the mothers slid in my direction. A large, breast-feeding matron made a jocular remark at my expense – in Xhosa, so I wasn't privy to it, but it provoked a burst of hilarity. Her nursing baby released the shiny black nipple and looked around, startled by the noise. Its mother smirked at me triumphantly, as if some score had been settled, and then fished another fistful of breast from the frayed fabric of her dress, and plugged her baby's mouth with it. I smiled ruefully, and busied myself with papers in my briefcase to hide my self-consciousness.

The shadows lengthened, the mothers grew bored with my presence. Melissa emerged from the surgery door periodically, but always avoided my eyes. I watched her closely from under my lids while feigning interest in my papers. I was struck by the lightness of her manner with her patients – she was neither timid nor patronising, and gave each one in turn her full concern and attention. She conversed, it seemed to me, in competent Xhosa or Afrikaans, although she assured me later that her command of the latter was halting and of the former abysmal. Each time she vanished behind the surgery door the room seemed to dim, each time she reappeared my heart flared in recognition.

One by one, the waiting room emptied. Three hours after I had arrived, the final mother carried her baby out of the door. Melissa made a point of helping the nurses tidy up (perhaps to divest me of any lingering delusions regarding my importance) and then offered me some tea.

I foolishly asked for coffee, and was presented with a thick china mug of discount-store, no-name-brand instant, sweetened with condensed milk. Melissa sat on a plastic chair opposite me, and appraised me over her teacup.

"So," I said, with slightly forced heartiness, as I tried to drink the muddy concoction without grimacing, "you've been fully briefed on the research project, I take it?"

I found her quite disconcerting. Her eyes were so very candid. Her skin was so flawlessly smooth. It was all I could do not to reach out a hand and brush her cheek, as she had done to the baby.

"Yes," she said. There was a silence.

"Well," I soldiered on, "what do you think?"

She hesitated. I could see she was trying not to be rude. "It sounds . . . interesting . . . great, I mean. I'm sure it'll be very beneficial."

"Your enthusiasm overwhelms me." I smiled to soften my words.

She smiled back wryly. "I'm sorry . . . Look, Mr McIntyre, my opinion really doesn't matter. My superiors feel that this is a good thing, and I assure you I'll do whatever is required of me to gather the data."

"James, please," I said. "And I can assure *you* that your opinion does matter. What are your reservations?"

She shrugged, and brushed back a lock of hair – not in any flirtatious way, but impatiently, as if brushing aside my question.

"I mean," I persisted, "I would have thought providing infants with formula could offer an ideal way to protect them from contracting HIV through breast milk."

"In theory . . ." She looked at me guardedly. Then, with a you-asked-for-it shrug, launched forth. "The thing is, most of the women who come to these rural clinics don't have taps. For many, their only water is a river two or three kilometres away, contaminated by human and animal faeces – and the only way to boil it is to collect wood and make a fire. They are HIV positive and some are developing Aids, which means they are sick, and usually tending to several other children – not necessarily their own. So hundreds of babies die every year from gastroenteritis. And the damage to the babies' immune systems by depriving them of breast milk, not to mention the harm done to campaigns to promote breast-feeding as the healthiest option after all that bullshit propaganda by formula producers . . ." She paused to draw breath. Her eyes burned a bright blue, as if to underline the sincerity of her concerns. "To be honest, I think it may be a bit of window-dressing."

"Window-dressing?"

"Well, you know, fiddling around with formula when what the government should really be doing is giving the babies AZT at birth and putting the mothers onto ARV's. They're making such a big production of the free formula at these clinics, but then they gloss over their grotesque failure to provide the most basic measures . . ." Her voice broke off.

I waited, but she did not continue. She flicked me a defiant glance, and stared out the window. She was a feisty girl, your sister. A less self-opinioned man than I might have packed up his offending documents and shuffled out of the clinic. But not me. Not when so much was at stake. Instead, I resorted to some patronising industry patter.

"I can understand your concerns," I said. "But isn't it so that a lot of the mothers in practice use mixed feeding rather than exclusive breast-feeding, which, as I'm sure you know, is worst of all? Because the formula irritates the lining of the baby's stomach, and makes it more susceptible to the virus when breast-fed. Which is also why this formula is potentially such a winner since it is less allergenic than normal soy or cow's milk."

"I *know* all that." She brushed her hair back again irritably. "Don't worry, you don't have to sell it to me. I can assure you I'll give it my support. It's just . . ."

She gestured vaguely around her, at the pile of case folders with their unending testimonies of insurmountable problems, the shabby fittings, the broken equipment, the grubby chairs.

I looked at her closely. There were shadows under her eyes, her voice was strained. It wasn't just the clinic, the doomed mothers and their babies, although that was overwhelming enough for a newly qualified doctor with little support. There was something else. And before I could stop myself, I'd reached over and brushed her cheek with my knuckle.

"Be careful, Dr Campbell," I said. "This work is not for those with sensitive skins . . ."

She stared at me, momentarily nonplussed. Tears sprang to her eyes, and I had a wild, hopeless vision of her collapsing into my arms. But she didn't.

She flushed, and stood up. "My skin is quite thick enough, thank you," she said tersely. "And now, perhaps you can explain exactly what you need from me. It is getting late, and I have a long drive home."

I had lost her. I berated myself for my clumsiness and stupid conceit. We limped through the business of the day, and I took my leave.

Outside, the ragged children were still gathered in a tangle of dusty feet and runny noses. A few clustered around me as I left, pestering me for small change. The call of wild geese flying overhead drew my eyes up to the evening sky – beyond this scene of rural desperation was a panorama of surpassing beauty.

I climbed into my car, and drove away. It had not been a promising afternoon. But, against all odds, my heart was singing.

Chapter 5

AS Easter approaches, Sam's foreboding grows in proportion to Maddie's enthusiasm. She fantasises about moving house and changing her identity so that Maddie can never find her. The nose would be a giveaway, of course. Perhaps if she wore a burqa?

But Khaya continues to challenge her at every turn, and in her heart she knows that this weekend may be her only chance of improving the situation.

So she tries not to think about it, and concentrates instead on the delicate art of negotiating each day without offending Khaya. Which is something like performing oral hygiene on a crocodile without getting bitten. He is insulted when she gives him juice in the wrong cup – a sin that can never be remedied by something as simple as putting it into the right cup; when she ties his shoelaces instead of letting him do it, even though he can't; when she can't make the sun go down and come up again because the day has gone wrong and he wants it to start over. And those are just the ones she knows about. Frequently, he refuses to divulge the cause of the offence, and takes further offence that she can't identify it without his help.

One Friday afternoon finds her encouraging him to complete his homework before going to the harbour for fish and chips. The task at hand seems innocent enough: colouring in a picture of bunnies gambolling amongst Easter eggs. Some children, Sam supposes, might even do this sort of thing for fun, although the one rabbit does have a rather nasty leer. But Khaya is offended to the core of his being.

"Bunnies!" he mutters disgustedly, as he scrawls furiously over them with purple and black wax crayons. "I *hate* bunnies . . ."

Sam watches with some alarm as he obliterates first gormless faces and protruding teeth and then whole bunnies, until the page is scored through. What emotional aberration will Ms Wilson read into this effort?

"I hate bunnies!" he bellows, scrunching up the paper and throwing it across the room, then glaring at her defiantly.

"Well, you're done now. Let's go to the harbour."

"Yukky harbour . . ." (He'd been begging to go half an hour earlier.)

"Well, I'm going," she announces grimly, making for the door.

"Yukky harbour!" he yells.

But he follows her to the car. And once they are there, he scampers along happily enough, pausing to admire the rusty, creaking hulks of the boats, or to watch the antics of the foraging seals, or to throw his chips up and watch the seagulls catch them in mid-air. Sam walks behind, breathing in the compelling smells of sea and fish oil and tar, reflecting on her regrettable history with Dylan.

Had she been pissed off because Melissa didn't need her any more? Probably more than she admits. Well, it's not easy, is it, being around people who only have eyes for each other? And it had drawn unwelcome attention to the barren landscape that was her own "romantic life" – with its huge tracts of celibacy broken only by a few stunted growths of one-night stands and fleeting affairs.

She'd told herself, for all those years after their parents died, that she had no time for such things, that she had to focus her energy on being mother, father and big sister to Melissa. But had there actually been any knights in shining armour champing at the bit to sweep her off into the sunset? She can't recall any now. When Dylan came along, Melissa no longer needed her. And when Melissa no longer needed her, she could no longer pretend that she was sacrificing a vastly populated and compelling love life to care for her sister.

And yet, in the unforgiving glare of hindsight, it seems as if she'd done everything she could to drive Melissa away. Her words come to her now, with horrible clarity, through the fish-and-tar harbour air and the intervening years. *Ridiculous . . .*

You're actually planning to keep it? . . . You think Dylan will be a good father? Dylan?! How these words had rushed out. How frantically, futilely, she'd tried to bolt the stable door in the wake of their thundering hooves. How helplessly she'd stood by while they trampled, wild-eyed and snorting, on all she cherished.

How could Melissa forgive her those words? They'd kicked down in a hail of falling stones the castle she'd built to keep away the demons of grief and loss. Worst of all, they'd forced her to choose between Dylan and Sam. And when Melissa rebuilt her castle, she had made sure that the enemy was firmly on the outside. There was no doubt. Melissa would never have abandoned Sam willingly – she'd simply had no choice.

Sam had hoped that it would all somehow come right when Khaya arrived, that she'd be able to prove herself so indispensable as an aunt that Melissa would realise she couldn't do without her. I can do babies, she thought. Even at twelve years old, hadn't she always been the one who could soothe Melissa? Oh, baby Melissa . . . . resting in her arms as light as thistledown, as secure as a hand in a glove. She'd wanted a baby sister her whole life, and when she finally got one it seemed as if her small weight, the sweetness of her breath, the tendrils of hair that clung to the tiny stalk of her neck could dispel everything bad in the world.

But when she held Khaya for the first time, he'd felt so alien, so disturbingly vulnerable. She was terrified she would break him if she held him too hard, and drop him if she didn't. He seemed to sense that he was in unsafe territory and began whimpering, then screaming . . . *Puce*, she'd thought, looking in horror at the violent shade infusing the outraged knot of his face. She'd hastily handed him back, before he turned into a pig, like the duchess's baby in *Alice in Wonderland*. She had been an aunt for two hours, she thought miserably, and she was already a failure.

So there they were. Melissa undermined and defensive, Sam excluded, Dylan bewildered, Khaya alternately hungry, cold, hot, wet, too tired, not tired, bored, overexcited, and conveying every emotion in astonishingly strident tones. And when Melissa announced that they were moving to Port Elizabeth, Sam's sorrow at her departure was somewhat tempered with relief.

In a twinkling, the whole catastrophe was gone. They'd packed themselves into Dylan's white '75 kombi, with the blue waves he'd painted on the side, and bobbed off into the sunset.

How did it happen, Milly? she wonders, perching herself on the harbour wall and dislodging a clamour of seagulls. *How did two people who loved each other so much suddenly become unable to breathe the same air?*

It happens. These things happen. It wouldn't have been a permanent rift; it would've resolved itself in time. But time was the one thing they did not have.

Sam was left with months of regret and an empty house, thrown back into her own life for the first time in ten years. She'd wandered through the house, her eyes bruised by the spaces left by Melissa's absent possessions. She'd tried to refer to Melissa's room as the "guest room", a fiction that might have been easier to sustain had she been able to populate it with guests.

How quiet it was. You could hear the clocks ticking, the flowers growing in the garden. Roots pushing aside soil. Earthworms munching and tunnelling. The whirr and click of a ladybird's wings. Your own life sighing and settling around you, like dust in an empty room.

Still, she had "moved on", as Maddie would say approvingly, as if the key to a successful emotional life was to be a perpetual nomad. The photography course . . . *Daniel* . . . Those trips to Namibia photographing the dunes, listening to him read poems by e.e. cummings and Dylan Thomas in their tent at night. The hair on his arms golden in the lamplight; the way he'd look up and catch her eye, and smile with his own until she seemed to disappear into his gaze.

"Stop reading poetry now, and come and ravish me . . ."

"Don't be so crass, woman, I am ravishing you with words. Now listen . . . 'in your most frail gesture are things which enclose me . . .'"

"Do I have frail gestures? It seems improbable, in one so robust."

"You're fishing," he had said, "but I'll oblige. The way you touch your throat when you are afraid of your feelings; the way your hands fly up a little when you laugh, as if you have surprised yourself; the way you'd lift a finger in acknowledgement when I caught your eye during lectures, a gesture so slight that it was almost gone before I saw it. Shall I go on?"

And she'd smiled the secret smile of a woman whose lover has passed a test and said, "No, that is enough. You may read me some more poetry now."

* * *

. . . in your most frail gesture are things which enclose me . . .

Of all the poetry he'd read, that line haunts her the most. It expresses so eloquently the fleeting lightness of love, and its tragic propensity to be blown away by the unforgiving winds of fate.

* * *

"Hey, HEY, can we take him home? His name's Crabby!"

Sam jerks out of reverie. Something smelly and repulsive is dangling inches from her nose.

"HEY!" Khaya says again.

She pulls her head back to get it into focus, and finds a long-deceased crab, its claws and four remaining legs hanging by unpleasantly visceral threads from the carapace of its body.

"Oh Khaya, throw it back, it's disgusting."

"'Snot disgusting. He's my friend. I want to keep him."

"He'll stink your room out. He already stinks."

"I like his stink."

Sam sighs. Sometimes she is too tired to do the right thing.

"Tell you what, if you leave Crabby here, where he is happiest, bobbing on the ocean wave, I'll buy you a chocolate ice cream."

Khaya eyes the crab thoughtfully, then fixes her with a calculating eye. "One scoops or two?"

"Two, you scheming little gogga," she laughs. "Come on, then."
"Okay."

He tosses Crabby unceremoniously over the harbour wall. Sam swings him onto her shoulders, marvelling as she does so that she'd ever found him alien. The feel of his body – the knobs of his spine pressing against her stomach in bed in the morning; his small bony legs clamped against her sides when she gives him a piggy back; the way he sinks into her, heavy with sleep, when she carries him from the car – has become like a second skin to her. They walk down the harbour wall, past the bobbing boats and sky-wheeling seagulls, with the salt wind in their hair and the promise of ice cream in their hearts.

* * *

Easter looms inexorably. Every phone call from Maddie to discuss the logistics of meals and egg hunts leaves Sam feeling more and more like Khaya's purple-and-black scribbled Easter bunnies.

She wants to take her own car in case she needs to run away, but the thought of driving so far is too terrifying. So Good Friday (Bad! Bad Friday!) finds her hunched over her long legs in the back of Maddie and Hamish's Toyota, being pelted with gobby bits of Mia's rusks and juice as she throws them around in outrage at being confined to her car seat for so long. Khaya, who is deeply offended because there isn't a seat belt for Hanky (*I suppose you don't care if he goes through the windscream!*), sits clutching his grey woollen elephant with the lumpy trunk, and glaring out of the window. Hamish is, as always, rather taciturn, locked, no doubt, in geological ruminations about astroblemes and batholiths. It is left to Maddie to fill the car with gay chatter, which she manages with her usual flair, in between soothing Mia with sticky bits of sugared dry fruit and playing "I spy" with Khaya.

But when they arrive, the cottage is everything a seaside cottage should be: thick whitewashed walls; piles of perlemoen shells on the stoep; old bookcases full of slightly mouldy hardcover Agatha Christies and jigsaw puzzles with lots of sky. The sea is a ribbon of light just beyond the end of the garden, and the pounding waves provide a soothing lullaby.

It is hard to be grumpy there, and as they tumble out of the car and colonise the small bedrooms with their belongings, Sam feels her misgivings dissipate. She takes Dylan's arrival a few hours later in her stride, relieved to have their stilted interactions carried along by Maddie's gregariousness and Hamish's gentle dry humour.

By Sunday morning, Khaya has released his fears and his fury, and is behaving pretty much like a carefree child. Maybe Maddie's strategy is working after all, Sam concedes (only to herself, of course) as they sit on the stoep chasing cream-cheese croissants with Hamish's painstakingly percolated coffee, and watch Khaya and Mia, stuffed with chocolate, scour the scrubby bushes for overlooked Easter eggs.

But wait. What's this? Hamish, dear, blundering Hamish, innocently opening a can of worms.

"So, Dylan, I hear you're working on some project up in Elandskloof . . ."

Sam shoots a panicky look at Maddie, but she is gazing out to sea, seemingly lost in another world. *I should go.* Yes, Sam, put down this delicious cup of coffee and get away from here. But some horrid fascination for what Dylan will say keeps her rooted to the spot.

"Eh, it's amazing what's being planned there," Dylan exclaims eagerly. And launches into a fervent description of the area, eulogising its seven biomes; its diversity, its ancient plants and cycads lodged high up in rocky crevices, the numbers of endemic species. Animal life too! What a multitude of beasts once roamed its plains . . . buffalo, mountain zebra, lions, leopards and, of course, the famous eland.

"The big animals and predators have been forced out by the farms. The reserve is shaped like a U, with a tongue of cultivated land running down the middle on either side of the river. That's where the grasslands would have been, which you need for the big herds. If that land were incorporated back into the reserve, it could sustain buffalo, rhino, lion, elephant even. The eland could come back to Elandskloof.

"My own patch is the rivers. If we pull this off, we'll have an entire riverine system in pristine condition. I'm doing a project to assess the damage done by farming."

He sounds less woolly than usual – quite authoritative. Despite herself, Sam glances up. Dylan and Hamish are sitting on a bench, Dylan leaning back against the wall, embroidering his discourse with cavorting hands. Hamish is leaning forward with his elbows resting on his knees, glancing back at Dylan encouragingly every now and then, but otherwise staring with apparent fascination at the ground between his feet. He is a small, wispy thing, Hamish, Dickensian somehow, with his mild grey eyes and a rather sparse goatee. An incongruous partner to Maddie, who currently sports a bleached shock of white-blonde hair standing up like a cockatiel crest. Maddie is looking at Dylan now too, evidently roused from her reverie by the absorbing content of his chatter, and seemingly quite oblivious of the thin ice on which everyone is skating.

"How do you measure the river's health?" she asks.

"The basic idea is to compare the river to what it would be like without human interference. It's quite challenging, because there are so many variables. Sorry, is this very turgid?"

"Not at all. It's fascinating," says Maddie, with irritating enthusiasm. But she is right. It is sort of fascinating, if one can pretend it isn't Elandskloof.

"So how have humans messed up the river?"

"Ag, the usual stuff. Irrigation, draining wetlands, overgrazing leading to silt run-off, planting aliens . . . Ironically, major damage was caused by the old Nature Conservation guys. They had a whole fishing thing going down, camping weekends and good old boys around the fire talking kak and comparing fish sizes.

"So they packed these rivers with alien fish, like trout and bass. They boast about it. They get all wounded when you tell them that they fucked up the environment. But that rapacious old bass has made major dents in the redfin, which are endemic to the area, and is messing up the balance of other creatures."

Redfin minnow. Sam's mind flips back to the sight of four feet – two white, two brown – gleaming through clear water, toes squished into mud, and the exquisite shiver induced by a flickering frieze of minnows nibbling your ankles. She and Chrissie cling together, laughing, daring each other to stand there for as long as possible, until they both collapse in an intimate tangle of limbs under the water.

"So how did the idea for the reserve come about?"

"Well, it's Jannie's baby – Jannie de Vries, who manages the Elandskloof Catchment Reserve. He's the guy who rents the house at Cedar Hills from Sam. He initiated the whole idea, and began fund-raising. He says I can stay with him while we're busy."

The words are slipped so quickly into the slipstream of his monologue that it takes her a second to react. But as she takes in their meaning, a dangerous prickle starts at the back of her head.

"What did you say?"

Dylan looks at her with a flicker of challenge. "I said I was staying with Jannie."

"At Cedar Hills?"

"Yes. What? Chill out, Sam, what's the big deal? Jannie's renting it."

"I can't believe it, Dylan. Didn't you think you should at least ask me?"

Dylan stares at her. "What do you want?" he asks quietly. "What do you want with Cedar Hills? That it should just vanish? Disappear? Crumble to dust?"

She wants it never to have been, she wants no one ever to step on its soil . . . She wants it to be kept in a glass case somewhere as a shrine to Melissa . . . Christ, she doesn't know what she wants. She just doesn't want Dylan living there. But she can't say that, because it will sound stupid. Because it is stupid, seemingly, and yet to her mind so profoundly logical.

Before she can answer, Khaya runs onto the stoep. "Look, we found a giant beetle, come look." He freezes as he sees the hostility on their faces.

"I hate you, you're all fat bums," he shouts, and runs off down the path, towards the sea. Sam starts after him, but Dylan is already leaping down the track with long-legged strides. He swings Khaya onto his shoulders and walks down to the beach. The wind billows the white fabric of their T-shirts, making them look like a tall sailing boat on a sea of pale golden sand.

* * *

Sam watches them, feeling as awkward and spiky as a stranded lobster. Then she swings on her heel and strikes out along the beach, determined to put as much distance between herself and the whole humiliating exchange as possible. She strides off resolutely, trying to lose herself in the white stretch of sand that rolls out unendingly before her, the sandpipers scuttling on stalk-like legs at the water's edge, the seagulls wheeling in the cloudless blue sky . . . But she cannot silence the furious dialogue with Maddie raging in her head. So that when Maddie herself comes running up after her, she feels almost as if she had conjured her up out of her imagination.

"I don't want to talk to you," she proclaims, as if talking to Maddie was the last thing on her mind.

"Well, I want to talk to *you*," says Maddie firmly. "Because you know what, Sam, this whole thing is just fucking ridiculous and I want you to tell me once and for all why you're so pissed off with him. I know he went off with your sister, and he's been patchy as a parent to Khaya, but does that really justify this fury?"

"Patchy? Jesus, you call deserting his son for six months patchy?"

"But he's tried to make it up. What do you expect from him? What'll it take to make you forgive him?"

"You don't understand. There are things I never told you."

"Well, tell me now."

"No, I don't want to talk about it."

Maddie grabs Sam's arm, and pulls her around to face her. "Sam, do you want Khaya to grow up completely fucked up?"

"Fuck you, Maddie. You really know how to stick the knife in, don't you?"

"Because I have to . . . because you're so bloody stubborn. You have to face it, Sam. If you don't resolve your relationship with Dylan, Khaya will carry the can. You *know* that – look at him today."

"Resolve my relationship? What kind of psycho-babble bullshit is that, Maddie? You just don't know . . ."

"What? What don't I know?"

"That night . . . that Dylan left. That night that he walked out on his deeply traumatised two-year-old son . . . he left me a note."

"And . . . ?"

"He said . . . fuck, I don't know, it was all just raving, but he said that he had to go away to find out 'the truth' about Melissa's death. He said he believed that someone else was with her in the car, who maybe caused the accident then ran away . . ."

"Why on earth did he think that?"

"He didn't say in his note, and I couldn't ask him, could I? I didn't see him for six months." Sam picks up a stick and hurls it furiously into the sea.

Maddie sinks down on the sand, shaking her head. "I just can't fathom it. It makes no sense." She absent-mindedly scrapes the sand into a small mound, and pats it to form a perfectly spherical dome. Sam watches the smooth, round egg of sand emerge from under her hands, fighting an urge to stamp on it.

"God, that's so bizarre . . . Did Khaya ever say anything? I mean, to suggest that someone else had been there, with him and Melissa?"

Sam shakes her head. "Khaya didn't say anything for about six months, although I knew from Melissa's letters that he'd started talking. He made weird noises, but the first recognisable word I heard him say, ironically enough, was 'Dadda' – when Dylan decided finally to show up."

"Did you ask him when he came back?"

"To be honest, I didn't really want to know, but I did raise it with him once. He said he'd been confused, mixed up by grief, he didn't know what he was thinking . . . When I tried to probe him on who he thought was there, he said he was mistaken. The whole thing was preposterous."

They sit in silence, watching the black oystercatchers running round the dunes on comical long red legs.

"But still," says Maddie eventually, "is that why you're so pissed off? I mean it's a peculiar idea, but it's not uncommon, you know. People who are bereaved often like to blame someone. Maybe because they want to be able to direct their anger at something tangible, or because they think that if someone caused this death, they can somehow make it right again."

"And maybe they also find someone to blame because they don't want to take the blame themselves."

"Take the blame . . . ?" Maddie stares at her, aghast. "Oh, you can't mean that. Are you suggesting that Dylan . . . No, you can't be."

Sam glares back. She is a consummate glarer, having inherited the gene from her dyspeptic great-great-grandmother, and honed the skill on hordes of fellow boarders at school.

"Of course I'm not saying that he killed her deliberately. But the whole thing was bloody strange. Why was she driving back to Port Elizabeth with Khaya, so late, without Dylan? Why didn't he check that she got home, or look for her when it was evident that she hadn't? *Why didn't he look for her? Why did he let her die alone?* I mean, even if they'd had a huge fight, and she'd driven off in a rage, through a pass like Grasnek, surely he would've at least checked that she got home safely? He didn't care, Maddie. He didn't even fucking care enough to go after her. Or his son. Khaya sat the whole night on that mountain while his mother died beside him. Jesus. What do you think that did to him? Don't ask me to forgive Dylan for that. *Ever.*"

Sam puts her head onto her upraised knees, and rails at the sand at her feet. "You never stop, do you? You just never bloody stop. You go on, and on, a dead horse to you is just an invitation to a flogging. Jesus, when will you just learn to leave things alone?"

She stands up abruptly and runs off, struggling to catch her breath amid the harsh sobs constricting her chest, shamed and humiliated by her outburst. She's never shared these feelings before, and she didn't want to now. They are hers, damn it, however mad they might be. Letting them out has diminished them. They look absurd, lying there exposed to Maddie's gaze. They've lost their dignity and grandeur. She knows Maddie is longing to suggest that she share them with Dylan, as if they could then indulge in some horrible confessional that will end in a mutual hug. The very idea is repulsive.

The bottom line, *Maddie*, is that she can't abide Dylan. Because of his conduct around Melissa's death. Because the loss of Melissa, far from being some kind of rope that binds him to her, is highlighted by his presence. Her loss is the negative space that dangles between them, a chasm that nothing can ever bridge. And now he is at Cedar Hills. And she isn't.

He is *there*, drinking the sweet waters of the rivers, staring up at the stars, breathing in the smells and the silence, while she rots away in that godforsaken Springbok Publishers. Or watches the developers in Hout Bay fell yet another forest or concrete over yet another wetland. Or is jostled by sweaty hordes of humanity along rubbish-strewn streets. Why is it so bloody easy for him, and so impossible for her?

She falls to her knees, and beats the ground, shouting, "Fuck, fuck, fuck!" A nearby gang of oystercatchers peer at her down their red beaks, apprehensively trying to gauge this performance. She stops beating when the pain in her hand finally communicates itself to her brain, then leaps up and runs into the waves fully clothed. She ploughs through the breakers and strikes out vigorously with some vague intention of swimming as far as she can, to Antarctica perhaps. But her waterlogged clothes weigh her down, and she soon wades, defeated, back to shore.

A pitiful performance all round, she thinks. But at least it has worn her out, and taken the edge off her rage. She peels off her clothes and lies naked, eyes closed against the sun, her heart hammering and chest heaving as her body struggles to return to equilibrium. She is tingling all over with muscular effort and the creeping warmth of the sun as it dries her.

* * *

She wakes abruptly, startled out of a dream. It feels much later. The light is tending towards early evening, and a cool breeze has sprung up, heralding the grey fog that is blowing in across the sea, and causing a forest of goose bumps to erupt on her skin. She reluctantly pulls on her damp clothes, which are encrusted with wet sand and salt, and not kind on the skin, and begins the long walk home.

Her mind travels back to that morning, three years ago, the day after Melissa's memorial service at Cedar Hills . . . lying looking at the stain on the ceiling of her bedroom at Cedar Hills. Trying to ignore that plaintive wail that rose and fell in the dawn light, with seemingly little hope of attracting attention.

Eventually she staggered out of bed and located the noise to a small, wet, malodorous bundle in a travel cot in the corner of her room, with Dylan's note "explaining" why he'd left Khaya in her care. Sam rampaged around the house searching for him, but he had indeed gone, along with the other mourners who'd slept over the previous night – two sylph-like girls with shaved heads and tinkling bracelets that made them sound like alpine goats as they wafted dreamily about the house, murmuring in the sotto voce of bereavement.

Now it was her and Khaya. The last survivors of the catastrophe.

Khaya's wail ascended to ear-splitting screams, great gouts of noise that flew through the air and smacked her in the face. She picked him up warily. For a moment he was silent, staring at her with appalled blue eyes, shocking against the bright red of his cheeks. Then he screwed up his eyes and screamed louder than ever.

She joggled him hopelessly, then lugged him to the bathroom and laid him on the floor. He arched his back and kicked his legs while she wrestled with his clothes. She tried dabbing at his mess with toilet paper, while he spread foul-smelling excrement all over himself and the bathroom floor. Eventually she ripped everything off, and ran the bath, and deposited him in it. She was choking with sobs all the while, and paused in the middle of this operation to throw up in the lavatory, in the process smashing her fingers with the seat.

After she had stuck him in the bath she sat hugging herself and weeping. She wanted a drink. She wanted to be completely insensate. She wanted to crawl into the dark cave of her bed and shut out this cheerless, Melissaless world. She wanted to run out the house and drown herself in the Elands River, just so that she did not have to listen to his awful screaming any more.

She became aware of silence, and cautiously lifted her face. Khaya was sitting in the bath, staring at her curiously. He held his hand to her, pointing to it. She bent forward to look at the spot identified by the small, black-rimmed finger. A tiny necklace of dried scabs lay on the smooth padded skin over his knuckles. He seemed to be waiting for some response. Sam smiled encouragingly. Eventually, Khaya bent forward and kissed his hand, and then held it out to her again. Sam took it gravely, and bent to kiss it. He nodded, as though satisfied, then sat back and smacked the water with both hands, showering her with drops and crowing with delight.

"All better," Sam whispered, staring at his laughing face in astonishment. The tears were not yet dried on his cheeks and here he was, creased in giggles.

"All better now," she repeated louder. Hopefully.

* * *

But it wasn't better. Not for a long time. She was completely inept with Khaya – she had no idea how to amuse him or soothe him, what he liked eating, what he was trying to convey with the myriad odd sounds he made with rising frustration. Half the time she felt as if she could barely even see him – she seemed to be in a thick fog, reaching out blindly to catch him as one would a drowning child in murky water. She'd drift into a frozen, catatonic state, with or without the help of alcohol, and suddenly realise that minutes or hours had gone by and she had no idea what he was doing, and she'd run panic-stricken through the house to find him. Once she found him chewing happily on a blister pack of Valium, but his teeth had not yet penetrated the foil.

She stayed at Cedar Hills for about five days – paralysed by a fear of stepping out the door, of attempting to barrel along the highway with a screaming Khaya in the back. But eventually she realised that she had to get out of there: she was running out of food, and she needed authoritative advice on how to parent an almost two year old. So, after yet another sleepless night, she threw her stuff and whatever things of Khaya's and Melissa's she could fit into the car, put Khaya into his car seat, which Dylan had thoughtfully left, loaded Mimsy and Richard (who'd also been left, presumably in her care), switched on the engine, put the car in gear, turned it around and headed grimly down the track.

The sun was just rising as they drove away, casting the rocky crags along the road in a rosy glow. The whole landscape was freshly minted by the dawn, as lambent as in the first flush of creation. Sam inched her way up the treacherous passes with only two thoughts in her head: *I have never seen a place so beautiful* and *I never want to set foot in it again.*

* * *

Sam shivers, pushing the memory aside. It's done, she tells herself wearily. Oh God, it's all so done, so final, so impossible to rewrite. But Maddie's right, fuck it. She has to find a way to . . . what? Forgive Dylan . . . ? Her mind recoils from the word. An awkward word with opaque connotations . . . the way it twists the tongue as it moves from the "or" to the hard "g", then causes the teeth to brush with brief menace against the lip for the "v". No, forget that . . . Love? . . . That's insane. Like? Tolerate?

Tolerate. Yes. That is the best she can do. Tolerate Dylan. Acknowledge his right to exist and to father his child. Quell hostility. Be dignified and restrained. Concede his right to stay at Cedar Hills. She owes that, at least, to Melissa, who'd have been *appalled* at her behaviour. And to Khaya.

But no more bloody weekends, Maddie.

* * *

The first test of her resolve comes rather abruptly when Dylan appears a few minutes later, looming out of the greyish mist that now engulfs the beach.

"Maddie sent me to check on you . . . make sure you weren't carried off by a giant albatross."

Thanks a lot, Maddie. She almost feels sorry for him – his discomfort is painfully evident, despite his clumsy attempt at humour.

"Thank you, I'm fine," she says stiffly, and through gritted teeth she adds, "And . . . um . . . Dylan, sorry about my outburst earlier. Of course you can stay at Cedar Hills if Jannie is okay with it."

Dylan stares at her in astonishment, and allows a real grin to break out. "Hey, kif, thanks. You won't regret it, Sam, we're doing amazing stuff there, I swear –"

"Yes, quite," she interrupts. "I'm sure you are. But, Dylan, I *really* don't want to know about it, okay?"

He holds up his hands in mock surrender. "Hey, that's cool, sister. My lips are sealed."

Which they are, mercifully, for the rest of the walk back.

Chapter 6
Confession of a Killer

I HAD much to occupy me in the weeks after my meeting with Melissa – contacting the other doctors who'd be helping to gather data, finalising research protocols, my lecturing programme at the university, plodding through literature. But my mind was primarily concerned with your sister.

First, some reconnaissance was in order. I discovered where she lived, and drove all the way out there one Saturday just to have a look. I sat at the white stones flanking the gateway to Cedar Hills farm, trying to find some trace of her mystery in their bland faces. An enormous tortoise foraging at the roadside peered at me with myopic disapproval. I considered going in on some pretext, but decided that whatever I said would sound flaky and make me look like some kind of sad stalker. And so I drove away instead.

I discovered too that she was married with a small child. This did not bother me too much. I'm sorry if that offends you, but that's how it was. Firstly, I knew from that tightness in her eyes that whatever was going on there, her married life was not in a state of unfettered bliss. Secondly, I am no stranger to fighting for what I want.

I have no intention of boring you with childhood sagas, but a brief biographical note is necessary. My father was a janitor at the Berkeley campus of the University of California, and he regarded its inmates as the lowest form of life. The shit of a professor (he was fond of telling me, waving a half-chewed fried-chicken drumstick for emphasis) smells no sweeter than the good, honest turd of a working man. Which seemed to suggest that there was something deceitful about academic faeces, and I was left in no doubt that he viewed intellectual pursuits as the masturbatory activities of limp-wristed pansies, which could teach you far less than the hard knocks of the University of Life. His contribution to my education was to make sure I got my fair share of these, particularly after a few too many beers on a Saturday night.

My father was not an imaginative man; his brutality was so routine it sometimes seemed to bore him. But it was persistent. And each clip across the ear, each bloodied nose, each blow of my head against a wall stripped one more inch of softness, leaving a steel-tipped core of enraged determination. I had certainly not been destined for the gleaming ivory towers of Berkeley, but I clawed my way up their slippery walls and went on to become the boy wonder of the microbiology department.

So, a failing marriage was a minor hurdle. A bigger problem was Melissa herself. I saw her on a few work-related occasions, but each time she presented a wall of cool indifference that resisted any efforts beyond perfunctory professionalism. And each time she weighed me up with those steady blue eyes, I could see the stereotype I filled: the arrogant American researcher, come to rake up whatever pickings he could from the wilderness of African deprivation. Determined to squeeze out whatever data served his purpose from the benighted bodies of his subjects, and to exact gratitude for his charity in the process. Her assessment was not entirely invalid, I suppose, but I was not just going to slink off.

You see, despite all that, she liked me. I was confident in that – when you have to fight for your place in a hostile world, your survival depends on your social perspicacity. No, not *like*. It was more primitive. Whenever I was near to her, I could feel an arc of electric tension between us that was not only one-sided. I would feel her eyes on me, although she flicked them away as soon as I looked at her. She was drawn to me in a way that she could not understand, and in conflict with all her better judgement. This response did not necessarily make it easier – on the contrary, it made her even more skittish.

I was wary, too. I did not want to scare her off. My years of tracking wolves in the forests of North Carolina taught me that a quarry should never be rushed – and the wilder it is, the more cunning and caution you need to display. I hope this metaphor does not suggest that this was some idle sexual conquest. Of course I sought to posses her sexually, but I wanted far, far more.

I need you to understand this, however trite or even perverted it may seem to you. You see, necessity drove me to reinvent myself. I changed my name, my way of speaking, my clothes, my diet. I cultivated a knowledge, and then an appreciation, of classical music and modern art. I learnt how to cook Thai food, how to debate controversial topics without hitting someone who disagreed with me, even how to laugh with that self-deprecating mockery that the entitled use to underscore their self-assurance. I read my way through classic fiction to improve my vocabulary and my grasp of literary references. I practised in the mirror – yes, I confess to that too. What a good mimic I was! How assiduously I studied the gestures and intonations of the world's beloved. How diligently I adopted them.

But in the still hours late at night, or in those sudden empty moments walking down long corridors, I was haunted by an underlying void. I'd lost myself. Or, more precisely, I'd never found myself. As a child I'd known only that the world my parents presented had no place for me. And yet, the more I strove to hammer myself into what I thought I wanted, the more I seemed to disappear into some phantom illusion. I was suspended between worlds – disclaiming all connection to my beer-swilling, Saturday-night-bowling origins, yet never quite embraced by the urbane intelligentsia to which I aspired.

The thing is, I believed – I still believe – that Melissa held the key to my salvation. Illogical, perhaps, but I convinced myself that she'd somehow bring meaning and restore my integrity. That if I stood in the right light, she'd see me for who I truly was, past my plasterboard childhood with its sordid bruises, past my over-eager pretentions, to that elusive inner self – and once she'd seen it, she'd reflect it back to me with love. Life had thrown into my path my one and only chance of redemption, and I had to do everything I could to ensure that I grasped it with both hands.

As the weeks went by, and my opportunities for seeing her diminished, I began to feel that this chance might never be realised. But late in March, fate dealt me a lucky hand . . .

Chapter 7

DYLAN is on his best behaviour when he arrives for his next visit. He gets Khaya to bed on time and actually helps with the washing up. Sam eyes him warily as he potters about the kitchen, meekly drying plates and wiping counters.

"You go and put your feet up. I'll bring you tea. And I bought us some chocolate – that black imported Belgian stuff. You like that, don't you?"

Put your feet up? Belgian chocolate? What the hell? But she obediently trots out of the kitchen and sinks down into the couch. Dylan brings out a tray with two mugs and a slab of Côte d'Or noir, sets it on the coffee table, and sits opposite her. He flings himself back in his chair, crosses one leg over the other, and bares his teeth.

She can't stand it any more. "All right, spit it out."

"What do you mean?"

"Come on, Dylan, you've been like a Jack Russell on amphetamines all evening. What do you want to ask?"

He looks a little wounded, and then grins. "Okay, you're right."

"So?"

"Well, I was just wondering, um . . . if, well, you know, I just thought that Khaya might really like a visit to, uh . . . Elandskloof, and I could . . . um, fetch him, and drive him up in his school holidays . . . well, if you think that's okay, I mean . . ." His voice trails off.

Sam stares at him blankly. He catches her glance and looks away, drumming his fingers on the arm of the chair.

"He can't go away this holiday," she says when she finds her voice. "He's got soccer clinic."

The words leap into her head from who knows where. The notice arrived a few days ago. "Do you want to go?" she'd asked.

"No! Yukky soccer," Khaya'd said.

"And an art workshop," she continues wildly. "I've paid and everything. You can't just spring these things on me, they have to be arranged . . ."

Dylan glances up at her. Something like hatred flares in his eyes. And then he finally says it.

"I think you're forgetting something. He's my son."

So, *this* . . . Something loud and dangerous drums in the back of Sam's head. But she has her own weapon of mass destruction.

"*You* were the one who forgot that, Dylan . . ."

The air crackles. His eyes are bright blue against flushed cheeks. He looks remarkably like Khaya when poised on the lip of a tantrum.

"I *never* forgot that. Ever. You know *nothing* of what I went through."

"Dylan, when you came back, we agreed that we'd do it together. You said you didn't want to try it on your own. You said Khaya needed the security I'd been able to offer him. Has something changed that I don't know about?"

"It's just . . . Jesus, it's so fucking claustrophobic. You don't trust me for one second . . ."

"You haven't given me much cause to . . ."

Everything is tilting now. The warhorses are gnashing their teeth and pawing the ground – who knows what'll be trampled next? Something hard and intractable is lodged in her throat. All these unsaid things. The whole teetering arrangement only made possible by so much tongue-biting on both sides that they barely have any words left for each other.

It is Dylan who retreats. He usually does. Sam has seen that as a sign of cowardice. But now she has a sudden uneasy thought that his compliance is driven not by weakness, but by his desire to make it work for Khaya's sake. That it is Dylan who crosses the line to meet her, and not the other way around.

"Never mind. Have it your way. It's probably a bad idea." He stands up abruptly. "I'm turning in. Good night."

"Thanks for the chocolate," she calls after him hopelessly.

"You're welcome."

He is gone. Sam stares at her tea cooling in the mug. How will she keep it all together? The spectre of *that* day, which has haunted her ever since Dylan came back into their lives, looms grotesquely . . . the day that Dylan will say, *He is mine. He is my son.* The day the whole arrangement is no longer tenable.

The very thought of it sucks all the breath out of her. Khaya is often difficult, and often exhausting.

But without him, she'd shrivel into dust.

* * *

The following morning, Maddie drags her off on a day's outing.

"You need to give Dylan some space with him," she announces on the phone. "And I want to see that William Kentridge exhibition at the National Gallery. Some culture will do you good. I'll pick you up in half an hour."

And the receiver goes down before she has time to argue. In some ways she is grateful for the opportunity to get away from Dylan. She's been hiding in her room since waking, but she can't hide there all day. Yet she's also nervous to leave him. *What if he kidnaps Khaya and takes him to Elandskloof?*

He wouldn't, would he? Still, the possibility haunts her all the way to the exhibition, and she struggles to listen to Maddie's chatter, or to respond with appropriate enthusiasm. Finally, as they walk through the overpriced shop to the exhibition rooms, it bursts out of her.

"Can you imagine? Dylan actually wants to take Khaya to Cedar Hills in the holidays."

She says it lightly, trying to hide from herself the dangerous crevasse that she and Dylan had skirted. She'd assumed Maddie would vindicate her refusal. But Maddie, as ever, has her own opinions.

"That's a good idea. Actually, that's a great idea. Why don't you go too?"

Sam stares at her in disgust. Really, she can be astonishingly dense sometimes.

"Don't make me laugh," she says mirthlessly.

Maddie shrugs. "Well, it would help normalise things for Khaya. You know, he'd be able to know where his dad was spending his time, and it might actually be really good for him to go back to Cedar Hills, to the place where he was last with Melissa."

"Yeah, or it might just drive him right over the edge. For heaven's sake, Maddie, it's an insane idea. What do you think it could do for him? Can you imagine all the associations he has with that place?"

"You're projecting," says Maddie, with her annoying bluntness.

"I'm not!"

Their interchange has so far been in hushed, gallery-appropriate tones, but now Sam's voice rises in indignation. A uniformed man sitting on a chair in the corner frowns at her, and she repeats in a hoarse whisper, "I'm not."

"You are," Maddie whispers back. "*You're* the one with the associations. Khaya probably doesn't even remember anything. It would demystify it for him – reassure him that his whole life didn't just vanish in a puff of smoke when Melissa died. I must say, I do like Kentridge's sculptures. They're so evocative – especially that one. It reminds me of you."

Sam glares at the offending sculpture – a long-limbed, hooded thing composed of what looks like dismembered gardening tools, stalking along with a predatory air. Maddie is right – there is something eerily familiar about it. Something about the way it holds its bladed arm aloft, in a futile effort to ward off the depravities of the world.

"Anyway, how'll Dylan keep him safe for a week in such a perilous place? Half the time he's stoned out his brain. It's all round a Very Bad Idea. And please don't mention it to Khaya."

But this is Maddie we're dealing with. The first thing she says when they come back – *the very first thing* – is, "Oh Dylan, I believe you have plans to take Khaya to Elandskloof?"

"Elandskloof?!" Khaya shrieks. "Elandskloof? We're really

going, are we going, Daddy? Are we going to see the mermaids and . . . and the stars . . . and the frogs, and the baby swallows and the rock that looks like the queen and . . ."

"Well," Dylan looks at Sam with something between terror and triumph, "that depends on Sam."

"Can I, Sam? Sammy-Sam, can I please please please?" Khaya flings his arms around her waist and butts her with his head.

"Um . . ." What can she say? Dylan has told Khaya a million stories about Elandskloof, until it has become a combination of Disney World (which he'd seen on TV), heaven (which his Grade 0 teacher told him about), and the Giant Land of his imagination, from where, of course, Hanky hails. Except that it is even better than any of these.

"Please please *please*," he looks up at her with beseeching eyes then burrows his head into her stomach. "Please, Sammy-Sam, I'll never be naughty again . . ."

"Well, I guess . . ." Sam casts a murderous look at Maddie over his head. And before she knows it, Maddie and Dylan have arranged the whole thing, while she stands reeling with disbelief.

* * *

Sam boycotts Maddie determinedly for some weeks after Dylan has left. Even though Maddie really is her only friend. *My only friend,* she tells her large-nosed reflection. *She's the most insufferably meddling person I have ever met and she is my only friend. I mean, how pitiful is that?*

Where have all her friends gone? She'd had some, hadn't she? There was Gill, from her teaching days; and Sandy and Brett, although they were more Daniel's friends; work colleagues with whom she had the occasional cup of coffee; her old university connections, but they were all in Johannesburg. She'd lost touch with people when she went to the States with Daniel, and she simply couldn't bear to reconnect with them when she came back after Melissa died. Half of them probably didn't even know she was in town.

No, really there is only Maddie, dear old Maddie, who's been her friend since high school, and seems to be the only person able to withstand Samantha's determination to scare everyone else away. And she will *not* see Maddie, she tells the mirror fiercely, she's just gone *too far* this time.

Her reflection gazes back from under beetling brows, with nothing redeeming to say.

* * *

The dreaded morning arrives, as dreaded mornings always do. Sam stands in the hushed gloom of the winter dawn, watching Dylan pack Khaya's suitcase into his bakkie. *This isn't happening,* she tells herself. Nobody believes her.

"Did you put in my extra Batman suits?" Khaya asks her.

"Yes."

"And Ellie?" This is the lumpy knitted elephant that keeps him company in bed each night.

"And Ellie."

How has it come to this? She wants to scoop him up in her arms and run so far away that no one will ever find them. She pictures herself as the Kentridge sculpture, silhouetted on the horizon, with Khaya in a bag on her back, her blade arms slashing away at any who try to stop them as they lope off into the distance. But she doesn't. She just stands meekly on the pavement while they settle themselves in the car and Khaya does up Hanky's seat belt. He doesn't need a child seat, he assures Sam, 'cos he's actually enormous.

"Khaya must wear a seat belt at all times, Dylan. Even when you're driving in Elandskloof."

He looks at her bleakly. "Do you really think you need to remind me of that?"

She shrugs. Dylan shakes his head in disbelief, waves goodbye, and climbs into the cab. She watches the taillights all the way down the road. Khaya doesn't look back.

* * *

The moment the bakkie has turned the corner, loneliness rears over her – huge, lupine and grey. It lollops after her as she goes inside, its yellow feral eyes glowing in the kitchen as she puts on the kettle for tea.

"You're not there," she tells it crossly. "I can't see you . . . la la di dah." She puts on the radio loudly and fusses about the kitchen, tidying away the mess left by Khaya's mad dash, banging cupboards, clinking cups, clattering dirty dishes. But loneliness just stands there, grinning, with its red tongue hanging out, and she knows that it will not leave her side until Khaya is back.

She finishes in the kitchen, and takes her tea to her bedroom. She takes off the tracksuit she'd thrown on hastily that morning, and, for the first time in years, stares at her naked body in the full-length mirror behind her wardrobe door.

Her body stares back, wryly. The puckered eyes of her nipples peer out from small, slightly sagging breasts. Her upper half is scrawny, sculpted by the protruding ridges of ribs, clavicle and sternum. Her lower half has a rather lumpy aspect, she decides, reminiscent of a melted candle around the buttocks and upper thighs, somewhat dimpled with cellulite.

She finds her legs are faintly pleasing – well, long anyway, although there is no countenancing those knees, clinging to their centres like ungainly flat toads.

She stares at this canvas of her dislocated life, rereading its tired old stories. The small recessed navel, linking her to her reluctant, long-departed mother. The wavy, thin-lipped smile across her lower abdomen, which marks the removal of her appendix twenty years ago in a hospital in Bloemfontein, after her medical-student housemate diagnosed acute appendicitis during a camping trip in the Drakensberg.

He'd been so convinced of the urgency of her condition that he'd wanted to whip it out in the tent, with a Swiss Army knife sterilised with vodka. In fact, there was nothing wrong with it, as the doctor in Bloemfontein had later informed Sam with pursed lips and a small, annoyed frown. As if she'd chosen to subject herself to painful abdominal surgery to liven up her holiday.

Your appendix was lily white, he'd said, accusingly.

Lily white. That phrase haunted her. It was so pejorative, implying a certain cowardice, as if her appendix lacked the courage for a full-bodied infection.

"Lily white," she says now, leaning forward to breathe the words into the glass. Cool words. A little papery.

The mist from her words fades to reveal the star-shaped scar on her chin, where Chrissie had pushed her backwards into the dam and she'd hit the wooden post of the pier going down. When she'd emerged from the water, she'd seen a rare panic in Chrissie's eyes, as she attempted to stop the copious flow of blood with Sam's shirt. Still, Chrissie would not humiliate herself by begging Sam not to tell.

She'd later eyed the three spidery black stitches Sam's father had inserted, and asked Sam what she'd told him. *I said I fell off the pier*, Sam had replied, waiting for Chrissie's outpouring of gratitude at her forbearance.

So, said Chrissie. *That's true. You fell off the pier.*

"Why are you here?" Sam demands of her reflection, with sudden rage. "Why are you even here? You should have died instead of Melissa. I don't even want you."

Her body stares back at her regretfully but, she thinks, with a certain mute defiance. Perhaps even something like pity.

Pathetic.

* * *

Sam turns away, and rummages through her closet to find some outfit vaguely befitting a "professional" woman, finally settling on her black corduroys, ankle boots from the factory shop in Salt River, poloneck white jersey, black jacket. The jacket is missing a button and the jersey has a hole, which is hidden by the jacket. The pants are worn at the knees. Actually, she realises once it is assembled, it doesn't really befit a professional woman at all. She looks like one of those lonely middle-aged women waiting at a bus stop who have no one to go home to. Which, she supposes glumly, is more or less what she is. As if it wasn't bad enough being one, without looking like one.

Twenty minutes later she is in her car coasting down Victoria Avenue from Llandudno towards Camps Bay, taking in the glorious expanse of the Atlantic Ocean on her left. It is a beautiful morning now that the sun is up – almost indecently beautiful, mocking her dejection. The recent rains have left the air crisp and sparkling, and the landscape is saturated with rich colours in the soft winter light, so different from the harsh bleaching of the summer sun. A smudge of bluish cloud lies like a bruise on the horizon, heralding a new cold front, but for now it is as balmy as a spring day, and almost windless. The sea laps mildly at the rocky coastline, offering a deep, still mirror to the cobalt sky, and as she passes Oudekraal she sees a school of dolphins leaping through the small waves.

"Don't cry," she hisses to herself, fiercely, as the sight of these wild, spirited creatures threatens to release the tears she's been holding back all morning. *Don't cry, don't cry, don't cry . . .*

But the tears spill over, and she snivels her way through the morning traffic, arriving at the huge parking lot behind her office building feeling like a soggy tissue. The parking attendant, a portly, pale brown man whose round, flat face and smattering of moles lend him the appearance of a chocolate-chip cookie, eyes her with his customary spleen.

"Ten rand," he grunts balefully, as if whatever miseries he has endured in life are entirely due to her existence. She shows him her monthly parking ticket, grudgingly admiring his steadfast refusal to recognise her – it is a ritual that they have acted out almost daily for the past two years.

She parks her car and trudges across the tarmac to the revolving glass portals of the publishing empire that employs her. She feels marooned, as if Khaya's departure has finally severed her from whatever fragile threads tethered her to the world.

She negotiates the elaborate security procedures in the lobby and enters the lift in a state approaching panic, then stands staring at the faux-wooden panelling, as if it might hold the key to the secret doorway that will let her back into her life.

Perhaps she should press the *Call Operator* button?

She glances around at her fellow travellers. A lime-suited receptionist with minty breath and pert breasts, a tea lady in yellow overalls glazed into immobility behind her trolley, two men in suits, brown moustaches and shiny shoes. They all seem possessed of a certain air of purpose, yet she thinks she can detect something haunted in their gaze. *Maybe, if we find the right button, the elevator will shoot us right out the top of the building (like Charlie's elevator in one of Khaya's favourite stories), and we'll float through the world until we find a kinder place to be.*

But the lift sticks to its schedule, the doors open and close, the people shuffle in or out obediently.

As does she, when her turn comes. What else can she do? She punches in the code at the office doors, and lets herself in as the lock clicks open. She'd hoped to sidle unnoticed past the receptionists, or at least to be consoled by a kind word from motherly Sannie Kruger, but no, Sannie isn't there. Instead, it is The Poison Arrow, as she has named the redhead with the coral lipstick, whose job description seems to include reading up on how to feng shui your house and guide your boyfriend to your G-spot (simultaneously, if possible), and exploring new avenues of nastiness.

The Poison Arrow looks up. Her eyes flare with malicious joy.

"Mr Potgieter is after you," she announces, and licks her lips as if she can taste his name. Sam's manager.

Sam plays it cool. "Really? Why?"

"You were due to meet him today, at eight o'clock."

Sam glances at the clock on the wall. It is ten to nine. Fuck, fuck, *fuck*! She bares her teeth.

"Oh that," she says airily. "Yeah, I know, but there was an accident on the road coming in. The traffic was backed up for miles."

The Poison Arrow smirks back. *Ha, ha, ha,* her smirk says. Sam turns her back on it, and plods wearily down the corridor to his office.

It is going to be a long week.

Chapter 8
Confession of a Killer

I WAS eating breakfast with Terry Baxter on his porch when her call came through. Rice Krispies and banana, I think – Terry is not known for his sophisticated cuisine. Terry's a vet in Kareedouw; I don't think you know him – he came here about a year before Melissa died. Big shambling sort of guy. Walks with a limp from when a charging rhino remodelled his leg a few years ago. He used to work on big-game reserves, but had to scale down after his injury.

I met Terry back in the late '80s in North Carolina, when we worked together on a red wolf conservation initiative at Alligator River Wildlife Refuge. He was part of the reason I came to the Eastern Cape – he'd been on at me for years to come and help with their fledgling leopard-conservation project in the Elandskloof, although I kept telling him that I'd moved from carnivores to microbiology. He was mystified by my desire to "sit around and watch bugs grow in a Petri dish" rather than track leopards, but we were still good friends, and I often spent weekends at his place.

"Bugger," said Terry when the phone rang. "Probably some sow with impacted piglets. Just when we were easing into a day of leisure."

But it wasn't a pig. It was Melissa.

"Melissa Campbell," he said when he came back. "Young bird up at Cedar Hills farm. You were asking me about her last night."

"Yeah . . . what does she want?" I asked, trying to stitch up my grin and hoping that Terry was too busy shovelling Rice Krispies into his beard to notice my poorly disguised enthusiasm. I prayed that she was on her way with a sick dog.

"She's in a hell of a state. Up walking above her farm this

morning when she came on a leopard in a gin trap. I just hope this baby's not too badly injured – if it's okay we may be able to collar it and release it. Move your ass, china. We're going leopard hunting."

We stopped by the wildlife hospital to pick up equipment and two assistants. An hour later we pulled into the gates of Cedar Hills.

She was waiting on the porch. Her hair was tied back, her skin translucent in the sunlight, the arch of her neck so exquisitely tender against the cotton collar of her shirt I had to thrust my hands into my pockets to stop myself caressing it. Her face was drawn tight with anxiety.

"Hi, howzit Melissa. You know James, don't you?"

She stared at me, nonplussed and faintly accusing.

"Hi Terry, thanks for rushing over. Hallo . . . James . . ." she added, tossing the words reluctantly in my direction.

"James is a friend of mine," Terry explained. "I brought him along because he's a useful bloke in a tight spot with a predator."

"Is he really?"

Terry looked at her curiously, then at me. I smiled blandly.

"I worked with Terry on wolf conservation in the States," I offered.

"Right, let's get going," Terry interjected into the unimpressed silence that greeted this revelation. "Where's this leopard?"

We piled into his pick-up – Terry, Melissa and I in the front, the assistants, Vuyo and Fransman, sitting silently in the back. Melissa became more animated in the cab, although she regarded me narrowly out of the corners of her eyes when she thought I wasn't looking. I tried not to look at her face, but I could feel when her eyes were on me. I fixed my gaze at her hand resting on her knee, so tantalisingly close to mine. No wedding ring . . . a band of paler flesh where the ring had been . . . *but no ring.* She had a scratch across the knuckles and a Winnie-the-Pooh Band-Aid around her thumb. That Band-Aid killed me.

The track was bumpy, and, despite her best efforts to avoid it, we were often thrown up against each other. I could hardly breathe.

"I came across it at about seven this morning," Melissa was saying. "I was walking through the bush above Rooikrantz and Mimsy – my dog – was running ahead when she suddenly started to go berserk. I thought she was being attacked, actually, because the leopard was spitting and snarling. I screamed for her and took off down the track. But when I looked behind, I realised the leopard hadn't moved – I went back and saw it . . . its foot . . . in that horrible trap. I don't know how badly injured it is. It looked pretty mangled but I didn't want to upset it more, so I just grabbed Mimsy and came back down as quickly as I could."

"Do you know who set it?" Terry asked.

"My guess is Neels Koekemoer. Rooikrantz is still his land, I think, although there is talk of a land claim by the Stuurmans. But I think the trap is beyond where his land ends, into the wilderness area. He's no friend of leopards. His family between them have probably killed more leopards than the other farmers put together – his father used to say he likes his leopards stuffed or skinned."

"They're bloody barbaric, those traps," grumbled Terry. "I'd like to put Neels in one for a night or two. I've seen leopards chew off their feet to get out of them."

"It could have been Mimsy who was caught," Melissa said. "I keep thinking about that. Or me, for that matter. That grass is long, and I'm sure it was hidden. I don't know why the government still allows them."

Terry gave a disgusted snort, but whether it was aimed at Neels, gin traps or the government was unclear. They carried on talking, mostly Terry regaling her with leopard tales that skated the edge of credibility. Terry can't help himself from crowing around young women. I kept silent and tried to keep my heart steady and to stop imagining running my finger down the pale satin flesh of her inner arm, or kissing her Band-Aided thumb.

We drove past a derelict old house and wound up into the hills. Eventually we had to leave the pick-up and continue on foot.

The heat mounted as we ascended the slope and followed the path through the scrubby mountain fynbos. We were silent now, oppressed by the dry heat, the screaming cicadas, the sullen clouds. Small flies persecuted our faces. Melissa walked in front, then Terry, then me, with the two assistants behind, carrying the cage. The bush around us seemed to bristle with the eyes of unseen leopards, their tails flicking softly in the yellow grass, their legs bunching to spring.

We plodded up the path, skirting the almost-dry riverbed below, until we entered a craggy gorge. The euphorbias clustered on the hillside above us, huddling suspiciously as if speculating on our intentions – or planning an ambush of their own. The heat closed in between the rocky walls, and sweat trickled down my face. Despite the discomfort, I did not want the walk to end. I could watch her undetected now, savour the way the muscles of her back moved under her shirt, the light swing of her arms, the damp tendrils of hair against her neck. I wish it had not ended. I wish I was still walking there, through the heat, before the leopard, before everything. But about fifteen minutes into the gorge, it widened slightly to form a more gentle slope, and Melissa held up her hand to stop us.

"It's there," she whispered. "Past those thorn trees . . . beside the anthill. Can you see it?"

It was just visible – a heap of spotted hide almost concealed in the grass. We withdrew slightly, to enable Terry to get the darts ready.

"Cover me with this," he said, handing me the .308 rifle he'd brought along. "You guys wait back here, just in case this thing goes sour. James and I'll go closer."

We moved forward slowly. I was cool now, all thoughts of Melissa out of my head, focused only on the animal before us. It was so still I thought it might have died, but as we drew near it sprang to life, whipping round with a yowl, burning us with blazing yellow eyes shredded with fury and despair. The trap gripped it by three toes on its back leg. Two were already half off.

"Fuck," muttered Terry. "This thing's bedonnerd. Keep it in your sights, pal."

I raised the rifle while he drew within a few metres of the animal, trying to find a good angle for the dart. The leopard tried to spring, but fell awkwardly as the trap gripped its leg. It scrabbled to its feet, gathered itself and sprang again.

This time it did not fall. Its foot was wrenched free from the trap with a sickening crunch. And then it was a ball of enraged muscle and claws, hurtling through the grass towards Terry.

"FUCK!" screamed Terry, letting off a dart, which flew past the leopard's hindquarters.

There was a loud bang and a jarring blow in my shoulder. For a moment I thought the leopard had jumped at me, and raised the gun to ward off its claws and teeth. But it was crashing to the earth a few feet away, its legs flailing. It thrashed on the ground for a horrible second, and then was still.

"Jesus," said Terry. "Thank God we spent all those afternoons shooting beer cans."

It was only then that I realised I'd shot the leopard.

I'd shot the leopard.

I put down the gun, and stared stupidly at the empty heap of carrion that had moments before been a thing of such exquisite savagery. A young female, not quite fully grown. I knelt before her, holding her paw helplessly. Two bullet holes in her chest leaked blood, which pooled in a sticky mat beneath her. Her tongue protruded slightly between her teeth. The remains of her toes hung off her back foot.

Melissa ran up through the thicket, then stopped abruptly, staring down at us.

"You killed it," she whispered.

I looked up at her, flinching at the abhorrence in her face.

"I'm sorry," I said.

"Why did you kill it?" she asked, impatiently brushing away the tears pouring down her cheeks. "I don't understand . . . why is it dead? I thought you were going to dart it?"

I stood up. "A dart takes at least three or four minutes to work," I explained, hating her for the bleak accusation in her eyes. "And Terry missed the first one. There wasn't time." Fuck. Did she think I'd *wanted* to kill it?

"He saved my life," said Terry, slapping my back. "This man's a bloody hero."

Melissa sank to the ground and hugged her knees, shivering. She stroked the leopard hopelessly. She was feeling it, I knew, the raw beauty of its life, the leaden weight of its death. The impotence of the aspirant saviour who could not, after all, deliver the victim from its fate. Even made it worse. Without our intervention, the leopard might have got free and survived.

I should have tried to comfort her, I guess, but I was bleached with fury. The whole fucking scenario sickened me. I'd driven here so full of hope and now all we had was a dead leopard and a woman who'd probably hate me forever.

It was a sober walk back. Even Terry was unusually subdued. Fransman walked before me, carrying the leopard like a child in his arms – Terry wanted to take her back for a postmortem to check her diet and health. I could see her head lolling over his arm, the trail of bloody drops in the dry dust at my feet. Vuyo and I carried the cage; Melissa walked silently behind. It was funereal, that slow, hot trudge through the thorn trees, the handle of the heavy metal cage digging into my hand. The raw smell of blood and death filling the air, the shrieking cicadas.

When we reached the pick-up, Melissa said she'd walk the rest of the way home.

"It's fine," she responded to Terry's concerns. "It's not far. I need to clear my head."

I watched her walk down the track, her back stiff and vulnerable. I wanted to run after her, to crush her to my chest, to shout I'm sorry, to grind the whole bloody day into the red dirt. She didn't look back.

The day dragged on, from one wearying activity to another. When we finally got back to Terry's place, I had a shower, hoping the water would wash away the fucked-up day as well as the dirt and sweat and smell of death that seemed to cling to every pore. By the time I stepped out, I knew I had to move.

"I need to head back to Port Elizabeth," I explained to Terry as I gathered up my things.

"Ag, come on, man, it's so bloody late now – it's getting dark already. And I thought you were planning to stay another night?" He fixed me with a wounded eye. I knew he wanted to spend the evening drinking whisky and reliving the events of the day. I could not bear it.

"I'm sorry," I said, feeling treacherous. "I've just remembered a presentation due by Monday. I have to get back to prepare."

But a little way down the highway to Port Elizabeth I turned off, and headed in the direction of Elandskloof.

I don't know what I was thinking, really. Certainly, Melissa had given no encouragement. I was fairly sure that she would not welcome me. I was not even convinced that I'd have the courage to go onto the farm. It was after dark – it's never a good idea to travel that long, difficult road after dark, and to travel it on the off chance . . . She may be with friends. It could all be so deeply embarrassing I'd probably have to just slink out of town and never be seen again.

My trepidation grew by the minute – but my resolve was stronger. I could not stop myself. The memory of that vulnerable, stiff back heading down the path was driving me crazy. Somehow I had to get to her and wipe that accusation out of her eyes.

As I approached the white boulders of Cedar Hills, my pickup swung up the drive, seemingly of its own volition. I bumped over the track, pulled up under the pepper tree, resisted the urge to turn around and drive off again, climbed out and walked around to the front of the house.

She was sitting on the porch in pretty much the same place we'd found her that morning, leaning against the wall of the house with her arm around her dog. That is the image of her that comes to me most often, on these star-filled, regretful nights. The light on her hair, the cloud of moths batting against the lamp above her head, a white skirt pooled around her legs like a snowdrift. The open paperback lying face down beside her.

That last moment before I was in her life. When I could have just walked away, or never come. Before her fate was sealed.

I stopped, unsure of what to say, feeling immeasurably foolish. She looked up at me expressionlessly, and seemingly unsurprised. Then she stood up and walked cautiously towards me. The dog followed, barking amiably and wagging its tail.

"Melissa . . ." I stopped, empty of words.

Her eyes were dark and unreadable in the starlight, but as she turned her head slightly I saw the glimmer of tears in the light from the porch.

"I'm so sorry . . ." she said softly.

I did not expect that. I'd expected recriminations, stiffness, hostility.

"I'm sorry too," I said. "It was wretched. I couldn't do anything else . . ."

She gave a small hiccup, a half sob, half laugh, and lurched towards me. What was her intention? What was mine? I don't know, but suddenly I had my arms around her, and I was kissing her.

She pulled away after a few seconds, and stared at me.

"Melissa . . ." I began, not knowing quite what I'd say.

She put up her hand to cover my mouth. "I don't know who you are. I think I might even hate you. But I've sat here all afternoon and evening going insane, and if you are not going to come in and make love to me right now, then please leave. Just . . . no words."

So that was the beginning. My life with Melissa began as it ended, with the cordite smell of violent death. I dream of it still, that slow, hot walk with the dead leopard. But as often as not it is your sister dripping blood in Fransman's arms. I wake up wishing that your lovely, intemperate sister had been more cautious that night. That she had run inside and bolted her door to me forever.

Chapter 9

THE days without Khaya stretch out like a lost road through the desert. Sam's only companions are loneliness, anxiety, the indifferent Richard and Mimsy, who offers some comfort with her wriggly, damp affection. She spurns Maddie's occasional attempts to invite her out for a meal or a movie, partly out of pique, but mainly because she is convinced that if she allows herself to be distracted and relaxes her vigilance for *one second* some horrible fate will swoop down and steal Khaya forever. Vivid images float through her mind in unguarded moments – Khaya going over the pass in a bakkie (obviously), being bitten by a snake, scratching himself on rusty barbed wire and dying of tetanus, drowning in the torrential flood that the Elands River can suddenly turn into with heavy rains.

In fact, when she contemplates the multitude of disasters that may befall a child in Elandskloof, she marvels that she survived her own childhood at all.

She has the Melissa dream every night, with new and horrid twists. Melissa headless, Khaya being devoured by insects before her eyes, a long worm crawling out of Melissa's mouth. She wakes, weeping, and creeps into the kitchen to make tea, watched by the red-crayoned eyes of a dinosaur on the fridge, which Khaya drew to look after her while he was gone. Its head is festooned with enormous spikes, and it apparently possesses the capacity to frizzle baddies with its spit, denoted by bright green stripes shooting from its mouth. As fierce and loyal a guardian as one could wish for. She is just waiting for it to leap off the page and deploy its spit on loneliness and anxiety, thus freeing her to gambol in the playing fields of life.

On the third evening after Khaya's departure, the phone rings. It sounds so obscenely shrill and urgent as she runs down the passage to the kitchen that she knows it can only be Dylan delivering bad news.

But it isn't.

"Hi, Samantha? Is that Samantha Campbell?"

Male, an American accent. For an absurd moment she thinks it is Daniel, as if he'd somehow acquired the intonation of his adopted continent.

"Yes . . ." she says, as her heart leaps to somewhere it doesn't belong, and interferes with her breathing.

"It's James here. James McIntyre . . ."

Oh. Not Daniel.

"I'm a fellow landowner in Elandskloof," he continues. "I have the farm behind yours . . . Skilpadsberg. I also worked closely with your sister."

"Oh," says Samantha, intelligently.

"I was so shocked to hear of her death. It was a great loss, to everyone of course, but for you it must have been untenable."

"Yes." Her voice falters slightly. She still wants to cry when people say things like that. *Untenable*. Does he mean insupportable, or uninhabitable? She supposes that either would apply.

"The thing is, I'd really like to meet up with you. Melissa spoke about you so much. I was hoping to run into you at Cedar Hills, but I believe you don't go up there much any more?"

"No . . . I . . ."

"But I also wanted to discuss the Department of Environment's proposals with you."

"Oh. Um . . . I . . ." Jesus, this man must think she is totally brain dead. Actually, maybe she is brain dead. Certainly, her mind seems quite incapable of devising an appropriate response to this conversation.

"I'll be in Cape Town this weekend. I wonder if lunch on Sunday would suit you, perhaps at Rhodes Memorial? I'm pretty sure I can find my way there okay."

"Well . . . um . . . I don't know . . ."

"So we'll say one o'clock then? Look forward to it. Cheers."

And he is gone.

Samantha sinks to the kitchen floor and sits leaning against the cupboard door, clutching the receiver. It feels like an alien object, unknown and probably dangerous. What the hell was that about? She's heard about pushy Americans, but this is ridiculous . . . he didn't give her a chance to say a word. Okay, admittedly words were not exactly tumbling out of her mouth . . . but still.

She tries to imagine this meeting. Sitting over the bobotie and beetroot salad at Rhodes Memorial, exchanging views on Elandskloof with this bombastic foreigner . . . No. It is *untenable*. She'll phone him right now, and tell him firmly that they really don't have anything to say to each other. Yes, that's what she'll do.

Except that he didn't leave a phone number. *Blast*.

No, she'll just have to grin and bear it. She could, of course, not turn up. But that would be rude, and the daughters of Daphne Campbell do not easily commit acts of rudeness. Even the rude daughter. Even in retaliation for rudeness.

Richard weaves around her, purring and waving his tail under her nose, presenting her with an unpleasantly close-up view of his backside.

"You're such a whore," she tells him. "You only suck up to me if you want food."

Meow, says Richard, shamelessly.

Around her the kitchen grows dark, until she can barely see Khaya's protective dinosaur and its green gob. Across the valley, people in Imizamo Yethu are firing gunshots, as they do every night. Precious (her char) tells her that the tsotsis do this when they get high-spirited in the shebeen. Sam listens to them, wondering whether a bullet fired in high spirits hurts less than one fired with malicious intent.

Perhaps it isn't people in Imizamo Yethu. Perhaps it's a white fundamentalist militia meeting secretly to prepare for Armageddon. Or visitors to the "high-class" brothel up the valley shooting each other in an orgiastic frenzy.

Perhaps it's just her own insanity ricocheting around her brain.

She should take command of herself . . . Turn on the light . . .

Feed the animals . . . Mop the floor . . . Go to bed. The normal things that people do to knit together the patchwork pieces of their lives. But she feels completely inert, as if the effort of getting through each hour since Melissa's death has finally sapped all her energy. No, not inert actually. More as if the universe has become such a perilous and unpredictable place that her only chance of survival is to stay absolutely still. The slightest movement might tilt her right through the rather nasty orange-and-grey linoleum squares of her kitchen floor into some nameless chaos that yawns beneath.

She glances at the fridge again. Below the dinosaur is a tattered scrap of paper stuck to the fridge, with the scrawled phone number of the psychotherapist Maddie's been nagging her to see for years. The writing has faded to a spidery brown, but it is still legible, although not in the dark. But she knows what it says.

Wendy Forrester.

She should change her name. How can you go to a therapist called Wendy? She'd try to sew your shadow back on, and tell you tales of Tinkerbell. She'd run her practice in a Wendy house. A windy house, as Khaya calls it. Full of hot air.

The clock ticks, the darkness settles around her. The distant traffic growls insistently. Richard gives up his mewing and begins washing himself. Mimsy watches her anxiously from under a wrinkled brow. The dinosaur drools on the fridge.

And still Sam sits, clutching the phone. Waiting for some indeterminate sign of redemption.

* * *

The week passes. Somehow, as she has learned, time keeps grinding on, even when it seems to have stopped, or actually to be going backwards. Otherwise she'd still be listening to Mrs Ritchie declining Latin nouns in her high-school classroom on a Thursday afternoon in 1978.

The week passes, and the weather obliges her for most of it by supplying lashings of wind and rain that mirror her disposition. And then at last (oh, at last) it is Sunday: the day that Khaya is due to return, at about five, and also (how the fuck did she get herself into this?) the day of Lunch with James.

Sunday dawns somewhat drizzly, although the storm seems to have finally worn itself out. Sam has a brief fuss about clothes before setting off, and then decides to just wear what she has on already, which is a pair of old jeans, trainers and a thick sweatshirt. Stuff it, the man has bullied her into lunch, she's not going to dress up for him.

She climbs into her Golf and gingerly negotiates the drive over Constantia Nek – she is still plagued by a pounding heart and clammy palms whenever she drives a road that twists, or strays near a cliff edge, or too close to trees, or does almost anything except roll out completely straight and completely flat. Mimsy sits beside her, eagerly scanning her surroundings – Sam plans to walk on the mountain above the restaurant after lunch.

Despite her misgivings about meeting James, once she's managed Constantia Nek she starts feeling quite buoyant, doubtless because of Khaya's impending return, and perhaps because the sun is breaking through the clouds and flooding the thickly wooded slopes of Cecilia Forest with a glorious autumn light, so that the last remaining red leaves on the chestnuts lining the road glow richly against the dark, wet branches behind them.

She parks her car, surprised to see how few cars there are, and climbs out. A man walks over to her. Is that him? He is tall, good-looking she supposes, although she no longer seems able to assess this sort of thing. An aquiline nose, a cleft chin, dark brown hair beginning to grey at the temples. Clean-shaven. He walks with an easy, loping stride, holding himself with a certain arrogance, as if unused to being thwarted.

He reaches her and extends his hand. "Samantha? James McIntyre."

Mimsy charges up to him as if he were a long-lost friend. Sam follows more cautiously, and warily shakes his hand. His eyes are disconcerting. For one thing, they are two different colours – brown and green. And there is something cool and impenetrable about them. There is a semi-circular scar under his left eye.

"I recognised you at once," he says, "from Melissa's descriptions. Although you're very different from her."

"Yep. Beauty and the Beast, that's us."

His mouth twitches. "Well . . . your sister was certainly a beauty."

She laughs. "Ouch. I guess I walked into that one."

He laughs too. "No, I'm joking. You're not at all beastly. Certainly not to Melissa – she thought you were the bee's knees."

Sam grins gormlessly. She can't imagine Melissa ever saying that, at least not with a straight face. *Bee's knees*, she whispers to Melissa. *Milksop*, Melissa whispers back.

"Did she ever mention me?" he asks.

Sam looks at him sharply. There is something in his tone . . . something to suggest it is more than just a casual question. He holds her gaze steadily.

She drops her eyes. "No, actually." Had she? She didn't think so . . . "Did you know her well?"

"Well?" He gives a small laugh, as if to dismiss the word as entirely inappropriate. Either because he hardly knew her at all, or because he knew her way beyond well. "Quite well, I guess. We worked together for about nine months on a research project in Elandskloof."

"The one to do with bottle-feeding the infants of HIV-positive mothers? Stompie Stuurman's granddaughter was on it, wasn't she? She died of an allergy or something – Melissa told me about it."

James winces. "Yeah, it was too bad. Melissa was very distressed. But it was nothing to do with the research programme. Melissa took things hard, as I'm sure you know . . ." He breaks off as he notices Mimsy, who's been running around him with wild joy for the last five minutes. "Good grief, is this Mimsy? Don't tell me . . ."

"Yes," she says, disconcerted by Mimsy's performance. The dog is friendly enough, but she doesn't perform for people like this unless she knows them well. Not quite well. *Very* well.

James glances up, and catches the question in her eyes. "I looked after her once when Melissa and . . . uh . . . Dylan went away for the weekend. We made good friends then, didn't we, Mimsy?"

Mimsy wags her tail in agreement.

"Look," he says, "the thing is, the restaurant's closed for refurbishment. I tried calling you but you must have left home already. So we could go somewhere else . . . or . . . I see you're dressed for walking, and I have some food in my car, so we could stroll up the mountain a bit and have a picnic. The weather looks like it's lifting."

Sam looks at him narrowly. Tried to get hold of her indeed. He must have known before that the restaurant was closed – otherwise why would he have brought food?

But she plays along, and they set off up the steep track leading away from the restaurant towards the Blockhouse and the contour path some five-hundred metres above them. For a while they walk in silence, then James asks her at some length about her work and she tells him about the riveting dramas of the Springbok Publishing textbook division. It is rare for her to be so talkative, but James gives a convincing impression of interest. And her nervousness is making her garrulous. What with the conversation, the incline and James's rapid stride she is quite out of breath by the time they reach the Blockhouse, and Mimsy is puffing like a Victorian steam engine.

Sam sits on the remains of the stone wall while James digs out the food. Cape Town is laid out at their feet like a picnic itself, freshly washed and brushed by the recent rains and winds. Far across the Cape Flats the purple range of the Hottentots Holland, usually lost in a pall of dirty smog, is etched sharply against the pale blue sky. The bustle of the city far below them is no more intrusive than the buzzing of the fat bumblebees amongst the fynbos.

Sam watches James extract a jar of olives, hummus, dolmades, an olive ciabatta, baby tomatoes, cream cheese, two glasses, a bottle of Boschendal Sauvignon Blanc and a bag of naartjies, with raised eyebrows.

"Some picnic. You always keep one handy, do you? Just in case?"

James grins. "Okay, okay, I confess. I found out yesterday that the restaurant would be closed. I just thought if I phoned you, you'd duck out of it. Would you have?"

Sam shrugs. "Probably."

"Well, I can't speak for the company, but you've got to admit the setting is pretty damn amazing, although I suppose you jaded Capetonians are immune to all that." He takes the bread out of its paper bag, slices it neatly with a penknife, then lays the pieces out on the flattened bag.

"No, I still find it pretty damn amazing, actually. I didn't grow up here, though, so maybe I'm less jaded than some. Which part of the US are you from?"

"San Francisco. Do you know it?"

"A bit. I travelled through there a few years ago – while you were working with Melissa, in fact. That's a pretty place too. What did you do there?"

She asks the question casually, but something in her tone may have alerted him, because he looks at her guardedly.

"I was in the Department of Plant and Microbial Biology at Berkeley University. Working with plant breeding."

"What did that have to do with infant formula and the transmission of Aids?"

"Well, nothing to do with HIV, but we wanted to run field trials on some soy we'd bred to be hypoallergenic, and we thought we could do some good and link up with an African study exploring the use of bottle-feeding to prevent mother-to-child transmission through breast milk. The company offered a good supply of infant formula in return. Tuck in."

James gestures to the food spread out beneath them. Sam obediently picks up a piece of bread, and furnishes it with some hummus and baby tomatoes. It's not a concoction that one can eat with delicacy, she discovers, although James seems to manage his without squirting a spray of tomato pips down his chin.

"Unruly little buggers, those tomatoes," he remarks, offering her a paper napkin to repair the damage, before pouring two glasses of wine. "Cheers."

Sam colours, and dabs her chin.

"So," she says, trying to regain her composure, "what made you turn your back on a successful career in microbiology for a farm in the backwaters of Elandskloof?"

He carries on eating his bread and sipping his wine without speaking, until Sam begins to wonder whether he heard her question. But then he says, "It's a long story. Let's just say that my career was becoming more of a liability than a blessing – whereas Elandskloof is only a blessing."

"Is it?"

He looks at her quizzically. "You don't agree?"

"Not really, but I have a complicated history with the place. So what are you doing there? Sheep farming?"

He laughs. "Hardly. No, I'm hoping to use my farm as a base to create a leopard sanctuary in the area. Both as a place where leopards are protected, and where we can do research, rehabilitation, public education and so on."

"A leopard sanctuary? That'll go down like a lead balloon at the farmers' association."

"Tell me about it." His face clouds with anger. "Mind you, it's a damn disgrace what those farmers do. Did you know that twenty-three leopards have been caught in gin traps in the last five years? Twenty-three! I know farmers think they're vermin, but a gin trap is the cruellest possible method to kill something – and other animals get caught in them too."

A picture comes to Sam's mind – the Koekemoers on their way back from a hunt one evening, a leopard strapped across the bonnet of their bakkie. Its dead eyes gleaming in the headlights of their car; its mouth still snarling its outrage to an uncaring world.

"Leopard-hunting parties were a regular feature of life in Elandskloof when I was growing up. My dad never participated in them, or any other hunting, but I guess it was easy for us to be moralistic about it – we didn't have livestock."

"Yeah, I know that the farmers need to protect their stock. I lost a foal to a leopard myself a few months ago. It was very upsetting. The thing is, leopards are so threatened now because of the loss of habitat. Farmers get pissed off, but there wouldn't be a problem if leopards had enough space, and if they'd left some game around."

"Why leopards? It seems a far cry from plant breeding."

"I guess. I've always been interested in carnivores – that was my first love. But I later developed an interest in microbiology. It seemed more cutting edge, more sexy I suppose, when I was younger. Now I'm pursuing earlier interests. In the US I was involved in research aimed at reintroducing wolves into North Carolina. More wine?"

"Thanks. You look like a wolf-man, somehow."

His hand jerks, causing the wine to miss her glass and splash her knee.

"I'm sorry. Did I say something wrong?"

"No. Someone used to call me that . . . a girlfriend. It startled me, that's all."

"What happened to her?"

"She died."

"I'm sorry."

They sit in silence for a few minutes. Sam watches a sugarbird hovering over a protea, probing the fat, furry flower head with its long beak. So this is what it's like, she thinks, to be one of those people who go on outings with others. He is right, of course – the setting is spectacular, offering one of those lavish, unstinting Cape Town vistas. And yet, as she looks down the mountain, the grassy slopes shiver like the skin of a frightened antelope . . . and when she lifts her eyes to the ragged cliffs of Devil's Peak, they seem to shimmer with the bodies of small children, dashed from the unforgiving heights by pitiless hands.

She feels his eyes on her. He is watching her with a small, amused smile, as if he's cut and pasted her into some personal landscape and is enjoying the effect. She feels a sudden jolt of resentment towards him, at the way he'd played out this whole thing, set up this elaborate scenario; manipulated her into it for some hidden purpose.

"This is a lovely picnic, Mr McIntyre," she says, somewhat acerbically, "but I believe you want to discuss something about the Elandskloof wilderness project? About which, I should hasten to add, I know very little, nor, quite honestly, have I taken much interest."

"Well, you'll need to give it some thought. It directly affects all the landowners in the kloof."

"And no doubt, when the department approaches me formally, I will give it some thought. But what specifically did you want to discuss?"

"Well, as I said, I am keen to establish a leopard sanctuary, but my farm is not big enough. We need to expand onto some of the neighbouring farms. I'm busy raising funds at the moment, and I think we could buy up a sizeable portion of land –"

"Whoa, back up a minute there. Are you implying that you'd like to buy Cedar Hills?"

"Well, it's an option."

"What on earth makes you think I would want to sell it?"

"I don't think anything. I am just asking a question. I heard that you seldom go there, so naturally . . ."

"I have reasons, you know. It's not that simple."

"Is it because of Melissa?"

Sam shrugs.

"Because, if so, do you think she'd have wanted you to have stayed away?"

She glares at him. "I have no idea. I haven't had the privilege of speaking to her for three-and-a-half years. Have you?"

"Okay, sorry, that was out of line. But even if you didn't sell, you could come in as a partner. Kobus Koekemoer is thinking of doing that."

"Kobus Koekemoer?"

"Yes, he owns Wanhoop next to Cedar Hills. You knew that, didn't you?"

"I'd heard so. But I wouldn't have imagined that he'd have been interested in leopards."

"Well, he's passionate about conservation, as a matter of fact. Unlike his brother Neels."

"Neels? What's he up to?"

"He's angling for a consortium of landowners to create a private hunting lodge. No predators except for a few leopards in an enclosed camp for tourists to gawk at or shoot if they pay enough."

Samantha leans back against the crumbling wall behind her, suddenly exhausted. She watches the ants scurrying about on the sand at her feet. Why are all these people fussing about the kloof? Why can't it just stay as it was, unchanged, so that she can carry on pretending it exists only in her dreams?

"How does all this fit in with the Elandskloof wilderness project?" she asks, with some reluctance.

James drains his glass, stands up and stretches.

"Neels is diametrically opposed to it. I'm reserving judgement. Frankly, I'm not sure that I want to relinquish the fate of the Elandskloof leopards into the hands of the Department of the Environment. Who's to say they won't screw up the management of the land, or sell out to some palm-greasing shithead with a plan for a golf estate? My plan is to go ahead with consolidating land for the leopard reserve, and then go in with the EWP if it looks like they've got all their ducks in a row."

Samantha laughs. "My, my, and I thought I was the cynical one. I'm sure that Dylan won't let them sell out to a golf estate."

"Ah, Dylan." He smiles patronisingly, and allows Dylan's name to hang for a moment, as if its foolishness is self-evident. "Well, he doesn't have much say, does he? In the end the whole thing will be decided on the basis of whether it serves some politician's interest, not whether Dylan is concerned about the frogs."

Sam squints up at him, suddenly irritated at his supercilious tone. Who is he to start throwing around judgements about the way South Africans did things? Swaggering around as if you could earn the right to have opinions about Elandskloof just by buying land. The fact that he is echoing many of her own reservations is beside the point.

But he clearly harbours no love for Dylan . . . Is that just personality, or something else? The way he spoke about Melissa . . .

so proprietary, somehow. *Had* he been in love with her? Well, even if he were in love with her, it would never have been reciprocated. He was too old for her, he didn't seem like her type, and Melissa was passionately in love with Dylan.

She stands up too, brushing crumbs off her legs, noticing with some embarrassment that the tomato pips have landed up on her jeans as well. Do these things know no bounds?

"So," she says, with as much dignity as she can muster, "you want to know whether I'll either sell you Cedar Hills or come in with you as a partner?"

"Well . . . that's jumping the gun a little. I really just wanted to get a sense of what you wanted to do with your land."

"Actually, I don't think that is any of your business. But if I sell it, I may let you make an offer. If I don't decide to sell it to the Elandskloof wilderness project . . . or Neels, come to that."

James looks alarmed. "Has he made you an offer?"

She smiles, pleased to have riled him.

He laughs nervously. "Right, you had me going for a second. Well, you're right, ma'am, it ain't none of my business and you've been mighty patient listening to me." She presumes the hammed up accent is some form of sarcasm.

James packs the picnic things away. A methodical man, she thinks as she watches him. Used to keeping things in control . . . those square fingers, with their well-manicured nails. She finds them disturbing . . . Is she experiencing a visceral dislike, or some kind of perverse sexual attraction? She's forgotten how to distinguish these feelings. She tries to picture him undressing her, probing her. Do people really do such things to each other? It is hard to imagine from where she finds herself now, stranded in some Arctic Circle of emotional detachment, far beyond the reach of normal human discourse.

"Naartjie?" he asks. She nods, and he throws her one, before closing up his rucksack, slinging it on his back, and turning to go down the track.

They make their way down the mountain in silence. Sam is glad to have some time to think, but she wonders at James's sudden taciturnity. Is he irritated that she hasn't shown unreserved joy about his leopard project? Not that she cares, of course. She couldn't care less what he thinks of her, she tells herself firmly. He's just one of those people who's good at making you think you care. Well, it won't wash with her.

When they get back to the parking lot, James recovers his powers of speech and turns to shake her hand warmly. A bit too warmly, she thinks, flexing her fingers afterwards.

"I'm glad to have met you at last, Samantha. Melissa told me how you took her in when your parents died – you sound like a pretty remarkable big sister."

Samantha looks at him searchingly. Is he trying to get her on his side? Surely he doesn't think she'll roll over *that* easily. She shrugs. "Any sister would have done it. There was nothing heroic about it."

"That's not how she saw it."

She walks to her car, aware of his eyes on her as she opens the back door for Mimsy. She climbs into the driver's seat self-consciously, glancing back on the pretext of checking behind her before reversing. He is watching her. He gives a small, ironic smile, and lifts his hand. She pulls out and drives away, flushed with a nameless embarrassment.

"Fuck you too," she says. But only Mimsy hears.

Chapter 10
Confession of a Killer

IT began with death. It ended with death. But I can assure you that everything that happened in between was alive with all the glory, abandon and savage tenderness that life has to offer.

We exchanged few words as we made love that night, but our bodies were eloquent enough. I responded to her with a ferocity that took me by surprise, despite my pursuit of her. And I knew that she felt the same.

"It's like running down a hill," she said, "and it's kind of terrifying because you don't know how to stop."

"You don't have to stop," I said. "Just keep running."

Later she said, "You have the eyes of a wolf . . . and different colours. One golden. One green. I noticed that the first day I met you . . . it's very unnerving. Like looking at two people in one body . . ."

"I am half wolf," I said. "Call me Mowgli."

"And the other half?"

"Pure lamb, of course. With fleece as white as snow."

She laughed. "Now *that* I find hard to believe."

"Ba-a-a . . ." I said, burying my face into her neck.

But when I reached for her in the dawn, she wasn't there.

I climbed out of bed, pulled on my jeans and walked out. She was sitting in her customary spot on the porch, wrapped in a blanket, gazing out into the waking world.

"Is this where you live?" I asked, sitting next to her. "I keep finding you here."

"Pretty much." She glanced up at me, but her eyes slid away. "James . . . I . . . it's not that simple."

"What isn't?"

"Me. You. I mean, I'm sorry if I misled you, but this is kind of a one-off thing."

"You sure about that? I don't want to be presumptuous, but last night you didn't exactly behave as if you wanted to be somewhere else."

"I know . . . I . . . Look!" she dropped her voice to a whisper and pointed.

A young steenbok stood at the bottom of the garden, just visible against the milky, early-morning mist hovering above the river. We watched it move along the lawn on tiptoe feet, nibbling the grass and the bushes, pausing now and then to gaze at the house with huge, liquid eyes.

When she spoke again, she sounded close to tears.

"Listen," she said, "you don't want to know, really. Last night was great, but I am carting around an awful lot of baggage right now. If you knew half of it, you would run a mile."

I suppressed a surge of irritation. Last night was "great"? *Great?* Like some fucking beach party? Last night wasn't great. It was life-changing. It was earth-shattering. And she knew it.

But I didn't want to scare her off, so I kept my tone light and said, "Come on, honey. I shot a leopard yesterday. I am not easily frightened."

She laughed sardonically. The steenbok lifted its head and melted into the bush.

"Now look what you made me do," she said. "Don't pull the macho wolf-man thing with me. It killed you to shoot that leopard."

Something stabbed my heart. She was looking right in there. The doors were so goddamn wide open she could have just walked in and taken whatever she wanted.

"You're right," I said. "It killed me. But I shot it anyway. I think I can handle a little baggage. Trust me. At least tell me what the hell you're talking about."

She turned her face to me. Her eyes were desolate and panicking. She was spooked, and stampeding away from me as fast as those beautiful legs could carry her.

"I don't want to talk about it. I'm sorry, I really am, but I need space, okay? I'm just not ready for this. Actually, I think maybe you should go."

I was defeated. She was running. All I could do was retreat and wait for her to come back.

I took her face in my hands. "Melissa, look at me."

She lifted her eyes reluctantly.

"You may not want to talk. But you *need* to talk. You're wound up like a bloody crossbow. If you don't want to talk to me, find someone else. But if you *do* want to talk – just that, nothing else, no expectations, no regrets – call me, okay? I'll come here, or you can visit me at my house in Port Elizabeth, but call."

"Okay," she said.

"Promise?"

"Yes," she said. To shut me up. Her eyes pleaded with me to disappear.

I kissed her lightly on the top of her head, and went inside. Next to her bed was a photograph lying face down. I turned it over. Her baggage, I discovered, or part of it at least, had dreadlocks and the face of an elf. A pretty boy, but he didn't look like much of a threat. I put it back, and put my card with my contact details on top of it.

I showered, dressed and fortified myself with a glass of water and some tasteless cookies that I found in the kitchen – Tennis Biscuits, they called themselves. I'd never seen such things in the US, but then again tennis parties were hardly a feature of my youth. It was not exactly the romantic breakfast I had hoped for, but I was reasonably confident this was not the end. We were united, you see, by the leopard – by its life, its death, that moment when everything had hung in the balance, when we were suddenly acutely aware that we were all composed of soft tissue and breakable bones . . . vulnerable matter that could without much force be ripped apart.

It had been infused into every second of our lovemaking . . . the blood-drenched fur, the mangled paw, the outraged eyes still mimicking life, the flies on the metal teeth of the gin trap, the vastly empty space between Terry and the leopard's claws, the bullets screaming through the air with only one intention. Each thrust of our bodies, each slow caress, was driven by a desire, perhaps, to banish these images – yet each drove them deeper into our flesh. For nothing accentuates life more than the proximity of death.

She was standing on the lawn when I went out, a lost fawn in the morning light. I smiled at her ruefully, and gave her a light, one-armed hug.

"I'm sorry," she started again.

"Melissa, when you get to know me better, you'll learn that I hate apologies. So don't be sorry. I'd not have missed last night for anything. Just call, okay?"

And then I climbed into my truck, and drove away.

I went home. I waited. I busied myself with this and that.

She didn't call.

I read my papers . . . reviewed and analysed data . . . attended meetings. I watched the sun go up and down. I ran along the beach until my legs buckled under me, then lay on my back, staring at the indifferent sky.

She didn't call.

She's frightened, I told myself. The volcanic intensity of that night. No wonder. She'll come round.

She's not interested, I told myself. It was just a blip on her domestic radar, and now she's gone scampering back to dreadlock-boy.

I tried everything to harden my heart against her, something I usually do with ease. I have learnt to walk away from hurt, from regret, from passion, to switch it off when it becomes self-defeating. But not this time. Her fire burnt brightly as ever, and threatened to consume me.

And then, when I'd almost given up, two weeks after the leopard, I came home from a beach walk one Saturday afternoon to find her sitting on my porch.

"Ah," I said, stopping myself with some difficulty from flinging myself on her and crushing her beneath my weight. "Porch-girl. I see you're exploring new vistas."

"Hi," she said tentatively.

We smiled at each other across a chasm of uncertainty.

"To what do I owe this honour?" I asked.

"I wanted to talk to you."

"Good. About time. Come in."

"Not about that . . ." she said hastily. "Something about the research project."

"I'm all ears, honey. Although, to paraphrase what a shirty young doctor once told me, you could have just faxed a report."

She laughed, abashed. "Okay, I guess I was also curious about where you lived."

"You should be careful of that. Curiosity can be fatal, as I'm sure you've heard. To cats, anyway. Come inside. Have some coffee. Or tea. Mind you, I don't think I have tea. I do have something called Tennis Biscuits though."

I'd bought these in the week before at the local convenience store. A tenuous link to her.

"No thanks, I don't really go for Tennis Biscuits."

"Oh? I saw them at your house, so I thought . . ."

"I only keep them at home for Khaya."

"Khaya?"

"My son."

"You have a son? That's wonderful. How old is he?"

"Fifteen months – well, just over."

"And where is he now?"

"With his dad. I just dropped him . . . uh, coffee is fine, by the way."

"Great . . . keep the coffee, can the cookies. You stay here and inspect my porch. Let me know how it shapes up to yours."

When I carried the coffee out to her, she was sitting hunched up with her face buried in her arms. She lifted her head when I laid down the tray and lowered myself onto the sunny step beside her. She forced her mouth into a smile, but her eyes were screaming.

"So," I said handing her the cup and pushing the milk and sugar towards her, "what is the first item on the agenda, Dr Campbell? The research project, or dreadlock-boy?"

She looked at me sharply, and then with dawning comprehension. "You saw his photograph . . ."

I nodded. She looked away. "I told you I didn't want to talk about that. Jesus, you're bloody presumptuous, you know."

"I wouldn't have got far in life without a healthy dose of presumption. Listen, Melissa, stop being so damn skittish. You pitched up on my porch looking like a gutted rabbit . . . If you don't talk to me now, you'll drive away feeling just as shitty as when you arrived. So I'll start you off. Where did you meet him?"

She looked at me warily, and sighed. "All right, you win. But don't say I didn't warn you. I met him on the R62."

"The R62? That's a good beginning. Very poetic."

"Have you travelled it? It's changing now – doilified for the tourists. But in those days it was a desolate thing, winding through barren mountains, past small-minded towns . . . a road populated by ghosts. Everyone in those towns had stories of the pretty female hitchhiker who vanished mysteriously ten minutes after you'd picked her up, or the headless one who'd suddenly appear and cause fatal accidents on empty roads.

"Dylan looked a bit like an apparition himself, like some kind of Pied Piper in a purple cloak, walking along the road miles from anywhere with his dog. We gave him a lift, which was kind of against our rules . . . but he looked harmless enough."

"We?"

"My sister, Sam, and I. Sam raised me after our parents died when I was thirteen. She's twelve years older than me. We were driving to Cedar Hills for a holiday. So we picked him up. He wasn't really going anywhere, just travelling wherever the wind blew. He somehow ended up coming back to the farm, and that was when it started."

"True love?" I asked. She looked at me narrowly, scanning my tone for sarcasm. I smiled innocently, attempting to convey that her feelings for Flower Fairy boy were no more pressing to me than the passions of the bugs that scurried beneath the porch.

"It *felt* like it," she said defensively. "He was so . . . I don't know, playful, I suppose. Life seemed to him just a never-ending lucky packet of possibilities. He was good for me, I think . . . that spontaneity. Whereas I'm nervous of surprises and tend to over-prepare for everything.

"A year later, I fell pregnant. Okay, so I guess I didn't over-prepare for that one. Sam thought I should have an abortion – I was in my final year, and Dylan and I were really not ready to have kids. But I didn't want to terminate. I don't know . . . maybe because Sam and I were orphans and alone in the world . . . I just couldn't bear to steal this life before it had even had a chance. To be honest, the pregnancy was not entirely an accident. And now that I have Khaya, I'm so glad I didn't . . .

"Anyway, the pregnancy was fine, only things were difficult with Sam. It was hard for her, I guess . . . she's very protective, and it had always been just the two of us. It was even worse after Khaya was born – Sam was so awkward with him. And I was so bloody determined to show her that I could cope, and too pig-headed to ask for help. Then Dylan got offered a job with an environmental NGO in Port Elizabeth, and I was interested in doing my internship at an Eastern Cape hospital, and possibly doing community service near Elandskloof, so we moved here."

She stopped talking.

"More coffee?" I asked. She shook her head.

"It's an unusual name, Khaya . . ."

"Dylan named him. It means 'home' in Xhosa. Dylan had a fairly fragmented home life, like me . . . I guess we both hoped that Khaya would bring us home . . . make us a family . . . Some irony, huh?"

"Is it?"

"Well, the wheels really came off after we got to Port Elizabeth. It was a bloody disaster. Internship was insane . . . the hours . . . the demands, the pressures, the fucking terror half the time because you were landed with cases way beyond your ability, endless nights on duty. The idea was that Dylan would work at home while looking after Khaya, and you can imagine how well *that* went. I had to give up breast-feeding because it was too hard expressing milk for when I wasn't around, and my milk dried up. And then I dried up too."

"You dried up?"

She nodded. "I did. Everything inside me just dried up. I looked at Dylan, this great love of my life, at my baby son's ten perfect toes, at the hollow desperation in the eyes of my patients . . . and I felt nothing. Just a great, ashy swathe of nothing. Even my son. Jesus, even Khaya, that beautiful, innocent boy. I was drowning, and the people I should have loved just felt like dead weights that would drag me down faster."

"Postnatal depression," I said. "It's not uncommon."

"Fuck, James. Don't patronise me. I know what it was. But it wasn't only that. You don't understand. It was all wrong. I'm not that person. I'm not the one who gets depressed . . . I'm little Miss Sunshine; I'm the girl who makes everyone feel better."

She sighed. "My doctor told me that I hadn't mourned my parents properly; that giving birth had reawakened all those old feelings. Maybe he was right. Sam and I had to make our way alone in the world, and she was only twenty-four . . . neither of us really had the space to fall apart.

"But I don't care how many labels you stick on it. The bottom line was, it was ugly, it was grotesque, and it just wasn't me . . . Sam always used to tell me this story about how, when I was born, I shone so brightly I kept the whole hospital awake, and they shouted, *Will someone please throw a blanket over that damn baby*. It was a silly story, but, you know, I could lighten people. I could always lighten Sam, and she gets pretty dark at times. I could lighten my dad, who could be a choleric old bastard when he wanted . . . and now suddenly, I couldn't even lighten myself. I was a big black bloody cloud, and I hated being anywhere near me." Her voice caught. She buried her head in her knees, to hide her tears.

"Melissa, if you think you can be the angel on the Christmas tree all the time, you're deluding yourself. You're not some singing canary put on earth to make people feel better about their sorry lives. You're a human being. You're complex, you've got issues, you've got pain . . . it *is* all part of you. It makes you who you are – it's not some growth you can just excise. And frankly, you'd be somewhat vacuous without it."

"Well, thank *you* very much," she said indignantly. "Vacuous. Mind you, maybe I could settle for that. Because dead man walking was fucking awful."

"I know it's fucking awful," I said. "So is burning yourself, but if it didn't hurt, we'd just keep walking into fires. Pain is learning. And you *do* still have a quality of light, by the way – it was the first thing I noticed about you."

"Well, that's kind of you to say so, but Dylan wouldn't agree. He told me he felt as if some joyless shadow had sucked out the real me and colonised my body. He said he didn't know what had happened to the woman he loved."

"He couldn't deal with it?"

"He tried, at first. But it totally freaked him out. I soon discovered that his apparent light-heartedness was often a way of avoiding thorny issues, and now I had blown a massive crater in front of his feet. And I didn't make it easy – I couldn't talk to him. I was too ashamed, especially about my feelings around Khaya . . . I just locked myself up inside my head and refused to let him in.

"So he ran away. He went out as much as he could whenever I was home. We basically never spent time together, and when we did, we fought. As sweet as it had been before, that was how toxic it became. So when my community service at the Willowdale clinic started, we agreed that I'd go alone and he would stay in Port Elizabeth. Well . . . it was my decision, really. I think Dylan would still like to make it work – but he just wants me back the way I was, and I can never go back to being that person again. Once you've seen a darker side to yourself, it changes you . . . you're less trusting, more reserved. And I really hated the person I'd become with him . . . so cold, so ungiving. I guess I needed someone who could give me space to work through my demons, and Dylan always seemed so . . . *wounded* and accusing, although maybe I was projecting my own guilt . . . Whatever it was, I just reached the point where I had to get away."

"And Khaya?"

"He spends alternate weeks with each of us. It's not great for him, but we don't know how else to do it. Dylan is a good father . . . a much better parent than I've been . . . and I feel so bad sometimes, because I know he'd much rather be around Khaya every day . . ." Her voice trailed off.

"But how do you feel about Khaya now? Still the same?"

She shook her head. "It's getting much better – lately especially. He's so quaint, you know? We walk around the garden together every morning and evening, and he potters along solemnly beside me, with his hands crossed behind his back, like an elderly English gentleman, totally absorbed in everything he sees . . . a stone, a leaf. And he's so painfully bloody forgiving . . . I just don't know how I'll ever make it up to him . . ."

She glanced at me, impatiently rubbing her eyes. That gesture. With the back of her hand . . . Do you remember how she'd do that? She hated anyone to see her cry.

"I just want to be *there* for him, you know? I owe him that . . . no distractions. It's one of the reasons I can't get into any entanglements. Apart from the fact that I'm feeling so fucking guilty and confused that I don't even know who I am."

"They're not necessarily mutually exclusive," I said.

She smiled wryly. "What happened last time felt pretty bloody exclusive, Mr Wolf-Man."

Our eyes met, held . . . I was drowning. I could not, would not let her look away. She *had* to feel it. We were rushing down a tunnel that had only one end.

She dropped her eyes warningly. "Don't," she whispered. "Or I'm gone."

I backed off. We talked more – a lot more. I promised her that Khaya wouldn't grow up with a big black hole in his soul because of her earlier feelings about him. I promised her that she would rediscover her light. Of course, I had no authority to make such promises, but she seemed to find them reassuring. We went inside, made a fire, made supper . . . and later, despite her very best intentions, we made love.

"Oh God," she groaned afterwards. "What've you done? You've bewitched me . . ."

"I've stolen your skin," I said, running my finger down the eloquent line of her collar bone.

"My skin?"

"Don't you know the story of the antelope and the hunter? The hunter saw a beautiful buck in a clearing. But as he was drawing his bow, the buck took off her skin, and out stepped the most beautiful woman the hunter had ever seen. He ran into the clearing, and picked up her hide, and begged her to come with him. She did not want to go, so he ran off with the skin, and she followed him home. He hid the skin. He promised her he would return it if she'd be his wife for a year."

"Did he give it back to her?"

"Of course not. But she found it, eventually, and put it on, and galloped back into the forest, never to be seen again."

"Is that what happened? Did you hide my skin?"

I smiled. "Perhaps."

She shuddered. "You *have* put some kind of spell on me . . . I'm not sure I like it."

"If I have, I'm only returning the favour."

She looked at me curiously.

"That first day in the clinic. You put something in my coffee, I guess. Maybe that's why it tasted so vile."

She laughed. "God, I thought you were such a prick."

"I know. An American know-it-all. I don't blame you, I was pretty overbearing."

Well she was right, wasn't she Samantha? I was overbearing . . . but she was falling in love with me, however reluctantly. And when she left me the next day, there was a spring in her step and a light in her eye that had been absent when she'd come to my door.

Before she left, we had a conversation, seemingly perfectly innocent. But it marked the beginning of a fatal sequence of events . . .

Chapter 11

SAM drives away thinking about James's last words . . . *A pretty remarkable big sister.* Did Melissa really tell him that? She has no recollection of being remarkable. She recalls – what? Standing in the middle of a supermarket with a shopping list and a feeling that all the towers of tins were cascading in on her . . . or skulking in the corner at a PTA meeting after a kindly "fellow parent" had asked her what standard she was in . . . or running out into the garden when Melissa couldn't stop vomiting, screaming abuse at her parents for leaving her with this appalling responsibility. And feeling convinced that she'd somehow brought about her parents' death, because she'd always secretly believed she'd be a much better mother to Melissa than Daphne was, and this was some cosmic payback for her temerity.

Come to think of it, much the same age and displaying much the same parental ineptitude as Dylan.

She was twenty-four when she became Melissa's guardian, and still bent on pursuing a lifestyle as annoying to her parents as possible in an old miner's cottage in Crown Mines. With Pete, Ziggy, Nomonde and a skinny redheaded nymphomaniac called Yolanda. All fabulously dedicated (when they weren't too stoned) to the overthrow of the apartheid regime (first) and capitalist fascist imperialism (thereafter).

A high old life, mostly – high on anything and everything. Still, by 1986 things were beginning to unravel, what with the government's "emergency" laws and its inclination to treat even its mildest opponents as treasonous. At the point at which her parents' aeroplane fell out of the sky, Sam's household had been shocked into some sobriety by Nomonde's detention; Sam herself was working for a group that ran drama workshops for township youth – hardly a blazing threat to the establishment, but seditious enough to attract the attention of bored security policemen on a quiet day in the office.

It was obvious that being Melissa's guardian would require some self-reinvention. Her Crown Mines house was, in their Aunt Rose's parlance, "distinctly insalubrious". Even Sam could see that: Ziggy's rent boys . . . Nomonde's detention . . . occasional raids by the security police. And that awful truck-driver boyfriend of Yolanda's who looked as though he'd be more than willing to sling a leg over a thirteen year old.

So she'd dutifully moved back into her parents' Johannesburg house. But as soon as she'd carried her sleeping bag and Pink Floyd record collection through the front door she was gripped by the panicky restlessness that always possessed her when she was there.

"I can't do this," she'd whispered, as she prowled the corridors late at night, trying to dodge the ghosts that leapt from every panelled doorway – her father's stern and bracing, brooking no such nonsense; her mother's with a small resigned smile, anticipating failure.

Two weeks after their parents' funeral, as she sat watching Melissa painstakingly colour in her biology diagrams for school, maddened by the way her green crayon refused to stray over the lines, she'd said, "Let's go and live somewhere else."

"Where?"

"I don't know. We'll just drive until we find somewhere we like."

Melissa colluded in this act of insanity, as usual. She was always a willing co-conspirator, despite her natural inclination to a measured life. Always ready to follow Sam into whatever mad prank she devised. She left the security of her neat room with its posters of wild horses galloping through a river, Bruce Springsteen dancing in the dark, Che Guevara in red and black (a present from Sam on her thirteenth birthday, when Sam decided that the Abba poster simply had to go), and the framed Desiderata calligraphed in crisp black letters on faux parchment.

They did not go placidly, however, but somewhat noisily and

hastily – flinging things at random into Fergus's station wagon (including his smelly old springer spaniel called Berty) and driving out amidst the early traffic into the smoky Highveld dawn with Bruce Springsteen blaring (*born to ru-u-n*) and Berty farting relentlessly on the back seat. They were in the grip of a mad hysteria, delighting in this defiance of their parents' authority, perhaps because defying their authority somehow allowed them the illusion that their parents were still there to exert it.

They drove around for four days, staying in the motels that would tolerate Berty, winding up, inevitably, at Cedar Hills. As they bumped down the darkening dirt road through the kloof, Sam knew she was doing everything wrong. Melissa was beginning to get a brittle light about her, as if she might spontaneously combust at any moment. But Sam felt powerless to stop it. She seemed to have lost her grip on how people construct their lives – she'd had a texture and a rhythm that sustained her in some kind of purposeful existence. But it had all blown away as swiftly and completely as a footprint in the sand.

It is hard to imagine it now, Sam thinks, as she cautiously negotiates the bends along Constantia Nek. Had she really been that wild, reckless person? How'd she shrunk into this timid ghost – too fearful half the time to even walk out of her front door?

Cedar Hills, when they'd arrived, had been shrouded in darkness – the electricity had been cut off by a storm the previous week. The storm had also blown in a window, and the lounge was a mess of leaves and twigs and broken glass and sodden carpet. Sam located paraffin lanterns but no paraffin, and there were few candles. The wood was damp, and they had no kindling with which to start a fire. She'd felt bewildered by her lack of preparedness – her father had always drummed into her the list of basic items one took to Cedar Hills. It was as if she had not journeyed there consciously, but had been blown in on some inclement wind, like the bedraggled little robin they'd found dead beneath the broken window.

"Even this house hates us now," whispered Melissa, as they

sat shivering in sleeping bags around a single candle, eating cold baked beans out of the tin. "It's a one-person house. It can only love Dad. It never even loved Mom, did it?"

And Sam had remembered her mother standing in front of the window that now gaped broken toothed in the rain, screaming at her father, "God, this place is a coffin. How do you expect me to survive here? You should have married a bloody Hottentot."

"Oh, Milly, don't say that," Sam begged. "This house loves us all. You'll see. Tomorrow everything will be fine."

Melissa began sobbing. "It hates us. It blames us for their deaths. It always felt safe here . . . now it's so empty. I can't feel them here, oh God, I can't feel them. They're just nowhere . . . they're nowhere in the world."

* * *

And so they travelled to Cape Town, and Maddie helped them, in her own haphazard and inimitable way, to stick themselves back onto the surface of the earth. They sold the Johannesburg house and bought a small Victorian semi in Gardens, found a school for Melissa and a job teaching English for Sam. They watched each other closely for signs of disintegration, and did their best to hide their own distress. Melissa couldn't admit to missing her parents in case Sam thought she found her inadequate as a guardian. And Sam couldn't admit to missing them in case Melissa thought she resented having to look after her. So they navigated the stormy seas of apartheid's dying days in a haze of mutual delusion, secretly congratulating themselves for each day that passed without disaster. There was no room, after all, on their shaky little craft, for anything as brutal and explosive as honesty.

Is that true, Milly? Sam asks now, as she winds down the narrow road into Hout Bay, past the old olive orchards and the historic oaks nudging the passing traffic. Was it all balderdash?

Oh Sammy, sighs Melissa. *It was nothing like that. We had such adventures. Stupid romantic movies, sunset picnics, catching the train to the beach. We were the happiest orphans in the world.*

But I was supposed to keep you safe, Milly. To protect you from ill winds and evil eyes, from malice, maladies and melancholy. From adversity, calamity, catastrophe, hornets' nests, thin ice, ruination and despair. I was supposed to keep you safe, and I failed.

You kept me from loneliness. You kept me from self-doubt. I just wish I'd been able to do the same for you.

But Sam doesn't hear this last part. For there were certain things, even when she'd been alive, that Melissa could never make Sam understand.

* * *

An hour later, Sam is in her driveway and Khaya is back. He's back! She hugs him tightly, relishing the press of his wiry arms around her neck, breathing in his smell. She can smell Elandskloof on him – the sun, the dust, the river water. She can smell it, and the scent brings such a wave of nostalgia that she thinks she might faint.

"Hey, you're squashing me." Khaya wriggles free and runs to Mimsy to give her an equally passionate hug. Richard watches them disdainfully from the garden wall.

She tells Dylan about her meeting with James later that evening, after Khaya has gone to bed. She is curious to see whether James's antipathy to him is mutual.

"What did he want to meet you for?" Dylan asks suspiciously.

"He wanted to find out if I was selling Cedar Hills."

"Are you serious? For that bloody leopard sanctuary of his?"

Sam nods. "I'd have thought you'd be in favour of it?"

"Christ no, he's just trying to fuck up the Elandskloof wilderness process. I bet he doesn't give two shits for the leopards. How can he care about leopards when he's into genetic modification?"

"Genetic *modification*? Whatever makes you think he's into genetic modification? He told me he was doing plant breeding."

"He's a microbiologist. From Berkley. Obviously he's into genetic modification."

"Dylan, your logic is hard to follow sometimes. Anyway, he said he'd given that up."

Dylan gives a hollow laugh. "I bet he has. I don't suppose he told you why, though."

"What is that supposed to mean?"

"He was totally discredited, that's what. I heard that he was fired because he'd been found to have plagiarised his research and falsified results. He's a snake, Sam. You can't trust him further than you can spit."

"He worked with Melissa, didn't he? What did she think of him?"

A painful spasm crosses Dylan's face. "She thought he was a big fat wanker," he says bitterly.

Sam says nothing. She regrets raising the matter. She realises that she'd wanted to lay it all to rest, that she'd hoped that Dylan's reaction would suggest that James was some harmless, dull work colleague of Melissa's who'd once looked after their dog. But there'd been something horribly like jealousy in Dylan's tone, and she doesn't want to know what's behind it.

Whatever it is, Dylan clearly has no more fondness for James than James has for Dylan. And frankly, dear Mimsy, Sam tells her dog as she takes her into the garden later that night, I don't want to know any more about it. Some silly boy thing. Melissa would never have been attracted to James, and if Dylan thought she might be, then he's an even bigger twit than I thought he was.

* * *

Sam watches with palpable relief as Dylan's bakkie heads down the road the next morning. She looks down at Khaya's small blond head beside her as he hops from one foot to the other because he refused to wear slippers and the tar still holds the chill of the winter's morning. He's back, and he's all hers, and he is wonderful beyond words.

"Let's have porridge!" she cries gaily, and swings him over her shoulder in a fireman's lift while he shrieks with delight.

"Yay, yay, porridge, I'm upside down," he sings, kicking his heels and squirming wildly so that for a moment she thinks she might drop him.

"Don't be so wild, child."

"I'm a wild child, I'm a wild child!" he sings, squirming even more.

But twenty minutes later, when she sets the steaming bowl of oatmeal before him, he pushes it away violently so that it skates across the kitchen table, and would have smashed to the floor if Sam hadn't caught it.

"Hey!" she says. "Why did you do that?"

He glares at her, his face a picture of mulish rage. "Don't want porridge!"

"Why? It's lovely. Look, I wrote K for Khaya in syrup. I know, let's give some to Hanky. I'll make him an H for Hanky, see?" Sam babbles away, hastily ladling out another bowl, and scrawling an H in shiny golden syrup over its surface.

"You stupid lady!" Khaya shouts. "Can't you see Hanky's not even here?"

"Don't call me stupid, Khaya. What do you mean he's not here? I can see him sitting right there."

"You can't see him, dummy. 'Cos he's not there. Liar, liar, your pants are on fire . . . you big fat bum."

"Khaya! Stop being so rude. What's got into you? If Hanky's not here, where is he?"

"He can't come back," Khaya wails. "He growed and growed and now he's too big to fit here!"

He leaps up, flings Hanky's porridge on the floor, and runs out of the room sobbing.

Sam stares after him, repressing the tide of fury shooting up her spine, and sets about picking shards of ceramic out of the sticky mess of porridge, while pushing Mimsy's eager nose out of the way.

"It's all Dylan's fault," she mutters.

But she knows it isn't. She knows all too well what Khaya is talking about – how hard it is to buckle yourself back into the constraints of city life after the limitless space and light and silence of Elandskloof. How the buildings seem to crowd in on you, determined to block your eye's natural trajectory to the horizon. How the sight of small plants struggling through paving makes you feel as if it is your own body, and not the earth's, that is being suffocated by tar and concrete. How the clatter of traffic and helicopters and lawnmowers and the whole relentless march of machinery batters your ears and ricochets round your skull. How people seem to pour out from every crevice, until they feel like an alien species that will trample you into the ground if you falter even for an instant.

She knows because she has been there a hundred times, each time she'd returned to the city after visiting Cedar Hills. Because now that the gates of Cedar Hills are locked to her, she feels permanently stranded in this state of claustrophobia and fear, with no hope of escape.

She scrapes up the lumpy mess of porridge with paper towel, and walks to the scullery for a bucket of water and a cloth. As she throws the paper towel into the bin, her eye is caught by a photograph on the fridge that Dylan has given her of Khaya at Elandskloof. He is leaping off a rock into the water at Smitskraal, wearing nothing but a Batman cloak that billows up behind him. The same cliff that she and Melissa had jumped off so often, holding hands and shouting with joy, daring each other to try the higher ledges. The water below is deep and still, reflecting with perfect clarity the red, rugged cliffs above, the flying boy, the sky and distant mountains. The sun flashes on his naked skin. He is so free, flying through the air with elation and terror, suspended forever in a moment of total abandon. A wild child in a wild place. A world apart from the bewildered, shuttered boy who so often awaits her when she picks him up from school.

Sam sinks into a chair, and rests her face in her hands. "Oh God, Milly," she whispers, "I'm really fucking this up, aren't I?"

But Melissa doesn't answer her. The kitchen is silent, save for the sound of Khaya's sobs from his room, and the distant drone of a chainsaw clearing forests for Hout Bay's latest gated community.

Chapter 12
Confession of a Killer

IT was while we were having breakfast the next morning that Melissa told me about Aletta's rash. It was the first time I'd heard Aletta's name. It would not be the last.

"She's one of the babies on the programme," Melissa explained while eating the papaya and mango slices that I'd prepared for her. I was finding it hard to concentrate on what she was saying, because of the way the light caught the skin on her throat when she swallowed. I leant over and kissed away the mango juice that was running down her chin.

"She's one of my favourites, actually," she continued. "Partly because she's so utterly appealing – all eyes and incredibly lush, curly hair, and a face that never seems to stop smiling. But we also have a long-standing connection to the family. Her grandfather lives at Cedar Hills, up in that wattle-and-mud house behind the koppie. He keeps an eye on the place when we're not there – he's been there forever, since long before my parents died. I used to play with her mother, Jasmine, when we were kids.

"Anyway, Aletta spent last weekend with us because I was on call, and Khaya's usual child minder wasn't around so Jasmine came to keep an eye on him. On Monday morning she asked me to look at Aletta because she'd developed a rash and a bit of diarrhoea. So I was wondering, do you think it's related to the formula?"

I reluctantly pulled myself away from contemplating her throat, and applied myself to the question.

"It may be an allergy. It's disappointing if it is, because we've bred the soy to eliminate the major allergenic protein. But there are other minor allergens, although it's rare for anyone to react to them. Have you recorded the details?"

"Yes, but it's odd. She's been on the formula for five months. Why would she only start reacting now?"

"That is strange . . . it's probably unrelated then – perhaps if she was staying with you, her mother used different soap or something."

"That wouldn't account for the diarrhoea, though."

"No, I guess not. Did you take her off the formula?"

"Yes, she's gone onto a dairy-based formula, and she seems to be okay now. It's a bit unnerving, though . . . the possibility that I might be giving them something that could harm them. There's nothing else in that formula that could be a problem, is there?"

"No, of course not. And if there was, you'd have seen signs by now. I think it was probably unrelated – if she's fine now, then I'd stop worrying about it."

There you are. That was it. An innocent little conversation. Quite dull, in fact. It went out of my mind almost instantly. Isn't it strange how so many of the momentous moments in our lives are predicated on such trivia?

Later that day we lay naked across my bed, in the slatted afternoon light, and I told her the story of a fisherman who had cast his net, and pulled in the skeleton of a woman.

"He was horrified by the hollow sockets of her eyes, her grinning teeth, by the worms crawling through her skull. He tried to throw her back, but she clung to him with bony fingers. He ran home, but she followed him, clanking after him with a dreadful clatter of bones. He slammed the door, but she slipped through the window and lay beside him.

"Sometime in the night, he began to think about this skeleton, about the poor drowned girl it had been, and began to weep for her. When he awoke in the morning, a beautiful young woman lay beside him. He had restored her with his tears."

"What macabre stories you tell," she said. "Stolen skins, and skeletons . . ."

"Are you afraid of skeletons?" I asked. "We all have them. Here, and here . . ." I traced the contours of her bones beneath her skin – the rippled ridges of her ribs, the rounded humps of her knees; the heart-shielding sternum, the hollow sockets of her eyes.

"It is the bones that make us interesting, don't you think? The hidden bones of our dark secrets. That is the message of the story," I added, kissing each cupped wing of her pelvis. "It is only when we embrace the bones of each other's darkness that we can have true love."

"You believe in love?"

"Of course. What else is there to believe in?"

She sighed. "I have no secrets from you. I told you everything. How did you make me tell you everything?"

"Because you knew I was not afraid."

"What about your hidden bones?" she asked. "Should I be afraid?"

"Ah, that is the tricky thing. Only you can know if you should be afraid. And you can only find that out by discovering them – but then it may be too late. You see, there is another fairy story that teaches us a different lesson – the story of Bluebeard. Do you know that one? He murdered his wife, and hid her in a room – hung her up on a hook. And then he married another girl, and told her she could go anywhere in the house, but she must never open that door."

"But she did?"

"Of course. When he came home, he could see by the blood on her hands that she'd found his secret. So he murdered her too. And the next twelve wives. They could never stop themselves opening that door. I think the last one escaped."

"But Bluebeard probably would have killed her anyway. So what killed her was trusting Bluebeard, not unearthing his secret . . ."

"Not necessarily. Some secrets are only dangerous if they are discovered."

She shuddered. "I don't trust secrets," she said. "Or ghosts, or skeletons, or things shrouded in mystery . . ."

"Then you don't like humans. We all have secrets – and usually guard them most fiercely from ourselves."

"Perhaps I don't like humans," she sighed. "Perhaps I like simpler things, like rocks and sky . . ."

"Nothing is simple, Melissa. The simplicity is only a function of your limits of perception. You can choose to make people simple if you refuse to see what lies behind their masks. But you're fooling yourself if you think anything or anyone exists that can be understood only on one plane."

"How do you know so much about fairy stories? Did your parents read them to you?"

I laughed at that. The only literature to be found in my childhood home was my father's beaver magazines and my mother's soft-porn romances.

"No . . . I read a book that analyses fairy tales to help you find the story that narrates your life."

"Do you believe that? I'd never have thought you'd be so whimsical."

"The old fairy tales are hardly whimsical. They're gruesome – and not afraid of delving into the shadows of the human psyche. I guess for that reason they have some insights to offer . . . Humans haven't changed much over the centuries. Our fundamental issues are still the same – and all our stories about the wonders of the world are, in the end, about ourselves. We're a very narcissistic species. Anyway, you should read the book sometime. Its title was what attracted me to it . . . it seems pertinent to you."

"What is it?"

"*Women Who Run with the Wolves.*"

She looked at me with sudden apprehension, then turned away. "I don't want to fall in love with you," she said.

I turned her head towards me, and kissed her slowly. "Nobody's forcing you to, my darling girl. But you might find it more rewarding to run with the wolves than to run away from them . . ."

She slept then, or pretended to. I lay watching the light changing on her body, the flickering of her eyes behind her lids, felt with my lips the dancing pulse at her collar bone, weak-kneed with gratitude that she was here, that all I need do to touch her was reach out my hand. Then I covered her with a blanket and sat beside her, working. Later I woke her with a tray of tea and boiled egg and toast. I watched her eat, watched her shower and dress, gather her belongings, trying to memorise each gesture, to frame and pocket each tiny movement so that I could savour them in the coming days. As she rose to leave, I felt a sudden dread at letting her go.

"It's so far," I said, putting my arms around her, and burying my face in her hair. The smell of her, the warmth of her body against mine . . . how could I stand to be without it? "Why do you have to live in such a wild and intemperate place?"

"I'm a wild and intemperate girl."

"Seriously, though, don't you find it lonely out there?"

"I did at first. I thought I'd go quite mad there. Sometimes just my breathing sounded like a howl of insanity. I'd run from room to room yelling, as if I could fill up the house with noise. But the silence afterwards was even worse.

"The space is good for me, though. I have lots of time to think. And I have Mimsy, and Khaya half the time, and when he's there his child minder stays in the house. And I get the odd visitor. Jannie comes around, or Kobus Koekemoer's neurotic wife."

"Jannie?"

"Jannie de Vries. He manages the wilderness area. You sound suspicious. Are you jealous?" She grinned at me with her wicked blue eyes.

"Not at all. Should I be?"

"No . . . he's got a girlfriend. Sometimes she comes too, then they get stoned and play guitar and we sit around singing old Bob Dylan songs."

"You don't get stoned?"

"No, I used to with Dylan, but I stopped when I fell pregnant. And ever since then my brain's been far too fragile to challenge it with mind-altering substances."

"I don't like getting stoned any more either," I said. "I'm scared of what might come running out of the woods."

"Well aren't we such goody-two-shoes? Or are we just cowards?"

"I have some creative suggestions for how to be bad and daring," I said. "If you'd like to come into the bedroom with me I could show you."

"Mr McIntyre, I'm shocked. What kind of girl do you take me for? Now I am going home, sir, and there is nothing you can do to stop me."

Sadly, she was right. I watched her car until it was out of sight, then turned and walked back into my empty house, Melissa's concerns about Aletta already long forgotten.

Chapter 13

THE weeks pass. Cape Town sinks knee-deep into winter, hunching its shoulders against the driving rain and wind. The mountain retreats behind a bank of cloud, tormenting Capetonians with the illusion that they aren't special after all, that they live in a dull, mountainless city like the rest of humanity. Each day, Sam drives home through the gusting squalls, running the miserable gauntlet of traffic-light panhandlers huddling numb-toed in the debris of passing cars, resisting the urge to load them into her car and drive them home for a hot bath. She knows, of course, that such kind impulses will inevitably end badly – being ripped off or inconvenienced way beyond her comfort zone. So instead she buys the jokes-for-change and *The Big Issue* and an occasional beaded bug, and otherwise grips her steering wheel and stares grimly ahead, willing the light to change.

On a bank in her garden, the aloes flare into bloom, reminding her of those that glow like coals on the slopes above Cedar Hills, or loom on its mountain ridges, silhouetted against the pearly winter sky like the scouts of an invading army.

"You should run away from here," she tells them as she passes on her walk from the gate with the morning paper. "This is no place for you. I'll open the gate, so you can run back to where you belong. Quickly, before it's too late."

But the aloes just wave their spiky arms at her wistfully, as rooted to the ground as she is.

Khaya settles into a reluctant routine. He returns to school at the end of the holiday with an air of resignation, and fewer battles over clothes. But his persistent efforts to persuade her to take him back to Elandskloof tug at Sam's heart. Apparently, he is obliged to a tadpole called Sneeze, whom he'd left in the stream that runs below Cedar Hills.

"I need to go and visit him very soon," he informs her earnestly.
"Okay, well, you can go again sometime."
"After breakfast?"
"No, another time."
"When?"
"I don't know, Khaya, sometime, okay?"

Whereupon he retreats to a corner and mutters to his woollen elephant. "Some people," he remarks, glaring in her direction, "just don't *care* about tadpoles' feelings."

But Sam shuts her ears, forcing herself indeed not to care about tadpoles or fish eagles or any other creature that might dwell in the Elysian plains of Elandskloof. She plods about her daily routine, enduring the evening traffic and Khaya's tantrums and Mr Potgieter's sneering tyranny with a kind of desperate obstinacy, hoping to somehow respin the suffocating but safe cocoon in which she has shrouded herself since Melissa's death. And perhaps she might have succeeded, despite Khaya's efforts, had it not been for Chrissie's letter.

* * *

It arrives at her office one morning in mid-August, when the rain has lifted briefly but the sky remains a dull pewter. The letter is waiting to ambush her amongst a slew of banal correspondence pertaining to copyright permissions and authors' contracts. There is nothing at all on the envelope to suggest it is anything other than yet another dull request or statement of information, and Sam is halfway through reading it before she quite grasps what it is saying.

Dear Samantha
You may remember me, or my family at least – we lived on Rooikrantz farm next to Cedar Hills until we were moved from there in 1973.

I am writing to you on behalf of my mother – Mariah. She used to run the clinic with your dad.

You may have heard that we have finally won our land claim, and we will be taking possession of the land on September 21. This is the day of the meeting in Elandskloof to discuss the future of the farms there, and to discuss the department's proposals to enlarge the nature reserve in that area – I am sure that, as a landowner, you are aware of these.

The thing is, my family is very confused about the decisions they need to make in this regard, and my mother is anxious to hear what you think about it. She is also very keen that you come to the celebration for the return of our land, which will be held on the same day, as she is very grateful to your father for the help he gave us at that time, and would like to thank you personally as the representative of the Campbell family.

I do hope that you do not find this a difficult request, as my mother will be sadly disappointed if you cannot come. She asked me to ask you, as she believed that you would be more willing to listen to me. I will be there too, and would like to see you again after all this time.

Yours truly,
Chrysanthemum Stuurman

Chrysanthemum. Chrysanthemum Stuurman and Sam the *bitteraalwyn* – the bitter aloe. Two flowers of Elandskloof who once flourished in the same garden until they found themselves uprooted and stranded on different sides of what seemed like an insurmountable wall.

The last time she saw Chrissie was in 1975 – two years after their eviction – in the Cash & Carry at Willowdale. Sam had been looking for a decent paintbox, scanning with little hope the small collection of wax crayons, chalks, plastic paintbrushes and notebooks, when she glanced up and saw Chrissie watching her. Her almond eyes were challenging as always, but also apprehensive. They'd stared at each other, locked into a moment of wordless confrontation, then Chrissie had opened her mouth to speak. But Samantha simply lacked the courage to hear whatever it was she had to say. She'd turned abruptly, grabbing something off the shelf to authenticate the charade that she'd found what she needed. She paid at the till with lowered eyes and burning cheeks. Tienie Fransman took her money, her gaze roving the shop because, Sam knew, she was checking to see if Chrissie was stealing something. And in an act of futile solidarity with her spurned friend, Sam stole something herself, lifting a small pink sharpener off the rack next to the till, unseen by Tienie who was too busy eyeing Chrissie.

When she got out of the store, she looked at what she'd bought: a small notebook with a painting of two kittens playing with a ball of wool on the cover. The only honourable option would be to wait for Chrissie and give her the notebook and the sharpener . . . But she didn't. She walked quickly to her father's car and lay down on the back seat to wait for him, digging the sharpener into the palm of her hand as hard as she could to try to drown out the flood of shame in her chest.

Sam drops the letter and walks to the window. A tiny portion of Table Mountain's flinty face is visible, almost squeezed out by Cape Town's modest crop of skyscrapers – the flat, ugly slab of the Civic Centre, the Shell and ABSA tower blocks. To her right, the long, army-green flank of Signal Hill broods over the city beneath a leaden sky.

She presses her forehead against the suicide-proof glass, and stares at the human beetles scurrying about fifteen storeys below. The air closes in on her. She imagines grabbing something – her computer perhaps – and lobbing it through the glass, flooding her office with oxygen and driving out the stale, man-made fibre and dirty feet smelling fog she must breathe. Instead, she grabs her bag and the letter and marches out of the office, barking some official-sounding pretext for her departure to the feng shui brigade filing their nails in reception.

Outside, the air is sharp and clean, blown clear by recent strong winds, and carrying the salty tang of the Atlantic. She walks to the parking lot and liberates her car from the sour clutches of the parking attendant, then threads her way through the early afternoon traffic to the Waterfront, parking beyond the V&A so that she can walk along the pier. She strides out on the concrete strip, relishing the crash of the waves against the concrete dolosse and the keening of the seagulls that wheel above her.

But Samantha's eyes are turned inward, as she finds herself back in the field with the dead donkeys, on the day that everything had changed in Elandskloof.

* * *

It was a week after Christmas, ten days before Sam turned eleven. One of those glowering summer days, when the air coats your lungs like hot, sticky toffee, and the leaves fry in the trees, and the whole landscape shimmers with the shrill chorus of cicadas.

Sam came upon them by chance, as she rode Oneway past Oom Hennie's lucerne field, and found a knot of Stuurmans standing at the gate, talking in hushed whispers. She reined in her horse, scrambled off, and approached the group. Stompie nodded to her briefly, but otherwise they ignored her, which was ominous enough in contrast to their usual friendliness. She looked past them to the field. Chrissie was kneeling beside two dark mounds – she thought they were piles of earth for a moment, and then realised they weren't.

They were donkeys.

She tied Oneway to the gate, and walked slowly across the field.

"What's wrong with them?" she called to Chrissie. "Are they sick? Did they eat too much?"

Chrissie glanced up, but didn't reply. Then she saw the bloodied holes. Ishmael had two – one in his neck, one in his head. Isaac had three, all in his chest. Big purplish splats of blood smeared the grass, like squashed mulberries. Their eyes were open. Sam stared at them, shocked at their opaque emptiness.

She sank to her knees next to Chrissie, who was stroking Isaac's ears.

"Baas Hennie," said Chrissie, abruptly. "He killed them."

Sam stared at the donkeys, taking in the brown dusty fur, speckled with bits of lucerne . . . the lips drawn back slightly from the teeth . . . the fur standing up in slick red spikes around the bullet holes. Her eyes skittered away from the holes, especially the one in Ishmael's head, because it was just above his eye and amongst the black blur of flies you could see pinkish-gray stuff oozing out and bits of white bone. She felt vomit shooting up her gullet. She retched, but nothing came out. Chrissie glared at her, furiously, as if it were she who'd pulled the trigger.

Raised voices made them look back to the gate, where Oom Hennie was now standing, locked in a noisy altercation with Stompie and Reggie and various other members of the Stuurman clan. Sam looked at the rifle cocked under Hennie's arm, and suddenly imagined him lifting it and spraying bullets into the Stuurmans, into Oneway, Chrissie, herself – into every living thing within his range. She leapt up and ran to Oneway, scrambling onto him as he took off as if hyenas were after him, with Sam clinging to his neck.

She half climbed, half fell off him as he clattered up her driveway, vomited her breakfast violently into the shrubbery, and then ran into the house shouting, "He's got a gun, he's going to kill everyone."

Fergus wasn't there. Sam's mother, laid low with yet another migraine, staggered out from her room, pale and confused. But when Sam explained, her face hardened with resolve.

"Come on," she said, grabbing her keys and heading for the car. Sam felt a thrill of treacherous excitement. It had been weeks since she'd seen her mother so animated. She felt gratified, as if it were she, and not the death of the donkeys, that had brought her mother back to life.

They were all still standing at the field. Daphne ran up to Oom Hennie, shouting, and grabbed his gun. She threw it on the ground, and screamed at him. He looked deeply embarrassed. Some of the Stuurmans were grinning to see big old Baas Hennie being berated by this small woman in her red and white polka-dot dress. But Sam was mortified – she'd never seen her mother scream like that, with tears running down her red face, her hair awry, dust on her dress. It was even scarier than Ishmael's leaking brain matter.

Then Fergus arrived and led her away, with Hennie shouting after him, "You need to keep your wife under control, Doctor." As if she were a dog.

He followed them to the car, raging on, ". . . been in my lucerne once too often . . . warned those bliksems . . . . sick of their animals running all over my farm . . . breaking fences . . . damaging crops . . . goats eat every damn thing in their path . . . bloody ridiculous, a Hotnot owning a farm . . . got it coming to them."

Sam shut her eyes tight and stuck her fingers in her ears, but Oom Hennie's words still felt like sharp rocks, falling out of the bright blue sky onto her face. A hailstorm of hate. He went on and on, as if he could use these word-stones to build a wall around what he had done, as if he could turn it into something else, something useful or decent. But every word just fell down and left the bodies of the murdered donkeys lying in the field for everyone to see.

* * *

Of course, it really began a week before the donkeys, when Oupa Jan Koekemoer died. And with him the gentleman's agreement that he'd made when he bought his land from great-grandfather Ian Campbell – including the land that wasn't great-grandfather Ian Campbell's to sell. The land that had been occupied by the Stuurmans for as long as anyone could remember. The land that Oupa Jan promised to let them continue to occupy as long as there was breath in his body.

But his son Oom Hennie had no patience with such nonsense. The Stuurmans were "Hotnots" occupying prime farming land, and from the moment the last rattling breath left Oupa Jan's frail chest, their fate was sealed. The shooting of the donkeys was the opening salvo of a war that, at that moment in history, Hennie had no chance of losing.

After the incident, everything seemed to hold its breath in the shimmering dust-blown heat, waiting for the sword to fall. A track of grim-faced visitors knocked on the Campbell's door (the Stuurmans and various farmers in the area, but never Oom Hennie). They gathered in Fergus's study, and Sam sat outside the window amongst the acrid-smelling blackjacks and thorn apple, listening to the sober murmur of voices, trying to decode the ghastly dramas that adults seemed determined to impose on their lives.

"It's a damn disgrace," she told the huge shiny songololos that ponderously crossed the baked earth, like miniature freight trains across the prairies, mouthing the phrases she'd overheard. "Damn disgrace . . . damn disgrace . . ." she sang. The millipedes curled into tight spirals, unimpressed.

The impending disintegration of the Stuurmans' lives was mirrored by the growing madness in Daphne's eyes. She spent her days on her bed with the curtains drawn and a facecloth with blue roses over her face. Grace would take her food, but she seldom ate it, leaving the untouched plates outside the door to gather flies. When Sam spoke to her, she seemed to reply from some great distance, and said obscure and frightening things. "I can hear the wind," she'd say, staring past Sam into some invisible pit of hell. "It blows the dust right through me . . ."

One night Sam heard a strange sound, and found her mother standing in the front room in a white nightdress, banging her head against the window, not hard, but steadily. It was the steady beat of that sound that somehow frightened her most . . . like a war drum portending unknown calamity. The glass shook a little with each blow, so that the moon shining through it seemed to dance. The window was open; the curtains blew around her like swans trying to fold her in their wings.

* * *

It took a week after Ishmael and Isaac's demise for Sam to brave Chrissie again. She chose the day of her eleventh birthday, hoping this might offer some immunity against rejection.

Chrissie was polishing the front steps of their house.

"Can I help?" Sam asked, resting her one foot on the other, and swinging Oneway's reins against her thigh.

"No. You'll make a mess. White girls can't polish."

Sam stood in the morning sun, watching Chrissie's shoulders

moving furiously through the threadbare pink fabric of her dress, and the growing sheen on the red-painted cement floor. Chrissie's dress was tucked into her knickers. Next to her was an open tin of floor polish, its lid bearing a beaming rising sun. There was a long, z-shaped scratch on the back of Chrissie's leg, which would normally offer a good topic for admiration and discussion, but her shaking back offered little encouragement to conversation.

"It's my birthday today," Sam announced, playing her trump card with hopeless desperation.

"So?"

There was a long silence, broken only by the clink of Oneway's harness as he stamped his hooves or shook his head to dislodge the flies. Sam finally slunk away, muttering, "Well, I guess I'd better be going then."

Chrissie did not even look up.

* * *

When Sam came back to Cedar Hills at the end of the first term of boarding school that year, her world had changed. The Stuurmans were gone, save for Bra Piet's family – his wife, Tannie Aletta, and their adult, one-armed son Stompie – who built a *blougombos* house on Cedar Hills and stayed there to help Fergus run the farm. Chrissie Stuurman's stone house was a storage depot for Oom Hennie's fertiliser and insecticide sprays.

Daphne had finally succumbed to that mysterious ailment common to "highly strung" farmers' wives – a "total nervous breakdown" – and was recovering in a clinic in Johannesburg. Fergus's Willowdale practice was suffering sorely because his efforts to help the Stuurmans had branded him as a communist *kaffirboetie*, and he could no longer run the clinic on the Koekemoers' farm. Oneway had been returned to the Koekemoers.

Within three months, Fergus would give up his practice altogether, and move to Johannesburg, going down only for holidays.

Daphne would never go back.

* * *

Sam sits on a concrete dolos, clutching her letter. *Dolos*, she offers to Melissa. *School-shoe brown*, Melissa says, *with a large bottom, and no sense of humour.*

A group of whales has gathered offshore – Sam watches one breach, its great stomach rising out of the water before it crashes to the side, sending a wild spray into the air. It rears out of the water three times, and then flips upside down and presents her with its y-shaped tail. *No wonder they're so pleased with themselves*, she thinks. The biggest things in the deep blue ocean, afloat in a medium that lets you drift through life instead of dragging yourself in defiance of gravity over the unforgiving ground. Whatever had possessed humanity's antecedents to leave the comfort of the sea?

She rereads the letter. What is its tone? Diffident? Hostile? Snide? Sarcastic? *You may remember me* . . . Brisk, probably. Yes, brisk and businesslike, and, as the Chrissie of yore, brooking no argument. Of course, no normal person *would* argue. They'd be flattered. They'd return the letter to its envelope, and begin making sensible arrangements at once to ensure that they honoured the request of an elderly woman who'd served her community with unfailing dedication and had been sorely abused by history. Sam tries to picture herself milling amongst the Stuurman crowd: Tant Aletta and Oom Piet – no, hold on, they'd both passed on – Stompie, who still lived at Cedar Hills, Sister Mariah. Chrissie's father, Reggie, who'd taught at the local farm school at Kleinspruit, with his owl-like spectacles and invetcratc brown suit . . .

Oh God, who is she fooling? She can never go there. Drive those passes? What a joke. It's hard enough driving over Constantia Nek. It was, as James said, *untenable.*

She pictures the deep ravine in the red rock that guards the entrance to Elandskloof from the west. *Die Slot*, it is called. The Keyhole. When she drove away from there with the motherless Khaya three-and-a-half years ago she'd thrown away the key. If she tries to pass through Die Slot now, she is sure she'll be met by an impenetrable wall of rock.

But Chrissie has asked her. Chrissie has swallowed her considerable pride, and, for the sake of her mother, has asked her. Sam feels the pink sharpener digging into her flesh. Oh Christ, she says to the seagull perched on a dolos and eyeing her speculatively, I'm going to do it again, aren't I? I'm going to turn my back on Chrissie and walk away. There is nothing I can do about it.

The seagull gives a derisive shriek and lifts into the air, hovering over her for a moment before flying away. Sam sighs, crumples the letter into her pocket, and turns to walk reluctantly back to her obligations.

* * *

As the days pass, Sam persists in doing nothing about it. Beyond her steadfast inertia, Cape Town sticks its head out from under the wet winter bedclothes and experiments with brief, tantalising flashes of spring before retreating under a blanket of cloud again. The ancient oaks on Hout Bay Main Road sprout a fuzz of apple green as new leaves begin to uncurl; the ericas and pelargoniums on the slopes of the Karbonkelberg blaze pink, purple and yellow. A pair of hadedas build a nest in her garden – a great shambling thing of loose sticks and leaves – and the mother hadeda sits on her eggs, peering over the curve of her enormous beak with lugubrious dedication, while her mate honks out to the world in pride.

And still she does nothing. She tries, a few times, to write to Chrissie to explain why she cannot go. But she simply can't find the words to explain the choking bubble of unspoken sorrow that clouds her brain whenever she thinks of the place. She cannot even conjure up a plausible lie. When an official invitation to the meeting arrives from the Department of Environmental Affairs, she drops it in the bin. When Dylan comes for his monthly visit, he makes a valiant effort to engage her on the matter.

"Did you get the invitation to the meeting?"
"Yes."
"Are you planning to go?"

"No."

"'Cos otherwise you can write a letter expressing your views . . . or I can convey these to the meeting . . ."

"I don't have views."

"Don't you think –"

"No."

And even Dylan lacks the nerve to pursue it.

* * *

September comes and Cape Town preens its feathers in the morning sun of a rash of glorious, balmy days. Seagulls swoop in cerulean skies and blossoms blaze white on garden fruit trees like freshly fallen snow, and even the most humble patches of ground lining the highways become carpets of small wild flowers. Khaya's school hosts a "pirates" picnic in Tokai Forest, an event he approaches with his customary disgruntled suspicion. But Sam is determined to make him enjoy it to disprove Maddie's assertions that she is imposing her own social ineptitude on the boy, and even agrees to accompany him.

"C'mon, Khaya, it'll be fun," she says hopefully, trying to conjure up some enthusiasm by drawing swashbuckling stubble on his soft cheeks with an eyebrow pencil, and tucking a wooden cutlass into his belt.

"'Snot fun," he mumbles, delivering a Captain Hook glare to his reflection. "Nina hurts my ears 'cos she screams so loud and Rory pushes me. And pirates are yukky. Why can't I be Batman?"

So the ubiquitous Batman cloak gets thrown over the pirate ensemble, and Sam endures two hours of sipping warm orange squash in the windy forest and trying to find things to say to the other mothers, while Khaya hides behind a tree and refuses to hunt treasure or sing sea shanties, preferring to dig holes in the pine needles with his cutlass. ("He's a rather *unusual* little boy, isn't he," smirks Rory's mother. "Have you had him assessed?") Nina's shrieks are indeed an assault on the ear, and as Sam's smile freezes on her face she's forced to concede secretly that the outing is "'snot fun" at all.

In the weeks that follow the picnic, Chrissie's letter lurks on the kitchen counter where she's left it, silently reproaching her whenever it catches her eye. It seems to gather even more in reproach after acquiring a ring from Precious's teacup and a smear of Marmite. And the more she ignores it, the harder it becomes to respond.

* * *

Nine days before the Elandskloof meeting, the phone rings just as she has collapsed in front of *The Thin Blue Line,* having finally cajoled Khaya into slumber.

"Hi, it's James McIntyre here. How're ya doing?"

Fuck. Why did she answer the phone?

"Oh, hi. Fine."

There is a moment's silence, then Sam blurts out: "I haven't decided about Cedar Hills, if that's what you're phoning about."

He laughs. "You're not a great believer in social niceties, are you, Ms Campbell?"

Sam laughs too, a bit abashed. "Sorry. I just thought you should know. I didn't want to waste your time."

"Or yours, no doubt. But actually, I was phoning to find out if you were coming to the department's jamboree on the twenty-first."

"Oh God, not you too . . ."

"Why? Who else has asked you?"

"Oh, well Dylan, and I also got a letter from Chrissie Stuurman asking me to go."

"Chrissie Stuurman? Well, then I take it you're coming?"

"What do you mean?"

"Samantha, you don't say no to Chrissie Stuurman. Even you aren't that contrary."

"Do you know Chrissie?" Sam asks, surprised.

"Yes, indeed. I had a meeting with her some time back, because I thought the Stuurmans might be willing to sell their land to the leopard project once their claim was settled – and she seems to be the spokesperson for the family. Boy, was I put in my place!"

"Where did you meet her?" Sam asks, despite herself. She is trying to conjure up a mental image of James and Chrissie meeting, but all she can picture is a young girl with cornrow braids standing on the top of the koppie above Cedar Hills shouting, "I'm the king of everything I see and everyone else is a *domkop spinnekop*!"

Actually, come to think of it, James and Chrissie are rather alike.

"In Paris."

"*Paris?*"

"Yeah, she's working for the United Nations in resource development. Didn't you know that? I was travelling in Europe, trying to raise funds for the leopards."

"Wow, she's come a long way!"

"Hasn't she? I'm not surprised, though. She's very formidable. So she actually asked you to come to this thing?"

"Yes, well . . . her family and mine share a lot of rather tricky history."

"Really? But then you must come, you know. You'll regret it if you don't."

"What do *you* know about it?"

He gives a small, bitter laugh. "Oh, I know about regrets, Samantha. That is one thing I do know about."

There is a silence. What does she say to that? Goodbye, probably. But something keeps her there.

"Well, I take it *you* are going?" she says, not that she particularly cares, but just to fill up the empty spaces.

"I suppose. It'll be a bit of group jerk-off, I imagine. At least, some people will be having their wires pulled and some people will be having their legs pulled. But I guess I should check it out."

Sam tries to suppress the image that this invokes. "That doesn't exactly inspire me to pack my bags and rush over there."

"Yeah? Would anything I say make you rush over here? Frankly, I don't really care either way. I'm just passing the evening. It gets kinda quiet out here."

There is another silence. This conversation is drowning her.

What the fuck does he expect? She listens to him breathing. *Say goodbye and put the bloody phone down* . . . but then her ears catch another sound – an odd, rhythmic percussion.

"Oh God," she says, "those are the frogs, aren't they?"

"Yep. Springtime, and the frogs are all a-wooin'. Quite something, huh?"

Sam pictures the velvet night, the canopy of stars, the chorus of frogs. She feels sick with longing.

"I've got to go," she mutters.

"At this hour?" he asks baldly. "Where're you going? Clubbing downtown?"

There is an edge of mockery in his voice. Does he *know*, Sam wonders, how she spends her nights holed up in her house, too terrified to move? How few friends she has? *Well, screw you too*, she thinks.

"Goodbye, James," she says firmly, and replaces the receiver.

She sits on the couch, trying to watch TV. But the phone call keeps intruding. Honestly. Phoning her like that. As if she owed him any explanations.

Who does he think he is, Milly? she demands of the photograph of her sister that stands on the mantelpiece – the last photograph Sam took of her. Melissa, Sam and Khaya are sitting in the hammock on the stoep at Cedar Hills. Sam did it with the camera timer, and they are all laughing, caught up with the excitement of getting into place before it clicked. Khaya is naked and chubby on Melissa's lap, holding a bunch of squashed flowers in one hand and reaching behind with his other to curl a lock of her hair around his finger. Melissa has one arm around his stomach, the other around Sam. All three are wearing bedraggled crowns of grass reeds and flowers, which they'd spent the morning making. They look like slightly crazed bucolic sprites. Here today, gone tomorrow, mocking you with their heedless joy, making you weep because of it.

Sam's eyes travel from the photograph around the room. It is like that hadeda nest, she thinks, suddenly appalled. A jumble of garden rubbish. The grey wall-to-wall carpet that came with the house is encrusted with stains, as is the couch and two boxy armchairs. She'd sold most of her furniture to pay for the trip to the US before Melissa died. The stuff she now owns was bought in a haze of grief after arriving back in Cape Town with Khaya. It all comes from one second-hand shop in Hout Bay. The couch is the worst – a great slab of lumpy brocade that lurches drunkenly to port like a worn-out old slapper. It is totally unredeemed by Daphne's striped hairy cushions with tasselled ears that rest unhappily on its threadbare surface like court lap dogs; or the blue Indian cotton "throw" that Maddie has tossed over its back to try to induce some style.

The few ornamental things are jumbled together as if they've just paused on the shelf on their way to a better place – a bowl full of unpaid bills, bits of Lego, lidless koki's, a piece of something that broke. Daphne's prized Dresden statuette of a boy with a calf stands deeply shamed by the half-bottle of cough medicine on one side, and one of Khaya's slippers on the other.

"Oh God, it's shocking, isn't it, Milly? It's the house of a refugee. Why have I never noticed before?"

Don't be so hard on yourself, says Melissa, who is suddenly sitting cross-legged on the floor peeling an apple, the light shining on her hair. *I always arranged our house. How're you supposed to manage without me, you sad old cretin?*

Cretin? Why, you truckle-nosed mongoose.

Splattered puke.

Nose hair.

Filibuster.

Quisling!

MILKSOP! *Here have a piece.*

Sam takes the invisible slice of apple, and bites into the crisp white flesh, closing her eyes to savour the sweet juice in her mouth.

"Milly," she says, without opening her eyes, "what colour is *regret?*"

It is the deepest indigo, says Melissa. *The saddest colour in the world. It is a dark, spiky word, with thorns that dig in your heart and never stop hurting until you stop holding it.*

Samantha snuggles into the unwelcoming lap of the couch

and buries her face in a hairy cushion, hoping to block out the world. She knows that if she opens her eyes Melissa will be gone. So she doesn't.

* * *

Sam has not heeded Chrissie's letter. She has not heeded James's phone call. Indeed, she might still be there, on that lumpy couch, frozen in the deepest indigo of regret, if something extraordinary had not happened.

She is woken by a loud crash some two hours later.

Sam sits up, her heart thumping. *The bad men,* she thinks. *They've come.* She waits for heavy footsteps down the passage. But there is silence. Should she phone armed response? Maybe she should investigate first. She walks cautiously down the passage in pursuit of the sound, sticking her head into Khaya's room on her way. He is sleeping soundly, a tangle of small-boy limbs protruding from his Batman duvet.

She finds it eventually: a shelf in her bedroom closet has apparently spontaneously detached its screws and come crashing down, spewing all its contents out onto the floor.

They lie in a jumble of old jerseys and scarves, photo albums, a tennis racquet, all covered with a strange grey powder. Sam stares at this, perplexed, and reaches out to finger the gritty substance. Then recoils as she realises what it is.

Melissa's ashes.

The box was on her shelf as she and Dylan had decided to wait to scatter them in some kind of ceremony when Khaya was old enough to participate.

Poor Melissa, thinks Sam. She got so sick of sitting on this bloody shelf, in a dark, dark cupboard in a dark, dark room, being peered at periodically by her dark, dark sister, that she summoned up some cosmic force to launch herself into space.

"Really, Milly," she says, "did you have to be so melodramatic?"

Melodramatic? This is nothing, sister! Wait till I'm a full-grown poltergeist. Then I'll really play havoc with your housekeeping – such as it is.

Sam feels a bubble of hysteria bursting out of her, and collapses onto the floor, laughing and weeping until she is exhausted. Mimsy watches her with a worried, faintly disapproving expression, and licks her ear. Sam pulls herself together, and goes to the kitchen in search of a suitable container. The brown cardboard box is all squashed, and she can't bear to shovel Melissa back into it.

Nothing seems right – Tupperware is definitely out, and anything transparent seems grizzly. At last she settles on an old tea tin with pictures of white elephants and Indian princesses – once decked in garish finery but now faded to a soft blur. Melissa had loved it as a child. Sam would tell her stories about the princesses, whom they named Nutmeg and Coriander. Sam can see her now – a small girl with wavy chestnut hair wrapped in Daphne's silk scarves, with a lipstick bindi emblazoned on her forehead, her eyes shining with the gravity and romance of her assumed identity.

Sam takes the tin back with a dustpan and brush, and sweeps up the ashes. The gritty bony chunks are manageable enough, but the grey powder clings persistently to the jerseys and scarves. What can she do with them? Wash them? She shudders at the thought – the last microscopic fragments of Melissa (the remains of her eyelash, or her left toe) swirling through the washing machine, and out into the city's drains, bobbing amongst the turds and condoms of Cape Town's citizens.

Forget it. Instead she goes out onto the moonlit lawn and dances around with them, hoping that the south-easter will blow Melissa's tiny bits to the four corners of the world. Mimsy joins in this game happily enough, but Richard is appalled, and charges furiously up the old yellowwood, hair on end, suffering even more outrage when his scrabby old legs can't support his sagging stomach and he slithers down the trunk in an undignified heap. The wind blows obligingly, setting all the trees and the racing scraps of silver cloud high above into a frenzied tarantella that echoes her lunacy.

She walks back inside feeling drained by this sudden outburst of bizarre euphoria, and sits in the lounge staring at the tin on the coffee table.

"I have to go, don't I, Milly?"
Well, duh!

And Sam – who's done nothing, and done nothing, and done nothing, who's embraced inertia with an almost messianic fervour, who's come within a whisper of losing herself in the dark forever – knows with sudden, painful clarity that it is time to do something. And this urge is so new and surprising that she has no option but to attend to it at once.

When Khaya wakes up and wanders into her room, he finds her busy packing.

"Are we going to Elands?" he asks, for the hundredth time, with little hope.

But this time, to his vast surprise and delight, Sam answers, "Yes."

Chapter 14
Confession of a Killer

DESPITE Melissa's insistence that she did not want to fall in love with me, our relationship grew steadily in the coming weeks. I saw her far too seldom, of course – she'd asked me to keep away when Khaya was there, and I could hardly pop down to Elandskloof after work. But while this frustrated me, I guess it made the time we did have even more precious.

It did not come right all at once. At first, she was often withdrawn or preoccupied, particularly after dropping off Khaya. And I'll admit there were times, when her eyes got that lost look, and her face became a blank mask of apparent indifference, that I wanted to shake her. Partly because of the chill I felt when she was emotionally absent, partly because I sometimes suspected that she was seduced by the power of withholding herself. But I knew that the more I tried to push her out of it, the more she would retreat. So I bit my tongue and forced myself to give her space to be, to sit and read, to go for long walks without talking, to lie beside me with her head on my shoulder and her thoughts somewhere else.

But these times grew less, and as I came to understand her better, I found I could usually make her laugh and make her feel good about herself. As the weeks passed, it seemed to me that I could feel her come back to life under my hands.

Do you remember how the dawn comes to your Cedar Hills garden? How the sun touches everything one by one as it moves over the hill? First, just the coral tree stands in a blaze of light, golden against the dark grass behind it; then the tips of the proteas, then the seed heads of the grass, until the whole hillside is gilded with flecks of light, and finally the giant fig near the river and the cascade of plumbago down the rocks.

Watching the joy creep back into her heart was like watching that. As for me, I'd never felt so content. I felt gratified knowing that I was the one who had brought her back into the light, and I liked the person I was when I was with her. I was . . . kind, I suppose. Mature. Magnanimous. Gracious. Just edgy enough to be sexy, but ultimately solid and trustworthy. Generous enough to be able to deliver her from her own demons, just as she, surely, would deliver me from mine.

It was not hard to slip into this role, because Melissa, once she'd confided in me, was eager to cast me in it. I just had to follow the lead of her expectations and play my part. It felt as if it was all unfolding, the happily-ever-after vision that I'd imagined that first day at the clinic. *This* was the man I wanted to be.

Our happiest times were walking the hills behind Cedar Hills, and we spent many hours exploring them, relishing our encounters with the wild animals and devising plans to save the leopards from blood-thirsty farmers. Mermaid's Pool was one of our most treasured places – I am sitting here now, writing, in the cave with the paintings, looking down on the pool. We didn't know about the rock paintings then – I only discovered those recently. But we could both feel the magic of the place, and when I look down at the water it seems I can almost see her there, sitting on a rock like a river spirit herself, the drops from her wet hair running down her back, her fingers trailing in the water, her secret smile as an iridescent dragonfly alights briefly on her bended knee.

It was here, as we lay together on the banks after swimming, that she lightly traced a circle around the scar beneath my eye and said, "Where does this come from?"

I shivered at her touch. I was going to tell her the usual story . . . a burning coal spitting out of a fire . . . but something in her eyes made me change course.

"When I was seven years old," I began, "my father, already on the wrong side of several cans of lager, told me to fetch another beer for him from the fridge. The can slipped from my hands as I took it off the shelf, and rolled across the floor. I'd no idea of what happens to beer in a can when it is shaken. I picked it up and took it through to him. He opened it, and the beer sprayed out all over his face and clothes. I was so terrified and appalled that I laughed. He put the beer down, and glared at me, and I managed to pull in my grin. Then he laughed too.

"'That was a funny sight, hey boy?'

"I nodded, warily, allowing the grin to creep back onto my face.

"'C'm here,' he said, still grinning. 'C'm on, kid, don't be so damn chicken. I want to show you something else funny.'

"I approached him slowly. He chuckled to show me it was just a bit of fun. As I got close to him, he grabbed my arm, picked up the cigarette that was smouldering in the ashtray beside him, and mashed it into my face.

"'Now that's funny, hey boy? That's a good joke. You wan' me to do that again?'

"I shook my head, tears pouring down my face, which hurt worse than I knew anything could hurt.

"'Then think twice before you take the piss out of your old man again. Now get your ugly mug out of my sight.'"

I didn't tell Melissa that that incident, more than any other meanness my father dealt out, was the making and breaking of me. As I grew up, whenever I looked at the scar, I'd remember that my father valued my face no more than the filthy ashtrays that littered our apartment. And I'd resolve to make myself fly so damn high he was no more than a speck of dirt on the floor. But it also fractured me, catapulted me into some cold, angry place that would always leave me on the outside looking in.

She said nothing when I'd finished talking, but as she leant forward to kiss it, I saw that there were tears in her eyes, and it seemed to me that her sorrow on my behalf could heal that fatal rift.

Against this gift of truth that I'd given her, this entrusting of the most shaming secret of my existence, my deception around the formula seemed like a small thing to me.

It'd never struck me as that important – I struggle now even to recall how it came about. Some committee of my sponsors thought it better to do a double-blind, so that the administering doctors on the programme didn't know the exact nature of the formula. I argued against this decision, which struck me as unnecessary and a bit sloppy. But the guy who pays the bills calls the shots, and my priority was getting the research done.

I guess if I'd known that I'd be involving the person most dear to my heart, I might have done things differently. But it was too late to change now – it had happened, and this was how it was. And as I came to know Melissa better, I realised that it would destroy her to know the truth.

This realisation annoyed me a little . . . it wasn't as if there was anything harmful in the formula, it was only the ignorant hysteria of popular opinion that had made it necessary to conceal its composition. There was part of me that felt that if Melissa truly loved me, she'd see that the benefits of what we were exploring far outweighed the minor deceit that it involved.

But in my heart, I knew she wouldn't. She wouldn't see it as a small thing . . . Like Bluebeard's wife, if she opened that forbidden door, her love for me would die a swift and brutal death – and a flood of self-hatred would sweep away all her new-found equanimity. I couldn't take the risk of losing her by telling her, nor did I want to plunge her back into her depression. It seemed, thus, that the kindest course all round was to keep quiet.

If all had gone as planned, she'd never have found out. But life was conspiring against us, as life often does. The time bomb was ticking, and one by one the cogs were falling into place.

Chapter 15

THERE are different homecomings. The journey home is never the same journey twice. Is it anticipation that predetermines the journey? Or the journey that determines the encounter at the end?

Sam has much time to brood on this and other matters as she and Khaya travel the R62. They have left too late – by the time she's organised someone to feed Richard, taken "family emergency" leave from work, seen to the car, phoned Dylan to let him know, et cetera, it is nearly eleven. And Sam's habitual chorus of paranoiac sibyls have reached a crescendo of lurid predictions – of car accidents, hijackings, earthquakes, uncontrollable bouts of vomiting or diarrhoea.

"I'm not listening to you," Sam tells them. "You've kept me locked up long enough. I'm leaving and there is nothing you can do about it."

Brave words. But she doesn't feel brave. And, as the road from Cape Town spools out behind them, her misgivings balloon in proportion to the distance she travels. Perhaps she should just drive the bloody car over a cliff and be done with it, she mutters to herself . . . but she doesn't, of course. That mysterious instinct of self-preservation keeps her glued to the road, however tenuously. *On our way home. We're going home* . . . John Lennon sings encouragingly on the CD player. *Little darling, here comes the sun . . .*

"Here comes the sun, li'l darling," echoes Khaya, from his seat in the back.

It is one of those early spring days in the Karoo, where the chill, dry wind seems to blow through one's flesh, desiccating it like the sinewy bushes that cling to life on the barren plains. The Spartan tones of the landscape are lifted by sporadic bursts of magenta flowers; the grey Langekloof mountains march alongside the road, mocking their small lives with ancient indifference.

Khaya is unusually quiet – a little apprehensive, perhaps, of the impulsive, unpredictable woman his aunt has turned into. Sam clutches the steering wheel and reflects on all the times she'd travelled this route . . .

After her parents died . . .

When she and Melissa first picked up Dylan . . .

To Melissa's funeral . . .

She drives slowly, too terrified to overtake the occasional trucks that block their path. The road beneath her feels as if it might dissolve at any moment, the passing sights seem to portend some unknown threat . . . the solitary man in the red woollen hat on the battered black bicycle; the child huddled amongst the sheep on the back of a bakkie; a shaggy white horse drinking from a small dam in the afternoon light, mouth to mouth with its perfectly mirrored image.

"Let's play 'I spy'," she suggests desperately to Khaya. "You can go first."

But he doesn't reply, and when she glances over her shoulder, she sees that he is fast asleep.

The sun is almost setting as they turn off the tarred road into Elandskloof. Pink Floyd is playing now – *Hello . . . hello . . . hello . . . is there anybody in there?* But there is no one in sight, save a few incurious sheep and an eagle circling far above them. The craggy slopes dream in lonely silence under the evening sky.

The jagged cliffs of Die Slot rear up, vermillion in the setting sun, presenting what seems to be an impenetrable wall of fiery rock.

"That's it, Mimsy," she says to the dog panting on the seat beside her. "We've tried. Let's turn around now and go back again."

But as they reach it, the rock seems to magically part, and they squeeze through. As they carry on, Sam has the eerie sensation that the walls have shut behind her. No turning back. *And we run and we run to catch up with the sun but it's sinking . . .*

The shadows deepen; the rutted gravel sighs and grumbles beneath their tyres. Small creatures dart through the undergrowth on the side of the road, anxious to get home before nightfall. A giant tortoise lumbers in front of them, and Sam waits patiently for it to cross. As night thickens, Sam switches on her lights, and watches the embodied shadows of bats caught in their beam. An owl swoops low in front of them.

The road winds on and on through the deepening dusk – wading rivers, skirting cliffs and traversing fields; past the candlelit *blougombos* houses of labour tenants and, further from the road, clusters of stone farm buildings under pepper trees and bluegums; past the astonishingly large and well-fortified police station, built in the seventies to stave off who-knows-what threat to law and order in this brooding backwater; past lucerne fields and ostrich pens and a few wistful cows. As night settles, the landscape fades into oblivion around her, although familiar landmarks and names suddenly loom out of the darkness, picked out by her headlights like signposts to another life.

She inches her car gingerly through eight flooded causeways, fighting the urge to lift her feet off the floor. The dark rivers lap the tyres curiously, testing them for taste and texture. "The great gig in the sky" is now playing – a wordless sobbing, both sorrowful and serene, that ushers them through the dark wilderness.

Towards the end, it begins to rain.

Was it always so long? They pass the gates to the old Koekemoer farm at last – the white kudu skulls nailed to the posts loom eerily out of the wet darkness. There is a new sign up: "Slanghoek Retreat" it proclaims in bold white letters on a dark wooden board, and underneath "safari, hunting, quad bike and 4X4 trails, farm cuisine". But Sam barely registers, because by now her vision has narrowed to a dark tunnel that can only encompass the gates of Cedar Hills.

And then, suddenly, there they are, the white boulders leaping into the light as she turns into the open gate. She bumps up the track, and pulls up under the pepper tree. As the front door of the house opens, spilling light and a welcoming figure into the garden, Sam lays her head down on the steering wheel and weeps.

* * *

"Hi – Samantha?"

A broad, open face, framed by a sand-and-silver beard and thinning hair, smiles kindly at her through the car window. She stares at him stupidly for a moment, then his name finds its way into her befuddled brain.

Jannie de Vries. Her tenant. Has she met him? She can't remember. An agent in Willowdale dealt with the letting.

She climbs out, feeling like a bundle of dirty washing, and shakes his hand. He politely ignores her dishevelled state and tear-streaked face. The house crouches in the dark behind him. Sam cannot quite bring herself to look at it, afraid perhaps that it'll catch her eye and flood her with reproach for her neglect.

Somehow they are bustled in, she and Khaya stand holding hands, blinking in the sudden light, staring around the front room like bewildered children delivered to a Place of Safety. She'd expected such a rush of emotion. But all she feels is numbness, underlaid with an anti-climactic sense of recognition.

"I haven't changed much," says Jannie, looking at her rather anxiously.

She'd been bracing herself to confront the fact that it was someone else's house now, that it would be quite different. But, remarkably, Jannie seems to have changed nothing at all. She looks around the room they'd always called the front room, which served as the "informal" lounge, entrance and general heart of the house. There is the grandfather clock, ticking ponderously in the corner. There is Fergus's old desk under the window, with its red leather blotter and old green-glass desk lamp. There are the crusty old Campbell forbearers, staring out of their wooden frames with varying degrees of outrage or regret. There is her mother's violent painting of flowers next to the kitchen door (the one of the red roses splattered beside white lilies that always made Sam think of gunned-down choirboys), and her print of Monet's water lilies above the fireplace, the bridge still going from east to west. The only sign she can see of any change is a guitar standing in the corner.

It is neat and clean, but harbours the sorrowful air of a place left behind by time, frozen around the lives that no longer inhabit it. The carpets are threadbare, the faded chairs sport shiny patches polished by multiple generations of heads and hands. Sam finds herself wondering about Jannie, about someone who could live in this museum to painful history with so little intervention to make it his own.

Jannie hovers, a man unused to company, grappling for the right note in these odd circumstances.

"Dylan was called away to Port Elizabeth for an urgent meeting. He'll be back tomorrow. Would you like some food? I've got some in the kitchen . . ."

Sam imagines sitting down to supper, fielding questions (although to his credit he has so far been remarkably incurious) and shakes her head hastily.

"No, I'm fine, we've been eating all day. I think we'll just go to bed, thanks."

But once she has read to Khaya and he has drifted off in Melissa's childhood bed, all prospects of sleep flee into the night. Sam lies staring up at the stain on the ceiling, just visible in the light from the passage. Splatty Island, she and Melissa used to call it. She'd make up stories for Melissa about the Splats – creatures formed from accidental spills that ran away to live there. The bed is deeply familiar, but not actually comfortable. The springs of the old-fashioned steel frame groan despairingly every time she moves. The white candlewick bedspread smells faintly of mothballs.

She can hear the moths blundering around in the dark, still disorientated by the light that had been on, the small sounds of their soft bodies hitting unyielding objects. Mimsy snores on the mat beside her.

"Well," she says rather crossly to the dark house, "you've got me here now. What are you going to do with me?"

But there is no reply, save the chorus of frogs down at the river and a sound like someone winding up a toy, which she thinks might emanate from a grasshopper.

"Milly?" Her voice is querulous and reedy in the dark, like that of an old woman calling into an empty house from her sick bed.

She thinks of Melissa's ashes in the tin in the suitcase under the bed . . . her sister in a tea tin.

Oh Milly . . .

* * *

She wakes with Khaya bouncing up and down on her.

"Hey, hey, let's go swim at Smitskraal. I can jump off the rock. I'm Batman! I can fly! Can Hanky come?" He leaps off and runs around the room shouting, "Come ON, lazybones, mazynones, bazylones."

"Oh Khaya . . ." she mumbles in protest. She doesn't want to open her eyes. She doesn't want to find herself here; she wants to be back in her eyrie where everything is safe.

But Khaya will not let her be, so she climbs reluctantly out of bed, throws on her clothes, and blunders down to the kitchen to forage for food. Jannie is out already, although the sun has barely cleared the horizon, but has left her a note inviting her to help herself "to whatever".

"What's this?" Khaya demands, pointing to the big iron Aga in the old fireplace.

"It's a stove."

"A stove. Wow. It looks like a train."

Sam laughs. "I guess it does. My father used to call it the industrial revolution."

"Why?"

"Well, I don't know really . . ."

"Where do you turn it on?"

"You don't. You use wood. You make a fire in it. In winter we used to keep it on all the time. The cats would lie on it at night to keep warm. Tant Aletta used to come on Tuesdays and Fridays to make bread for us."

And there is long-dead Tant Aletta at the kitchen table, her smell of dust and sweat and paraffin mixing with the yeasty odour of the bread, the dewlaps of her upper arms wobbling furiously as she pounds the dough into submission.

"Knead it, meisie, knead it! It's dough, not a kitten. You can't hurt it!" she roars, her sides shaking with mirth at Sam's feeble efforts. Afterwards, Sam and Chrissie sit on the back step in the morning sun, eating hot bread and *waatlemoenkonfyt*. The sticky, gingery jam, mixed with melted butter, runs down their chins.

"Tannie Aletta makes the best bread, nè?" Chrissie says, licking her fingers slick with grease.

"Ja, but it's not *real* bread . . ."

"What do you mean?"

"It's not *proper* bread, like you get at the Willowdale shop. In a packet."

"Ag, *Aalwynkop-spinnekop*, what do *you* know." And she jumps up and stalks off down the track.

"Come back, Chrissie, don't go off, man . . ."

But she doesn't come back. And Sam sits eating her bread alone, left once more to the company of the dogs and the toktokkies tapping out urgent messages in the veld.

* * *

As they eat their breakfast on the stoep, Sam surveys her world. It is unreal to her, like a two-dimensional painted film set. Nothing seems to have substance . . . the house, the backdrop of hills, the river running below, the mountains behind all feel like a landscape cobbled from memory that'll fall over if she pushes it.

What did she expect? Some dramatic epiphany that would either tip her into total madness, or enable her suddenly to make sense of her life? Or, at the very least, that heart skip that she used to feel at the space and the light and the rolling hills? That feeling of slipping back into a space that was created for her alone?

She looks at the aloes and euphorbias on the opposite slope, holding out their arms to her in a futile gesture of reconciliation. Behind her, the house folds its arms against her. And she remembers Melissa saying, after their parents died, *This house hates us.*

This is it, she realises. What she'd most dreaded in coming

back here. Like the day you realise you are no longer in love. Only, worse. Because Cedar Hills had been her portal of meaning into a world that could seem so futile and cruel.

She is locked out from the heart of Cedar Hills as effectively as if Die Slot had indeed closed up its red granite walls against her, and her first instinct is to once again run as far as she can.

She glances up to see Khaya watching her anxiously from the corner of his eye, gauging her response to the place, seeking permission to feel the joy and freedom he'd felt before.

So she beams at him encouragingly, and when they have eaten and washed their bowls, she says, "Come on, Batman. Let's go exploring. Maybe we can find your old tadpole friend."

Chapter 16
Confession of a Killer

ONE of the more curious agents to seal our fate was a West African nun called Sister Dorothea. I arrived at Cedar Hills one Friday evening for what I hoped would be a romantic evening with Melissa, armed with wine and song (I'd bought her the new Michael Franks CD) and a good dose of lust. I was somewhat put out, therefore, to find a very large nun sitting at the kitchen table.

"Hi James," Melissa beamed at me. "This is Sister Dorothea, from Gabon. The priest she was staying with was unexpectedly called out of town, so I invited her to spend a few days here. Sister Dorothea, James McIntyre."

"How lovely," I bared my teeth at her and shook her hand with scant enthusiasm, "I'm delighted to meet you."

"Sister Dorothea works on the Catholic church's food-garden programme," Melissa explained. "She'll be helping us with the vegetable garden at the clinic."

I'd seen the so-called vegetable garden. It was a sorry thing, a straggly row of worm-eaten cabbages plagued by frost, porcupines and the township's free-roaming black pigs. It needed all the help it could get, and frankly I thought Sister Dorothea should get back there as soon as possible and carry on with the job.

Sister Dorothea's face split into a delighted grin. "Do you know what my secret ingredient is, Mr McIntyre?" she boomed at me.

"James, please. No, I have absolutely no idea."

"Rubbish!" she said triumphantly, and smacked her hand on the table to stress the point. I thought she was challenging my reply, but then I realised that this was her secret ingredient.

"Rubbish, that's what it is. I go around collecting it from all the white ladies in Willowdale. Vegetable peels, old newspapers, anything that will rot. It's all gold to me. The taxi drivers call me Sister Rubbish-Bag." She held up her hands to me and waggled ten plump digits. "That's all you need to grow all the food you can eat, Mr McIntyre. Did you know that? Ten fingers, God's sunshine and rain, and a good load of rubbish."

I tried to display a suitable degree of amazement at this disclosure. Inwardly, I sighed. It was going to be a long evening.

After a lot more gardening talk, Sister Dorothea asked if she might make a phone call. When she'd left the room, I rounded on Melissa.

"You might have told me."

"I know, I'm sorry, it was a spontaneous thing. I was with her this morning when she heard that the priest was going away. But I wanted her to come anyway because I need advice on growing a vegetable garden here. It'll make a huge difference to those mothers if we can get them some decent nutrition. And she's really interesting, James. I thought you'd like to meet her."

"But Melissa, we have so little time together – it's not exactly the evening I'd had in mind."

She laughed. "Oh, stop being so stuffy, Mr Wolf. I'll make it up to you later, I promise."

"Are you sure that having a bride of the Lord under your roof won't cramp your style?"

She leant over and did something pleasant to my ear with her tongue. "Just you wait and see," she whispered.

"Do that again," I whispered back, but then Sister Dorothea swept through the door in a flurry of wimple, brandishing something in her hand.

"Where does this come from?" she demanded, flinging it down onto the pitted wooden surface of the table.

Melissa and I gazed at it. It was a small square notepad, with the name of NuGrowth and their sunflower logo printed in pale green on each page.

"I have no idea," said Melissa, looking nervously from Sister Dorothea to the notepad. "Why do you ask?"

Sister Dorothea sucked in her breath, and stabbed the offending item with one of her ten gardening implements.

"These people," she announced, "were put on earth to do the devil's work."

Melissa flung a panicky glance in my direction. I gave her a you-asked-for-it look back.

"Really?" she said faintly. She eyed the notebook with new respect.

"NuGrowth," announced Sister Dorothea ominously, pronouncing the name with as much distaste as if it were Beelzebub himself. "You don't know about them? The biggest biotech company in the world. Responsible for Agent Orange and most of the pesticides choking our planet. And now the main proponent of genetic engineering."

She turned her fierce black eyes on me. "Tell me, Mr McIntyre, what are your views on genetic engineering?"

"Oh, I'm pretty vague on the subject," I said, ducking the sharp look Melissa shot me across the table. "But I'd love to hear yours . . ."

She did not need to be asked twice. "Well, it's the arrogance, first of all. Thinking you can create life better than God. God never intended the genes of a strawberry to meet those of a salmon. Look, I'm not a creationist . . . I know about evolution. But genes evolve in their own sweet time – nature does not mash the genes of unrelated species together any old how. Start doing that and you're looking for trouble."

"But it could be beneficial, couldn't it?" asked brave Melissa – you had to admire her. "I read somewhere that they are developing drought-resistant crops, and crops that are more nutritious. That's good, isn't it?"

Sister Dorothea sighed, and shook her head. "Always the same old lies. You must read between the lines, my dear. What causes world hunger? Wars, urbanisation, climate change, unfair trade . . . You think that giving a multinational company monopoly over the very kernels of life will solve those problems?"

Melissa shook her head. Even she would not dare to think such a thing.

"As for these drought-resistant crops, it's a myth. There aren't any. Most of the crops are engineered to be resistant to a weedkiller called Clean-Up. Which, guess what, NuGrowth makes as well. Did you know that there are over ten thousand edible species of plant in the world," she barrelled on, eager to get all her points down before the world ran out of food and we ran out the door, "but only thirty species provide ninety per cent of the world calorie intake? NuGrowth would like to limit that to five – all engineered by them."

"It's too terrible," I put in helpfully. "God made the world in six days and on the seventh NuGrowth came and stole it."

Melissa kicked me under the table, but Sister D released a great belly laugh and said, "Oh, don't worry, young man, they haven't stolen it yet. And there are plenty of us who will make sure they don't succeed."

"I am glad," I said. "I'll sleep better at night knowing that."

"Maybe you should go to bed now," Melissa suggested with an acid smile. "You look very tired."

"Don't be silly, darling," I replied. "I haven't had my dinner yet. And I am *so* enjoying the conversation."

"Dinner!" cried Melissa gratefully. "I'm sure it's ready, let's eat . . ."

In the ensuing bustle of table-laying and dishing out, the topic was forgotten, and as we chewed our way through the lentil-and-bean curry, Melissa made sure it was not raised again. She plied Sister Dorothea with questions about her work in different parts of Africa, and Sister D was happy to oblige. She was kind of interesting once off her hobby horse, and the evening passed pleasantly enough. But when we'd finished and the plates were cleared away, the conversation headed once more into dangerous waters when Melissa told Sister Dorothea about how well the babies were doing on the soy formula.

"That's marvellous," she said. "One of God's little miracles, the soybean. So nutritious. Of course, NuGrowth are trying to patent that one too – about half America's soy is genetically engineered."

"Really?" said Melissa desperately.

"Yes. They've even engineered soybeans with Brazil-nut protein . . ."

"Brazil-nut protein!" Melissa exclaimed in horror. "But Brazil nuts are a major allergen . . ."

"Of course," Sister Dorothea replied complacently. "And needless to say, people with nut allergies reacted to it . . ." Would nothing shut this woman up?

"Excuse me," I said, standing up abruptly. "I am really sorry, but you'll have to excuse me. You're right, darling, I'm bushed – I've had one hell of a week. I'm sure you will forgive me if I head off to bed."

"What the hell got into you tonight?" Melissa demanded when she climbed in next to me some two hours later. "You were so rude. And what do you mean by saying you're vague on the subject of genetic engineering? You're a microbiologist, for Christ's sake."

"I just didn't want to get into a debate with her. Come on, Melissa, you promised to make it up to me, remember?" I reached for her and tried to pull her towards me. As I touched her, a wave of desire washed over me. All I wanted was to melt my body into hers and forget about Sister Rubbish-Bag and her hectoring ways. But Melissa would have none of it.

"Don't brush me off, James. You must have an opinion on genetic engineering . . ."

I groaned, and sat up. "Jesus, can't we be done with this already? Who cares what I think? Who cares what she thinks? Genetic engineering is here to stay whatever our opinions. Human beings are curious, that's why nowadays we drive cars and watch television instead of sitting in caves bashing our breakfast with a club. It was only a matter of time before we started fiddling about with genes."

"So you think it's just an expression of the human imagination?"

"Of course, what else? For the alchemists it was the elixir of life. Scientists are still searching for that one. But this is the next best thing: creating new life forms to suit your purpose. It is a spectacular feat of the imagination – at least as significant as the discovery of evolution."

"Or, equally, a failure of the imagination."

"How so?"

"A failure to foresee consequences. Those things she was talking about – the demise of the honeybees . . . the loss of indigenous knowledge on saving seeds . . . the loss of biological diversity . . . Indian farmers killing themselves because of debt. Either a failure of imagination. Or an act of staggering arrogance and self-interest."

"I suppose that might be regarded as a failure of imagination. But it is that same flaw that has driven virtually every single technological advance. Had humans been able to foresee the long-term consequences of discovering fire, we might still be gnawing on roots and steak tartare."

"And probably a lot healthier for it. We wouldn't be facing extinction from global warming."

"Come on, Melissa. You prescribe antibiotics every day. How many of your patients would die if they didn't have them? You know the damaging consequences of excessive antibiotic use. But you use them responsibly. Genetic engineering only becomes a Frankenstein if used in the wrong way for the wrong purpose."

"An antibiotic can't go off and reproduce itself outside of a laboratory. You yourself said this was a total breakthrough. It is not comparable."

It went on. She could argue, your sister, she really could. She was also young enough, I suppose, to imagine that having a strong opinion on genetic engineering was a vital act of social responsibility. As if it would somehow reach the ears of the NuGrowth henchmen and make them reconsider.

But much as we danced the dance, we both knew where it was going, and eventually she forced herself to get there.

"Anyway, if you're so enamoured with genetic engineering, why aren't you involved in it? You seem like the kind of guy who likes to be at the forefront of things."

A brave question. But she was not brave enough to say, *Are you involved in it?* . . . She didn't really want to know what lay behind that door. She wanted my reassurance that I had no dark bones after all. So I gave her what she wanted.

"Indeed I am," I replied. "And what I'm doing at the moment is very much at the forefront of things. Microbiology does not begin and end with genetic engineering, you know."

"That was your notepad wasn't it?"

"I believe it was . . . I probably picked it up at the university. NuGrowth funds a lot of research – not only into genetic engineering."

"And the Brazil-nut thing?"

"That's a red herring. A totally dumb idea, obviously, but it was only intended for animal feed, and they've withdrawn it now, anyway."

"So there's no chance . . ." Her words faded, but we both knew where they were going.

"Melissa, don't even ask that question. Because if you do, I am getting out of bed right now, and driving home."

"I'm sorry," she sighed. "You were just so . . . odd tonight. So jumpy and sarcastic . . ."

"I was thwarted. And a thwarted wolf is a jumpy animal. Look, if it makes you happy, I will debate GE with the good sister from dawn to dusk tomorrow. But please, please, my darling girl, if you have any heart at all, don't thwart me any more."

Thankfully, she didn't. But Sister Rubbish-Bag's visit had driven another nail in your sister's coffin. And, God forgive me, I have heaped a thousand curses on her wimpled head ever since.

Chapter 17

AS they walk along the path above the house, Khaya gripping her hand firmly as if he thinks she might suddenly float up into the blue sky like a big red balloon, Sam finds herself telling him about Chrissie.

"Chrissie's house was the best place in the world."

"Better than your house?"

"Yes."

"Why?"

Because there was always someone there to make a joke and pat you on the head . . . because no one was locked in their bedroom tormented by migraines and madness . . .

"Because . . ." she hesitates, ". . . because of Tant Aletta's garden. She had the best garden in the whole of Elandskloof. Yellow and orange chrysanthemums like giant pompoms, and sunflowers taller than me, and plumbago as blue as the sky, and red poppies and pink geraniums and white daisies, and black-eyed Susan climbing over the fences. And she also grew vegetables, great big juicy tomatoes and huge pumpkins and herbs to cure people from sicknesses. When you saw Tant Aletta's garden you had to wear sunglasses because the colours were so bright. And there was a coral tree with a tyre swing, and Chrissie's ouma would sit under there in the afternoons and tell us stories . . ."

"What stories?"

"Oh, all sorts of things . . ."

Terrifying stories about the malevolent water sprites that lived in Mermaid's Pool, waiting to drag the unwary into the lair of the river serpent . . . or of the witches that rode hyenas at night, looking for naughty children to crunch between their great teeth, as sharp as the long white thorns of the acacia trees, and hard as stones. Sam could hear the rasping wheeze of Ouma's chuckling, the odd guttural or whistling sounds she'd make to imitate the animals and birds, and see the way her hand, wrinkled as a pickled walnut, would dart through the air transformed into the head of a snake, or a flying bird, or the sharp nose of a marauding jackal.

"Can we go there?" he asks.

"I guess so. It's just over the hill . . ."

And for a moment it feels as if it is indeed just over the hill, as it had been thirty years ago. The white-washed, mud-brick house dreaming under its green tin roof amongst the wattle-and-daub homes of the others; the tyre swing in the coral tree; scrawny red chickens cluck-clucking amongst the weeds; Ishmael and Isaac dozing floppy-eared by the stream. Stompie Stuurman's legs sticking out from under some stricken vehicle that a farmer had brought to save himself an expensive trip to Fanie's Auto Repairs and Sales in Willowdale; Bra Piet's white goats winding down the ledge on the red cliffs behind the homestead, gleaming in the sun like her mother's string of pearls . . .

But when they come over the rise, it is nothing like that at all.

The brick house was torched nine years before in a lightning storm. Blackened twists of rusted tin roof lie fallen in the house; the walls are dark with soot. The other huts are ruins.

"Is this it?" Khaya looks around in surprise. "Where're the donkeys and the chickens?"

"They've all gone now."

"Why?"

Why? Why? Why? "Uh, it's a long story, Khaya. Some bad people made them move."

"Did they make Chrissie's house broken?"

"No, it was lightning that broke it."

"Can we go down there?"

"I guess so . . ."

They walk down slowly, threading their way through the blackjacks and nettles and thistles, climb the four steps to the porch, and step inside the door. There is nothing there but some rusted bedsteads, a few coils of barbed-wire fencing and a pile of broken animal harnesses, green with mould. A copper-coloured cobra, startled by their arrival, slithers rapidly across the floor and pours itself out through a crack in the wall.

Khaya steps back. "What's that?"

"A cobra. Be careful, they're very poisonous."

"A cobra? Wow, a cobra. A cobra . . ."

He clings to her hand, awed by this evidence that the things of men are not impervious to time.

"A cobra . . ." he says again, wonderingly.

* * *

"Hallo."

Sam swings round. A woman is standing in the ruined doorway, her face obscured by the bright sunlight behind her.

"Can I help you?" The words are sharp edged, as if she has found them rummaging around in her kitchen without invitation. As she moves further into the shade Sam can see her more clearly. A trim figure in jeans and a cotton shirt, with a heart-shaped face and flashing almond eyes, her black hair tied in a bandana.

"*Chrissie* . . .?"

"Sam . . . is that you? My God!"

They laugh, and lurch towards each other as if to embrace, but as Sam gets close she is overcome with shyness and sticks out her hand instead. Chrissie looks at it, nonplussed, and shakes it with a wry smile.

"Well! So you came . . . Did you get my letter?"

"Yes, thanks, I'm sorry I didn't reply. I wasn't sure what I'd do, but, well anyway, here I am."

"Yes, here you are . . ."

They look at each other, silenced, suddenly, by the weight of history. Outside, a guinea fowl scolds raucously from the pepper trees. Sam feels tongue-tied and tremendously tired, as if the charred beams of the roof are resting on her shoulders instead of lying amongst the wreckage of the house.

"We saw a cobra," Khaya announces, importantly. "It's poisonous," he adds, lest Chrissie underestimate the drama of this revelation.

Chrissie nods. "Plenty of snakes in the grass . . . some human ones too."

Sam laughs nervously.

Khaya looks quizzically at Chrissie. "What's a human snake?"

She smiles. "Well, some humans behave like snakes . . ."

"Do they wriggle on the floor?"

"No, I . . . gosh, are you always this exacting, young man? I don't think I know you. I'm Chrissie, pleased to meet you." She holds out her hand, which Khaya shakes gravely. "And what is your name?"

"Khaya. Sam said you were a little girl who liked skipping, but really you're quite an old lady."

"Khaya!" interjects Sam.

Chrissie laughs again. "Well, I still like skipping. Do you skip?"

"No, that's what girls do . . . I fly like Batman."

"I guess that beats skipping."

Khaya loses interest in them then, and begins rummaging about in the weeds.

"Is he your son?"

"No, he's my nephew . . ."

"Oh ja, my mom told me about your sister. I'm so sorry."

"Thank you."

"So . . ." Chrissie's voice tightens, "here we are at the old homestead . . ."

"Is this the first time you've been back?"

"Since we left, do you mean? No, I've been a few times. It's still a bit of a shock, though. I think some part of me keeps expecting it to all magically rematerialise."

"Yes, I know what you mean. I was thinking that when I was walking here, I kind of expected it all to still be here . . ."

Chrissie looks around, shaking her head. "It's so strange . . . being here. You know, on the day Hennie Koekemoer came to evict us he smacked my father in the face. For no reason. My father said, 'But Mr Koekemoer, there have been Stuurmans here for at least six generations', and Hennie said, 'That's six generations too long, Hotnot', and slapped him. Right here on these steps where we are standing . . . His glasses broke, there was blood on his lip . . .

"Later I said to him, 'Pappie, why did Mr Koekemoer smack you?' And he said, 'Because he was ashamed'."

She looks at Sam, squinting against the sun.

"Do you think he was ashamed?"

"I don't know. He should've been . . ."

"I don't think that man was ashamed. He couldn't have done what he did if he had any shame." Chrissie shakes her head.

"Ag well," she sighs, "now Mr Hennie Koekemoer is drooling in an old-age home in Humansdorp, and my father is getting his land back, so I guess what goes around comes around. But he'll never get his lost life back."

Sam stares down at the big red ants scurrying along the cracked steps. She has nothing to say.

"Hey," yells Khaya, "I found the sun, I found a sun tin, look . . ."

He runs to Sam, holding out a battered old round tin. An improbably optimistic rising-sun face, undaunted by the ravages of time, beams out through the rust, bright yellow on a red background. SUNBEAM RED POLISH, it proclaims proudly, its message still decipherable although most letters have partially succumbed to oxidisation. WITH WONDERSHINE. SHINES BRIGHTER, LASTS LONGER.

Chrissie stares at it, and then her face lights up like the sun on the tin.

"Oh my God! Sunbeam polish. Do you remember how I always had to polish our steps? And if my mother couldn't see her face in it, she'd tell me to do it again."

"Can I keep it?" asks Khaya anxiously, as if afraid that Chrissie will use her floor-polishing history to lay claim to it.

"Of course you can."

"Yay! A sun tin! Here comes the sun, li'l darling," he sings, sitting down on the steps with the tin and stroking its pitted sun face.

"You were polishing the steps the last time I saw you here," says Sam, looking out at the hills opposite.

"I know."

There is silence again. *Piet-my-vrou*, a cuckoo calls from a nearby tree. Or maybe, *It's-not-so*.

Then Chrissie says, "But I saw you again in Willowdale, in the Cash & Carry."

Sam forces herself to look up and meet her eyes.

"I know. I remember. I'm sorry . . ."

And Chrissie suddenly breaks into her first real smile, and reaches out and tousles Sam's hair – slightly awkwardly, for Sam is now a good head taller.

"Ag, don't look so worried, *Aalwynkop*! It's *ou stories* now."

* * *

Ou stories . . . is it that easy? Perhaps, perhaps not. They chat for a while, in the morning sun, sketching in briefly the details of each other's lives, not saying far more than they do say, as is the way with these encounters.

"Where are you staying?" Sam asks eventually.

"Right now? In Neels Koekemoer's guesthouse, actually."

"No! That's some irony, huh?"

"I guess so."

"I'm surprised you can even talk to him after what his dad did."

"Why? I'm talking to you, aren't I?"

Sam flinches. "It's a bit different . . ." *For God's sake, Neels used to call you "Stinky black jelly baby" and rub cow dung in your hair. I was never* that *bad.*

"Is it? His dad kicked us off the land, your grandfather sold it illegally from under our feet . . . it's not so different."

So. *Ou stories*, but still with a sting in their tail.

"*Great*-grandfather," Sam mutters.

"Either way, it wouldn't be fair to hold you accountable for his actions, would it? So why should I blame Neels for what Hennie did?"

"No, you're right, of course. Only, most people aren't so noble."

"It's more a question of survival than nobility. If everyone held everyone accountable for their own actions, never mind their ancestors' actions, we'd all have slaughtered each other long ago . . ."

Sam smiles vaguely, feeling nonplussed. Is this a lecture in forgiveness, or a backhanded reminder of her own family's role in the Stuurmans' mishaps? A caution to her not to think that she had any special standing in the Stuurman annals because of her childhood friendship with Chrissie, or, for that matter, because of Fergus's efforts to help them? She flails around, trying to find a bridge to that simple world where she and Chrissie were just two small girls poking around in the dirt of Elandskloof.

But of course nothing was simple. Even then.

"How is Stompie?" Chrissie asks. "I was on my way to see him when I came past here."

"I haven't seen him yet," Sam replies, grateful for the distraction. "I'll come with you."

* * *

They walk up the hill in silence. Sam thinks about Stompie, who has lived in the same *blougombos* house on Cedar Hills for over thirty years, with a succession of relatives, wives, children, grandchildren and girlfriends. He took over the management of Cedar Hills, with varying degrees of dedication and incompetence, after the death of his father. But he was so appalled by Fergus's death that he absconded completely for about six years. When he returned, he regaled Sam and Melissa with a Gothic saga of his decline, but assured them that Jesus had been kind enough to show him the light in the urine-saturated darkness of a police cell in Humansdorp – and never again would the devil's brew cross his Christian lips.

As they come over the brow of the hill the house lies before them – a long, low structure comprising a frame of stripped gum poles supporting vertical reeds, the gaps caulked with mud. The floors are mud and cow dung, stamped into a hard, polished surface; the windows unglazed holes, flanked by wooden shutters with peeling turquoise paint. The yard itself is neatly swept and tidied, with a vegetable patch, a stand of ragged mielies, and the rusted carcases of the Campbells' old Mercedes, a bakkie and a tractor. Stompie has retained his passion for these machines, even though it was a tractor that had so ungratefully deprived him of his arm while he was trying to fix it.

Tant Aletta's legacy is visible in the row of bright sunflowers lining one side of the fence. A donkey dozes in a nearby stand of acacia trees, twitching its long, fur-tipped ears to ward off the flies. As they approach, a small yellow dog of indeterminate breeding, sporting two chewed ears, hurtles itself out from the shade of the house in a volley of barking.

"Shut up, *bliksem*," a voice calls, and Stompie himself appears, a wavering figure in threadbare grey trousers and white shirt. The fabric flaps around his skinny limbs, which fill his sleeves and pants only slightly more substantially than his phantom arm. He waves his other arm at the dog, which slinks obediently back to the house.

Stompie's face dissolves into a mass of creases, gathered around a huge mostly toothless smile, as he recognises his visitors. His fall from grace is etched deeply into his face – a mess of scars on his forehead mark where he's tried to remove the charcoal, ink and urine tattoos carved into his skin during his spell in prison and he has the gaze of one who's been in hell and will do whatever it takes to escape it.

"Chrissie! Miss Samantha!" he cries. Sam has never been able to persuade him to drop the "miss".

"Samantha," she mumbles, glancing obliquely at Chrissie. Has she noticed?

He brushes the tears from his one good eye with his one good hand. "Ai, ai, ai, Meisie, *kom kyk wie's dit*! Come see the distinguished visitors that the Lord has brought to our door today!"

Meisie's upper half appears briefly above the stable door. She is a recent addition to the household . . . a new girlfriend? Although the term hardly seems appropriate for this squat sextuagenarian, who is eyeing them with the good will of a poisonous toad. She sizes them up through the thick folds of flesh around her eyes, expresses her verdict in a guttural sniff, wipes her nose with her hand, mutters something, and retreats.

Stompie seems unfazed by her lack of enthusiasm.

"Come sit, come sit, would you like a drink? Meisie, let's get these good people some nice coffee, sit a bit, where did you come from? Aiyee, if Dr Campbell could see you girls now, such grand ladies, I still remember when you two laaities used to play so nicely, and look, look who's here, who's this fine boy? No! Doctor Melissa's boy! Yo, but you're a little man now . . . *arme ou seuntjie* . . ."

He keeps up a steady monologue as he ushers them to a blue-painted wooden bench in the shade of a small overhang above the door. Soon everyone is furnished with a mug of acrid coffee, infused, it seems, with Meisie's disgust, and barely redeemed by viscous globs of condensed milk. Stompie disappears inside, and comes out with a scrapbook.

"Doctor Melissa gave it for us," he says. "When the Lord took our little Aletta. My Jasmine loved this book, but now Jasmine is too in the arms of Jesus."

Sam and Chrissie page through the book, looking at the photographs which Melissa must have taken of Aletta, Stompie and Jasmine. There is a newspaper clip from the local newssheet, with a story about the study and a photo of Melissa, Jasmine and Aletta with the other mothers and babies, standing in front of the clinic in Willowdale. And James, she suddenly realises. Hovering self-consciously, and looking as if he'd like to join the half of his body that the photographer has cut off. And then there are the cards of condolence, with their praying hands and gilded angels and copperplate homilies.

"You remember my Jasmine? My *laatlammetjie* . . . ?"

"Of course. She was such a pretty girl. Clever too." Sam remembers the child with the elfin grin, a couple of years younger than Melissa. She'd left the farm after Fergus died, and Stompie had gone on his walkabout.

"She came back to live with me when she had the baby. Her mother was rubbish."

"*She* was rubbish," Meisie yells triumphantly from inside the door. "She got the Aids."

Stompie ignores this interjection. "When that baby died the

light went out in Jasmine . . . she was never the same. She died from a broken heart."

"She died from the Aids," cackles Meisie.

Stompie lifts the book and cradles it against his chest. "A broken heart," he repeats. His tone is defiant, but his eyes are pleading.

"I can believe it," Sam says. "Aletta was such a beautiful baby."

Stompie smiles gratefully.

"Ja . . . but they were very kind, those people, you know. They gave us a lot of money – eight thousand rand – after Aletta died. Can you imagine that?"

"Why?" asks Chrissie sharply. "She didn't die because of the research, did she?"

"No, no, no!" Stompie looks shocked at the question. "She is allergic, you see. To nuts. That's why she died. They just gave it to be kind, but poor Jasmine was already passed away that time. I used the money for a nice headstone for them both. So you see, the Lord takes away, but the Lord also gives."

Sam glances at Chrissie, feeling a sudden coldness. Was it possible? That something in the research had caused Aletta's death? But surely Melissa would've told her if she'd found anything like that?

She looks over the images of Aletta as if they might provide answers. But the child smiles back enigmatically, holding the secrets of her brief life to herself.

* * *

Sam walks back to the house alone – Khaya found a litter of black and white kittens on the back seat of the Mercedes in Stompie's yard and refused to leave, so Stompie offered to bring him down later. She thinks uneasily about what Stompie said about the donation by the "kind people".

Eight thousand rand. About a thousand US dollars. Moderately generous as an innocent gesture.

An insultingly paltry sum if someone was concealing culpability . . .

Chapter 18
Confession of a Killer

THINGS settled down after Sister Dorothea took her rubbish bags and green thumbs and repaired to other food gardens. Melissa did not raise those thorny issues again. Was she afraid? Or had she made the decision to trust me? I looked into her eyes for traces of suspicion, but her gaze was candid enough – although she seemed unnerved by my scrutiny.

"Why do you look at me like that?" she asked once, pushing me away – only half playfully.

"I want to see right inside you," I said. "I want to know everything about you."

"It's disturbing . . . it makes me feel exposed."

"Do you have secrets, little wild thing?" I whispered, grazing her shoulder with my teeth.

"You told me that we all have secrets," she said.

But she didn't. Not really. Her eyes were incapable of lying. She'd chosen to trust me, I'm not sure why. Perhaps because I'd helped her rediscover joy, because I'd pressed her hand to life's beating heart, and set her own pulse racing, or just because she believed that trusting someone made them trustworthy. Because she hadn't yet learnt life's most salient and brutal lesson: that our greatest betrayals are always at the hands of those we love most.

The Brazil-nut issue receded, equilibrium was restored. We walked and talked and made love; we laughed, we told stories, we tramped the length and breadth of Cedar Hills, swam in Mermaid's Pool, built fires on cold nights and drank wine beneath the stars, we worshipped each other's bodies with our mouths and hands and eyes. Every second weekend was mine, a poor ration, but I made the most of it to weave the strands that would capture your sister's heart and bind it to mine.

One day Terry told me about a leopard cub that had been found by farm workers – he suspected that the farmer had killed its mother, although they weren't saying. I took Melissa to see it at the wild-animal hospital in Kareedouw.

She held it on her lap and fed it with a baby bottle, entranced by its woolly little head, its baby leopard eyes.

"It's so beautiful . . ." she murmured, laughing softly as it batted her hand with a soft paw.

"We're naming it after you," Terry said with a self-congratulatory grin. "It was James's idea . . ."

"We're planning to rehabilitate it and release it in the kloof when it's old enough," I explained. "So you'll have a little wild sister to look out for."

That was when we started talking about creating a leopard sanctuary – buying up more land in Elandskloof so that we had a proper base there, educating farmers, bringing in cage traps and sheep collars and breeding Anatolian dogs to protect the sheep . . . Life was rich with possibility.

Melissa even began to talk about introducing me to Khaya. Our life together was taking shape, and seemed to roll out before us endlessly into the future. But destiny had set us on a darker path, and its shadows were soon to reach us.

A few weeks after Sister Dorothea's visit there was a party at the clinic for all the Willowdale babies on the programme. There was good reason for celebration: only eighteen per cent of the formula-fed babies had tested HIV positive (they'd probably contracted it at birth), while the average mother-to-child transmission for breast-fed babies in previous studies was around twenty-five per cent – even higher if they were sometimes given a bottle. The results were good news for me too. Aletta was the only Willowdale baby to have developed an allergy, and I was pretty sure that was not linked to the formula.

Melissa invited me to come along. My reception was friendlier than on that first day I'd wandered into the clinic. Only the babies and their mothers were allowed into the clinic grounds, but there was quite a crowd gathered outside to pick up the scrag-ends of any celebration. They parted way for me and ululated encouragingly, making me feel like a reluctant and counterfeit member of the royal family. But when a similar welcome was extended to a pale-skinned delegation from the local Dutch Reformed Church, I realised that I was not as special as I had believed.

The proceedings kicked off with interminable prayers and speeches, relieved by regular outbursts of noisy singing and dancing. Melissa was presented with an appliqué quilt, which apparently depicted her treating a baby being brought by a mother. The baby was almost as big as the mother, and had a blue face – I assume this was artistic licence, rather than portraying a consequence of Melissa's doctoring. I was presented with a small, beribboned basket full of sugary dried fruit.

I spent most of the afternoon with what I hoped was a benign expression on my face, pretending that I knew what was going on. In fact, I could understand virtually nothing that was said – much of it was in Afrikaans or Xhosa, but I even struggled to understand the heavily accented English. Nonetheless, most people seemed to look upon me quite kindly, for which I was grateful.

I watched the participants from my state of bafflement, making a special note of Aletta Stuurman after Melissa pointed her out to me. I'm not good at assessing the merits of babies. But even I could see she had charm. She was a dense package of vivacity, decked in a pink dress sporting an improbable array of frills, who treated everyone she saw to a wide-mouthed, gummy grin. Her dilapidated grandfather was clearly besotted. He paraded her around, regaling whatever audience he could pin down with an inventory of her apparently astonishing achievements. She seemed equally taken with him, and patted the ruins of his face with small hands, cooing with evident delight.

The afternoon wore on. People began to drift off, after shovelling whatever koeksisters and sandwiches remained into their pockets and handbags, until, by five o'clock, most of the throng was gone. I helped Melissa and the clinic staff tidy up, then stood outside in the late afternoon sun while they finished. The red dust hung in the warm air; the brown dog that was tied up across the road dozed on the sun-baked dirt. The evening light seemed to soften the distant sounds of children playing; the clatter of pots as women prepared their meals; the raucous laughter of the men gathered on the corner for a smoke and a few cartons of sorghum beer; the revving engine of some township hotrod; the ubiquitous wails of infants.

I'd just lost myself in speculation about how Melissa and I would spend the night ahead when my reverie was shattered by the urgent roar of a vehicle as a battered bakkie pulled up outside the clinic with a squeal of tyres and a cloud of dust. Stompie Stuurman half climbed, half fell out of the back, his face a grey mask of terror. His granddaughter lolled weakly in his arms.

"*Waar is die dokter?* Where's the doctor?" he screamed. I ran forward to take the child, and Stompie collapsed to his knees.

"*Save* her, mister, in God's name," he whimpered. His hand – a withered claw of distress – clamped to my arm as I took her.

I gently released my arm and ran into the clinic with her. Her lips were blue, and her face swollen. She was unconscious. Melissa grabbed her from me and rushed her into the surgery.

"Call an ambulance," she shouted over her shoulder. "The number's next to the phone."

I did as instructed, and then followed her into the surgery. Melissa and two nurses were fluttering around the small body – far too small, it seemed, to sustain or indeed survive such frenetic attention. The nurses were performing CPR; Melissa was saying, ". . . adrenaline's not working. Her airways are closing. I'll have to do a tracheotomy. Bukelwa, get me a sterilised scalpel. Sannie, take over the heart compression."

She took the scalpel, swabbed the throat and plunged the blade into the child's windpipe. It was shocking, like some scene out of a horror movie when doctor turns to butcher. I realised later that it was the only chance of saving her, but at the time the plunge of that flashing blade flung me into a nightmare world of unreality. Melissa thrust a small tube into the hole she'd made. She breathed into it, while the nurse pushed lightly on the sternum.

It went on – for hours, it seemed, although it could only have been a few minutes. I think another adrenaline shot was applied. There was agitation and urgent requests for instruments, and Aletta's small, grubby feet (the only part of her I could clearly see) jerking mutely to the rhythm of the CPR. And then I became aware that the pace was dropping. A veil of despair was creeping in, shrouding the former urgency, as the realisation dawned: It was too late. And suddenly, everything in the room stilled.

"She's gone," said Melissa quietly. She pulled the bloodied gloves off her hands, held the stethoscope to the child's chest, looked up at the nurses, and shook her head.

"Time of death," she said wearily, looking at her watch, ". . . 6.03 pm." Then she laid her hand lightly on the child's forehead.

"I'm so sorry," she whispered.

They stood gazing at the tiny corpse. There seemed to be an air of expectation in the room, as if we were waiting for some signal from Aletta herself. Perhaps the expectation was only mine . . . it seemed, after all, so improbable that a child who'd been so fiercely alive a few hours ago could now be dead. I became aware that Melissa and the two nurses were holding hands. All three were weeping. I felt a sudden envy that they knew what was appropriate; that they were united in some common expression of sorrow or regret. I was just a block of wood propping up the wall.

As Melissa drew a sheet over Aletta's face, the siren of the approaching ambulance could be heard, bewailing its futility.

Chapter 19

IT rains all night that night, a soft rain like a young girl weeping, a gentle drumming on the tin roof. Despite its soothing sound, Sam's dreams are unhappy, tortured things.

She is climbing the cliffs above Mermaid's Pool, where the swallows nest in the small hollows scooped out over centuries by the vagaries of wind and rain. She is trying to follow Chrissie, who is moving rapidly, her bare legs catching the sun. *Wait, Chrissie, wait . . .* But Chrissie just looks down at her, laughing, and pushes something off a ledge. It falls towards her, rolling over. Melissa, baby Melissa, wearing her blue dress with the yellow buttercups, tumbling over and over, as she falls, while the swallows swoop and twitter around her. Sam tries to catch her, but she slips past, the yellow buttercups floating on the blue of her dress, Melissa smiling sweetly as she plummets to earth.

Wake up, wake up, wake up before she dies.

And then she is awake. And Melissa is dead.

Sam climbs out of her bed and into Khaya's, burying her face in the warmth of his back. He moves away, muttering in protest.

Bugger you, she shouts silently to who-knows-what demons hiding in the rain-swept darkness. She'll reclaim it, she decides. She'll claw her way back into the heart of Elandskloof, as she had clawed her way up the cliffs of her dream, inch by inch if necessary. And she'll start with Mermaid's Pool tomorrow.

* * *

She sets off late the following morning, leaving Khaya and Mimsy with Dylan. It is one of those still, faintly ominous, sunless days where everything seems to be holding its breath. The only sounds are rainwater dripping off trees, the liquid calls of the golden orioles, the squelch of her feet on the hard sand.

The path is narrow, and her shoes are soon soaked through by the long, soggy grass on either side. But her feet are content, feeling out a path that they know so well, happily recognising each familiar turn, each rock, each mossy enclave in the bank. As she walks, she hears Chrissie's ouma telling them about the mermaids: *Their hair is black as night and long like the roots of the old fig trees. Their skin is like honey, but they are the devil's things. When you hear their song, ah, their song is sweeter than a thousand birds, but if you listen, they'll steal you. They'll pull you deep into the cold, dark water, and feed your bones to the water serpent. Beware when the moon is full, children, for then the kloof fills with the song of the water spirits, and those with one foot in the spirit world will hear it and be unable to resist its call.*

"How does she know?" Sam had asked Chrissie later.

"'Cos it happened to her sister on her wedding day," Chrissie said.

"Did the water serpent crunch her bones?"

"Yes. All they found was her wedding dress, floating in the water, and her heart. That is why the water is red – it is still stained with her blood."

"Why didn't the water serpent eat her heart?"

"Because it was pure. The water serpent can only eat the heart of sinners."

"I bet she just drowned," said Sam, the doctor's daughter, who'd learnt that science was a reliable antidote to terror. But science was no match for the logic that drove Chrissie's underworld. She rolled her eyes in disbelief.

"Don't be so dumb! Don't you remember when Tollie Ockert drowned? They found his whole body, didn't they? If they only find your heart, it's the water serpent."

"Do hearts float?" Sam asked her father at dinner that evening, hoping for some refuting evidence before she faced the black well of night. He looked at her blankly, as if she'd asked him a completely inappropriate question (Does the sky sing? Do stones fall in love?), and told her to eat up her vegetables.

The tales are easy to believe of Mermaid's Pool – a ragged oval of deep burgundy suspended between two waterfalls, opaque as wine. Or blood, although Sam knows now that the colour comes from the roots of the fynbos that grows on its banks. It is so different from the other mountain pools, with their mosaics of jade and golden rock and pebbles glowing beneath the clear water. And even now she half expects to find floating on its surface a white lacy dress and a bright red heart, as pure as a young girl's piety.

But when she reaches the path above the pool, its wine-red surface is quite empty. She makes her way down, pausing when she spots the rounded spoor of a Cape clawless otter. She holds her breath, and creeps forward around a huge sandstone boulder bearded with grey-and-orange lichen. And there it is. Poised on the large, flat rock next to the pool, crunching a crab. Sam feels an electric jolt of recognition, as if she's rediscovered a part of herself she'd lost. *Yes . . . thank you*, she breathes softly, as the skin of Elandskloof's wild heart opens and lets her in.

The otter eats its crab with infinite delicacy, holding it between its forepaws and sucking flesh from its legs. The sun pushes its way through the sullen clouds, sending fingers of blue-black rays from the sky to the earth. Sam dissolves into it, becomes the rock, and feels the warm, wet weight of the otter, the brittle shower of fragmented crab shell. She is river, tree, sky . . . she is the otter's silken fur as it slides off the rock, the cool rush of water past its tiny ears, the joyous swoop and surge of its rolling body.

The otter raises its head above the surface of the pool, creating a synchronised dance of expanding ripples as the water drips from its whiskers. A small spider rides the wash of waves. The sun casts rays of golden light through the leaves of the surrounding trees, illuminating tiny details – a grey leaf here, a skating water beetle there, a hovering blue dragonfly – endowing each with a brief moment of radiance. Sam is weightless, without substance, a borderless sphere of reverence.

And then she sees James.

* * *

He is standing on the other side of the pool, on a small sandy cove below the steep jagged cliffs that plunge into the pool alongside the waterfall. For a moment, she thinks he is an illusion, a trick of light and shadow. He stands so still, not seeming to breathe, his eyes fixed on the pool where the otter surfaced a moment before.

As if suddenly conscious of their presence, the otter slips out of the pool on the other side, slides noiselessly over the rocks, dives into the water again and disappears downstream. Sam watches it go, feeling it all drain out of her – the river, the sunlight, the otter. She is empty, and cast out. Once more an outsider, with her face pressed against the glass.

She watches James picking his way over the rocks and crossing the rudimentary wooden bridge unhurriedly towards her. Her father built that bridge with Piet and Stompie Stuurman so that they could cross the river and hold picnics on the little sandy beach . . . All the railings and some of the slats have washed away in floods over the years, but it still offers a way over the deepest part of the river as it runs between the rocks.

As he draws closer, she feels her resentment growing. Why did he have to fuck it up for her just when it had almost come right . . . ?

"What are you doing here?" she asks sharply as he approaches, but he doesn't hear over the roar of the waterfall – or chooses not to.

"Well, hello! I see you made the trip after all . . . well done."

She nods cursorily.

"I used to come here with Melissa . . . it's beautiful, isn't it?"

Her annoyance deepens. She doesn't want to share intimate memories of her sister with this man.

"God! That's quite a look you've got there, Samantha. Are you related to Medusa by any chance? Look, I'll make a deal with you. I'm sorry if I disturbed you here, but I've found something close by which is pretty bloody amazing. If you stop scowling at me, and come across, I'll show you."

"What?"

"Nope, not telling. You have to trust me. Or not see it. I don't mind."

He swings on his heel, and walks back over the bridge and the rocks across the pool.

"It's above the pool on this side," he calls over his shoulder.

That side is his land, Sam realises, with a flush of embarrassment – the river at this point marks the boundary between their farms. She hesitates, but in the end, curiosity wins out over pride, and she strides after him.

They climb in silence away from the pool, following a track that winds up through the thicket of spekboom, crassula and thorn bushes covering the surrounding slopes. The steep path was created by animals on their way to the water and it often disappears altogether. Thorns and twigs scratch her legs and hands, her feet slide on loose rocks. Beyond the shade of the pool the sun beats down fiercely, and Sam is over-warm in her jeans and fleece-lined top.

They finally ascend the cliff, and backtrack through the scrubby fynbos along the edge towards the waterfall, watched by a disdainful steppe buzzard perched on the white branch of a dead tree. After about three hundred metres James scrambles back over the edge, and makes his way along a narrow ledge. He has not said a word. Sam follows uneasily, remembering her dream of the tumbling Melissa in her buttercup dress. Death comes easily in a place like this: a falling rock, a misplaced step, a sluggish puff adder . . . A small boulder dislodged by his foot careers wildly down into the depths, mocking her fears. Then James lifts a curtain of hanging vegetation, and disappears.

She hesitates, then pushes the creepers aside and follows him into the dark space beyond. As her eyes adjust, she finds herself in a large sandy cave – high enough for her to stand upright – with smooth sandstone walls the colour of pale honey. The whole of one side is covered in paintings.

There are several reddish-brown mermaid-like figures, some clear, others faded. One figure is serpentine, with a head and arms and a long, wavy, legless body, which seems to form a thread connecting the others.

Further along the cave is a painting of an eland. It is upside down, with wavy red and black lines emanating from its body and its mouth. It is outlined in black, filled in with red ochre. It is apparently dying, yet vividly brought to life by expressive, simple lines.

They stand in silence, breathing the smell of the dusty leaves and branches overhanging the cave, listening to the forlorn cry of a fish eagle and the distant roar of the waterfall. The cave sighs with the ghosts of the long-dead artists. She imagines them mixing their paints, applying the colours – what would they be? Blood? Ash? Clay? The marks look so fresh – as if their creators have just stepped outside for a moment, and somehow forgotten to return.

She becomes aware that James has left her to sit on the ledge outside. She stays for a long time, staring at the pictures, tears running down her cheeks. Who is she weeping for? The long-dead eland, the lost San, the tragic narratives inscribed in the rock seams of the kloof? Her sister? Or her own lost self?

By the time she emerges, the sun is turning to late afternoon, dipping low over the western hills. Mermaid's Pool lies some twenty feet below them, offering a perfectly mirrored world of cliffs and sky. High above, the fish eagle circles lazily against the shredded clouds.

"It's incredible," she says, sliding down onto the ledge next to him.

"Yes."

"I can't believe I never knew about it. I've been to Mermaid's Pool so often, and I never had any idea . . . How on earth did you find it? You'd never see it if you didn't know it was there."

"I was tracking a leopard . . . It was sheer luck, really. I stumbled against those overhanging bushes, and when I put my hand out to stop myself falling, the bushes gave way and I landed in the cave."

"It's lucky you didn't fall the other way."

"Yes, it is, isn't it?" He smiles at her ironically.

"Did you find your leopard?"

"I found traces of her. I've been trying to get her in a cage trap for weeks – we want to weigh her and collar her, but she's really canny. The males just walk into the traps. I think she hangs out around here . . . she was here not so long ago. Look." He points to the damp sand at the edge of the cave, which holds two well-formed leopard spoor. "That's pretty fresh. It was certainly made since the rain this morning . . . she's probably watching us right now."

Sam glances around, half-expecting to find a pair of yellow eyes staring at her. James laughs.

"Oh, you won't see her. Unless she wants you to."

"That painting . . ." she says. "It's strange, isn't it, that there are mermaids in it? Perhaps that's the origin of the name for Mermaid's Pool. Chrissie's ouma used to tell us stories about the water serpent and the mermaids that steal people to feed it."

"Possibly, although those stories might have also come from people who came here later, saw the paintings, and invented tales about it.

"There is a similar painting in the Southern Cape, which was shown to one of the Bushmen that Wilhelm Bleek worked with. He said the people with fishtails were 'rain-people' who protected people from the anger of the rain bull, which used to travel on earth as an eland. This painting may be recording a ritual to protect people against those violent floods you get here occasionally. The fishtail is metaphoric, I think. It refers to the trance state that shamans would go into, because being in a trance is like being underwater."

Sam stares at him in surprise, a little annoyed that he should know more about it than she does. "You've been doing your homework!"

"There are quite a few paintings on my farm. I became interested in them and did a little background reading. It's fascinating, really . . . they had such a different world view, the San. As if there were no boundaries between them and their environment, as if spirit, self and the natural world were in a constant state of flux . . ."

Sam gazes out at the scene below her. "It is easy to imagine that here. If you try to separate yourself from the landscape, try to pit yourself against it, you can only destroy yourself."

James shifts his position, sending another small rock plummeting down the cliff. It bounces off the rock walls and lands in the pool. "That's what drew me back here, to Elandskloof. I've spent a lot of time in wild places, but this place was the first that made me feel truly oceanic."

"Oceanic?"

"It's a Freudian term. That state of being where there is no boundary between yourself and the rest of the world. He said that infants and mystical people felt it, but not scientific people."

"So would you classify yourself as mystical or infantile?"

"I'd dispute his assessment. If science has taught us anything, it is that the more you try to define matter, the less material it becomes. Take electrons, for instance: no one really knows whether they are waves or particles or something else entirely. All we know is that all matter consists of moving energy and 99.9% empty space. Looked at this way, the boundaries between oneself and the rest of the world are somewhat illusionary..."

Oceanic... yes. That's what she's been longing for since Melissa's death, what she'd experienced fleetingly while watching the otter. As if that brutal event has flung a hard shell around her, sealing her off – from the earth, from love. From life.

"The weird thing is," he said, "I feel those boundaries so distinctly when I'm with other people, and yet they seem to disappear in places like this... maybe that's what draws us loners to the wild... that escape from alienation..."

She glances up, disturbed that he is echoing her own feelings so closely. He is watching her intently. She looks away, but not before she has seen something in his eyes – something calculating, but also sombre. As if he'd taken her measure and knows that it is not enough to save either of them. *Oh, I know about regret*, he'd said.

She doesn't care to know of his regrets. She has sufficient of her own.

A flash of iridescent blue and orange catches her eye as a malachite kingfisher darts beneath them. It drops, snags a fish, and flies up towards a nearby branch. But before it reaches it, the fish eagle swoops down with a soft whoosh of wings above their heads, and snatches the kingfisher in its talons. The fish drops back into the water.

"God!" she exclaims, glad of the distraction. "That was something!"

"Yup. Doesn't do to be too complacent around here. Even the predators are prey." He stands up. "Talking about predators, we'd better get moving. Leopards see a lot better in the dark than we do."

She stands up too, and brushes the leaves and dust off her pants.

"My house lies back over the cliff. Can you find your way back down to the pool without killing yourself?"

"No problem. And James, thanks – those paintings are extraordinary."

"You're welcome. By the way, I haven't spread the word around about them – I'll let the right people know, eventually, but I'd like to keep it secret a little longer, if you don't mind."

"Of course."

"Well, so long then. Just watch your feet going down. And watch your back."

She scrambles down the path to the pool, and crosses the rocks. As she reaches the other side, she looks up. James is silhouetted against the evening sky, watching her, flanked by two aloe sentinels. He lifts his hand to wave.

She waves back, and turns to make her way back, feeling his eyes on her. She trudges on down the path through the darkening hills. She doesn't feel oceanic now, despite the aching beauty around her. She feels prickly and haunted by unspoken questions.

Chapter 20
Confession of a Killer

IT was an allergy that killed her. On the way back from the party, apparently one of the children gave Aletta a biscuit with nuts in it. By the time her face had started swelling and the pick-up had turned around and driven back to the clinic, twenty minutes had been lost. She had a nut allergy that no one had discovered until it was too late.

Melissa took it surprisingly hard. This little hamlet was no stranger to death, after all. She'd buried many young patients who'd succumbed to the implacable twins of Aids and TB, and the graveyard where Aletta was interred sported a rash of freshly turned mounds.

The funeral was tortuous, as you can imagine – Stompie Stuurman hunched like a broken-winged bird in the dirt, his mouth a black square of grief. Saliva, mucus and tears poured out of him in an incontinent torrent as his body convulsed at what he had lost. Jasmine was too ill – or too distressed – to attend.

I stood beside your sister, painfully aware of the tender fragility of her neck, as we bowed our heads while the priest committed Aletta's body to return to the dust from where it came. As if to claim its own, the gritty red dust rose in small eddies around us, coating the polished shoes of the men and the white paint of Aletta's small coffin. Goats grazed amongst the neighbouring graves, unmoved.

"She was a symbol," Melissa tried to explain when I questioned the depth of her sorrow. "I know a lot of babies die here. But she was one who had cheated HIV, and she was a symbol of hope for people who have only hope to keep them going.

"And I've known her family all my life . . . I used to play with Jasmine when we were children . . . Stompie lives on our farm . . .

they are like my relatives. And we have a complicated history with them."

Then she told me the timeless, tragic tale of the Stuurmans, the Campbells and the Koekemoers.

"You can't keep taking on the sins of your forefathers," I said. "You can't erase what they did by forestalling any tragedy that might darken the Stuurman door."

"Don't be trite, James. I know that. But I was her doctor. I could at least have forestalled this one."

But of course the biggest shadow hanging over her was the concern that Aletta's death was somehow linked to the research project.

She didn't discuss this with me – perhaps she was afraid to voice her fears – but I knew it was eating away at her. One night at Cedar Hills I woke alone in the early hours. I walked through the house, and found her sitting at your father's desk, her face like an underwater thing in the glow of the green desk lamp. Her hair was tousled by sleep; her legs were tucked up under her. She was unbearably beautiful. I mean that – unbearable. My whole being suddenly ached with sorrow at seeing her, as if I'd had some presentiment of her death.

As I drew nearer, I saw that she was reading through medical notes. I was not surprised to see that the name on the pink case folder next to her was Aletta Stuurman.

"What are you looking for?" I asked.

She jumped, and swung round. "I don't know . . . I'm just trying to understand it."

"What is there to understand? She died from an allergy. It was pretty straightforward."

"I know. I just . . ."

"You're worried that something in the formula contributed to it."

I'd said it. The words hung there, suspended in the ticking of the grandfather clock. She looked at me searchingly.

"Should I be worried?"

I quelled my impatience. "No. Of course you shouldn't. How could it be related? Even if there was something in the formula, she hadn't even been on it for months. And none of the other babies have reacted."

"Dr Jansen from Humansdorp said one of their babies had also shown a mild reaction a few months ago – about the same time she had that rash. They tested him – he wasn't allergic to soy, but he also seems to have a tree-nut allergy. Seems a bit of a coincidence, don't you think?"

"Not really. Tree-nut allergies occur in about one per cent of the population – and there are six hundred babies on the programme. Two out of six hundred is only about 0.03%. If they both have allergies, possibly both were exposed to traces of nuts, perhaps from sucking their mother's fingers or something. Or just from birth. There is no way the formula could have contained nuts."

"It couldn't have been contaminated in the processing?"

"Of course not. Nuts are nowhere near those factories. But we'll get it tested if you're concerned."

"Would you?"

"Of course. I'll pick up a tin from the clinic tomorrow and take it through. But they won't find anything."

She sighed. "I know, I'm being stupid. I'm sorry. But it would make me feel better."

She picked up the stethoscope that was lying on the desk. "This was my father's. I can't stop myself feeling that by letting Aletta die, I let him down."

I put my arms around her, and kissed the top of her head. "Your father would be so fucking proud of you he wouldn't know what to do with himself."

She looked up at me. "Really? How do you know? You didn't know him."

"No, but I know you. If you were my daughter, I'd run down every street in the world with a loudhailer proclaiming it for all to hear. But I'm glad you're not, because otherwise I'd have to commit incest."

She gave me a shove. "Get away, you old pervert."

"Seriously, Melissa, you have to stop blaming yourself. It's a form of narcissism, you know."

"Narcissism?" she said, indignantly.

"Yes. You're playing God . . . if you take the blame for Aletta's death, you're implying that you could've done something to save her. But you couldn't. It was just one of those things. You're an extraordinary person and an excellent doctor and extremely dear to my heart. But in the end you're just a woman. You did your best, but it wasn't enough. And if you can't live with the harsh realities of that fact, then you're in the wrong profession."

Does that sound brutal? Perhaps . . . but I was trying to save her. I could not bear the darkness that was creeping over your sister's heart. She was retreating back into the shadows, and I was determined to keep her in the light. And if you are wondering whether I had to quell my own misgivings to reassure her, the answer is no. At that point I was completely confident that nothing in the formula could have contributed to Aletta's death.

I did have the formula tested – as I expected, no traces of nuts were found. Melissa didn't raise the issue again. But I could see she was uneasy. And much as I tried to silence Aletta's little ghost, I had a niggling feeling she'd be haunting us for some time to come.

CHAPTER 21

ON the day after her expedition to Mermaid's Pool, Sam and Khaya ride in Jannie's double cab down to Viskraal farm to release the eland. Sam sits in the back, trying to pay attention as Jannie and Dylan eagerly fill her in on the intricacies of the negotiations around the wildlife reserve. But things keep distracting her . . . the way Jannie's ears waggle when he smiles . . . the small pimple next to Dylan's nose . . . a bug squashed on the windshield. This is not intransigence so much as overload. Just being in Elandskloof is sapping all her emotional resources. All she feels capable of is sitting in the cave above Mermaid's Pool, with the paintings and the San ghosts, and staring into darkness.

Still, some words drift through her consciousness, trailing images of her childhood neighbours – now "stakeholders" – as they grapple with new challenges: the farmers gathering at the Willowdale Arms, dipping their moustaches into the foam of Lion Lagers and muttering about "land take-overs" and "the Zimbabwe situation" under the glassy stare of the stuffed springbok, around whose neck an irreverent patron once hung a Willowdale Rugby Union tie; the dispossessed clustered around *papsakke* of cheap sweet wine in dusty back yards, expressing variously the hope of long-awaited salvation, or the cynicism of those whose suffering is considered only fleetingly around election time. While wives slap washing contemptuously against the rocks in the river, and jeer at their men for believing they have choices.

It's hard to take in. The Elandskloof of her memory is a place of limitless silence. Every living thing, it had seemed – her larger-than-life parents, bullet-faced Grace who worked in their kitchen and harboured obscure and terrible grievances, their enormous dogs, the doe-eyed cows – all were swallowed into nothingness by those long, hot afternoons, fat with the buzzing of flies, when she lay on the lounge floor kicking her feet in the sweltering air, and wondered if anything would ever happen again.

But now there is this agitation. How do they come to grips with it? she wonders. Most of them are deeply entrenched in lives that have experienced little change, even from one generation to the next. No wonder they're scurrying around like ants who've had the anthill kicked.

She'd not anticipated this, foolishly. She'd imagined, if she'd imagined it at all, a landscape populated only by ghosts and frozen in time. A physical manifestation of her own emotional geography.

Dylan is explaining something (how he loves to explain – those cavorting hands, those nostrils that actually flare) about a model conservancy project . . . alien clearing . . . restored riverine vegetation alleviating flood damage . . . extra employment . . . twenty kilometres of fencing taken up. (Twenty kilometres! How long it must have taken the farmer to bang those posts into the ground, and stretch the unforgiving wire between them. How many blistered hands and blackened fingernails?) She tries, at least, to listen, and not to begrudge his enthusiasm, his inability to grasp that this place is not just a conundrum of ecology versus development, but some deep and ancient narrative destined to break the hearts of all who dare transgress it.

Jannie is pointing out the white-thorned acacia trees surrounding the road. "These are Pioneer trees – they're like nature's nursemaids for convalescing bushveld. They grow quickly, providing shade and cover for the struggling shrubs and indigenous grasses beneath. They attract birds, which bring seeds from all over to repopulate the earth. Then they die after about twenty years, and decompose to provide nutrients for the slower-growing forest trees."

"They're not pinier trees," says Khaya firmly.

"Why not?" asks Jannie, startled.

"They haven't got pine cones."

Sam laughs. "Let's see you explain that one, Jannie."

* * *

The eland are housed in a high-walled boma fenced with striplings and hessian. Sam sits on the bakkie roof with Khaya, lost in the great curves of their humped shoulders and dewlaps, the backward-spiralled thrust of their horns, the long contemplation of their noses, the silent pools of their almond-shaped black eyes beneath the matted triangle of fur. Their eyes seem to harbour a sorrowful wisdom, as if they know the fate of the world.

"They came a few days ago, from a game farm up near Craddock," Jannie explains. "I think they're settled enough to go out now."

They undo the poles. One or two animals move forward cautiously, and step through the entrance. They glance around, ears and tails flicking. Then they begin to move off, at a slow trot and then a run. And suddenly the whole herd streams out in a thunder of hooves and grunts, and a strange barking. A river of horns and warm brown bodies and wild eyes rushes past them to the hills above.

Khaya and Sam look at each other and grin.

"So there you are, Khaya," says Sam. "The eland are running free in Elandskloof again!"

"Yay! The eland are free in Elandskloof, the eland are free in Elandskloof . . ." He does a little dance on top of the bakkie. "Can I keep an eland in my bedroom?"

"No."

"Why?"

"'Cos then it wouldn't be free."

Khaya thinks about this. "But it would be cosy," he says. "I could give it bikkies."

"Sometimes," says Sam, wondering if she means it, "it is more important to be free than cosy."

* * *

Sam sits drinking tea in Kobus Koekemoer's front room. She has come to fetch Khaya, who is playing with Kobus's children. But also because she has a question.

He sits opposite her, a large man with a purposeful, slightly lumbering gait suggestive of some kind of agricultural machinery. His face is baked red by weather and scoured into deep furrows around his eyes and mouth; his stomach – like his father's – is an expansive balloon. His smile is different from Oom Hennie's, though – a kind of sideways tug of the mouth, a small crinkling and twinkling of eyes, ironical and a little shy.

She glances around the room as he pours the tea. They are in a square of yellow face brick, with small windows offering niggardly glimpses of the panorama outside. It is neat, but harbours the slightly forlorn air of a man unused to creating his own home – Kobus's wife left him some months ago. The couch on which Sam sits is a modular dark brown block of foam, dotted with stained, faded cushions and two Jack Russells. In the middle of the room is a wicker-and-glass coffee table piled with old *Landbou Weekblad* magazines and a glass ashtray set in a miniature Firestone rubber tyre. An overflowing toolbox stands in one corner; the brightly coloured plastic detritus of small children litters the floor. The stucco walls are enlivened with photographs of his children, and framed jigsaw puzzles depicting an Alpine mountain scene, fishing boats in a Cornish harbour, a North American forest in autumnal splendour.

"My wife did those," Kobus says, following her eyes. "She sat up all night, putting all these little bits together. It drove me nuts watching her do those things. I shouldn't have got irritated, though. It's a hard life for a woman, being out here."

"It depends . . ." Sam automatically rises to defend her sex. "I wouldn't mind living here."

Kobus smiles at her sceptically. "Really? Then why don't you?"

Sam shrugs. "I have to earn a living. Cedar Hills was never viable as a farm."

"Ag, we all have hard-scrabble farms out here, Samantha. Since the seed market went belly up, we're all scraping a living.

That's why I agree with your pal Jannie. This reserve is the only thing that will save the valley. I don't know why the farmers don't just take the department's offer and get out. They're lucky to find a buyer for their farms."

"Are you going to sell?"

"No way, Josè! Can you imagine me living anywhere else? This place is stuck in my bones, man. No, I'm going the conservancy route. What about you?"

"I haven't decided yet. I heard you were going into the leopard thing with James McIntyre."

"Well, I thought about it – it's an interesting project he's got going there, but it's too pie in the sky at the moment. The department can offer me more concrete benefits now, so I scheme I'll go in with them. Biscuit?" he suggests, offering a platter of Lemon Creams. Sam declines.

He nets two Lemon Creams in a meaty paw, baptises them in his tea and delivers them to his mouth.

"Ja, well, people are also confused by my dear brother Neels, filling everybody's heads with this idea that they should run their own game farms."

Kobus rattles his cup as he lowers it onto the table. Sam wonders suddenly if he finds her presence disconcerting.

"That idea doesn't appeal to you?"

"Ag, it's rubbish, man. Look, you can't get the whole ecosystem dingus working properly when there are fences everywhere. The animals have to be able to roam free, you know, especially the big guys – kudu, buffalo, eland. And you have to let the land recover properly if you are going to sustain big herds without supplementary feeding. In Neels's setup, the most you can hope for is a few *springbokkies* and impala. Neels is even talking about getting some lions in a camp for the tourists to take a potshot at. Canned hunting! It's sickening, man."

Sam looks at him with surprise, recalling the prolific assortment of stuffed heads, leopard skins and mounted horns in the Koekemoer *voorkamer* . . . and that prized photo of Hennie and his three older sons posing with the carcase of what must have been one of the last eland in Elandskloof. Holding its head up as if it was really still alive, as if they were all just having fun for the camera.

Kobus catches her look. "Ja, ja. I guess you think that's funny coming from a trigger-happy Koekemoer, hey? But, you know, my old man would never have gone for canned hunting, uh-uh. He had too much respect for animals."

"So, you landed up buying Oom Kleinhans's farm. You didn't want to change the name?"

He smiles. "Ja, 'Wanhoop' is hardly optimistic, hey? Mind you, that old Oom Kleinhans was a miserable old bugger ever since his son died. Do you remember when we were laaities? We were always daring each other to steal peaches from his orchard. We were convinced that he would shoot any kid he found on his land."

"He did – don't you remember? He shot Klaasie Stuurman's backside full of birdshot."

Kobus makes a curious noise, rather like a rusty gate being swung to and fro – it takes Sam a few seconds to realise that he is laughing. "Ja, ja, I'd forgotten. We used to pay him a tikkie to take down his broeks and show us his bum. *Ja wat*, but that old Oom Kleinhans came to a sad end, you know. He went completely bossies. Ended up living in an old sharecropper's cave in the mountains. Just with an old cooking pot and a blanket. He chucked rocks at anyone who tried to get him out of there."

"What happened to him?"

"Ag, shame, he died up there. The bush pigs got to his body before anyone else. One of his farm boys found him – or what was left of him."

Kobus's daughter comes in, carefully carrying a lump of mud on an arum lily leaf. "Here, Pappie, have some cake."

"Mmm, what's this? Chocolate cake? My favourite!"

The little girl giggles. "No, it's mud cake," she shouts.

"Mm, mud cake, even better, that's my real favourite! I pretended I wanted chocolate cake but what I really wanted was a lekker oozy slice of mud cake."

She shrieks with delight. "Eat it! Eat it all up!"

Kobus waves it under his mouth and makes chomping noises. "Mmm, *heerlik*!" he says, slapping his prodigious gut.

"Can I have some?" says Sam. The child looks at her with surprised distaste as if she were a bug floating in the milk. "No, it's all for my daddy," she says, and scampers out of the room.

Sam laughs. "Cute kid."

Kobus smiles proudly. "Ja, they're great aren't they? I really miss them when they're with their mom, but what can you do?" He shrugs, and carefully lays his mud cake down on the table.

Outside, the afternoon light deepens into the gold of early evening. It is time to go. Sam takes a deep breath.

"Kobus, I don't know if I ever thanked you . . . you know . . . for rescuing Khaya . . . after the accident."

"Ag, you don't need to thank me for that, Sam. I just did what anyone would have done . . . I was grateful to your sister, you know. She was very kind to my wife, Erika."

A silence blossoms in the darkening room. One of the Jack Russells utters little yips and twitches his miniature legs, chasing who knows what in his dreams. Outside, the children laugh and squeal. Khaya and Kobus's son are playing a game involving marching up and down banging stones together and shouting what sounds like "bingy bom bat".

"I just wondered . . ." she is trying unsuccessfully to sound casual, "whether you saw anything that may have suggested that someone else had been there with Melissa . . ."

He looks at her thoughtfully. "Actually, it's funny that you should ask that."

Her heart jolts. Does she really want to know this? "Why?"

"Well, when I got there, there was an aloe lying in the road."

"An aloe?" This is not what she'd expected.

"Yes, uprooted from the bank at the side, by the look of it. That's what made me stop, actually, because I had to move it, you see. That's when I noticed the car tracks going over, and then I looked over and saw her car. I might not have seen it otherwise.

"I didn't pay much attention, once I saw the car and . . . your sister, of course. Then I was just concerned with bringing little Khaya back. But I did mention it to the police."

"What did they say?"

"Ag, they didn't seem to make much of it. They said that there had been rain the day before, and the aloe probably fell over into the road – maybe she'd swerved to avoid it, and that's why she went over. They said that maybe she thought it was an animal, or something, in the dark . . ."

"But you didn't think so?"

"Ja, well, I wasn't sure. The aloe looked to me like it had been dragged across the road a bit – there were marks in the mud. And who'd go over Grasnek to avoid hitting an aloe? But I guess if she'd come round the corner and seen it, suddenly like, she might have just jerked the wheel slightly – that's all it would take on a road like that. I don't know . . ." He breaks off as he catches the horror in her face.

"But you know what, Sam?" His tone becomes brisk. "I think the police are right. I mean, who'd have put that aloe there, and gone off? It makes no sense. *Ja nee*, I'm sure they are right. It just came to my mind when you asked me that question, but I don't think you should read anything into it."

"No, no, of course not," agrees Sam.

* * *

She lies in bed that night thinking about what Kobus said. An aloe? It is so bizarre.

She stares through the open curtains at the dizzying cluster of stars that hang like iridescent fruits in the branches of the pepper tree. There are eland out there, she thinks suddenly. Wild eland roaming Elandskloof for the first time in decades.

It is more comforting to think about wild eland than misplaced aloes. But the aloe has been dragged across her mind, bringing with it the appalling possibility that someone might have wanted Melissa dead.

And all the eland in the world cannot remove that thought now.

CHAPTER 22
Confession of a Killer

TWO weeks after Aletta's funeral, I had to return to the US to finish writing up my research and process the data. Melissa dropped me at the airport. As we said goodbye, I held her against me, feeling the fluttering bird of her heart against my chest.

"Come back soon," she said, with a bleak smile. I thought from her voice that she might cry a little after I'd left. It was about the closest she'd come to a declaration of love.

As I walked away from her into the squat, unprepossessing building, my heart felt as if I'd tipped it out and let it fall onto the unforgiving tarmac. How could I leave her? Especially now, when she was so fragile, a wild flower in the wind.

I felt such desolation. I don't believe in premonitions, but it was as if I knew that by the time I returned the trust and tenderness now shining in her eyes would be erased forever.

I suppose it is time for me to explain to you the nature of my research. The formula we were using was genetically engineered – I'm sure you've worked that out. But it was not some crass Frankenstein cobbling together of genetic material, like the Brazil-nut soybean or the salmon strawberry (which was why I took such umbrage at Melissa's inferences). No. The soybean I'd developed was a thing of beauty – elegant, streamlined, working not in defiance of nature but alongside it. Taking it by the hand and gently nudging it into a more pleasing form.

At the risk of boring you, let me give you the bare bones of the process. I'm sure you know that food allergies are caused by proteins – that is one of the reasons why injudicious planting of foreign proteins in food crops can lead to an increase in allergies. Scientists have been working for some time to find ways of reducing the allergenicity of soybeans, using both plant-breeding methods and transgenic methods, such as Buchan's work with thioredoxin.

But none of these were really successful. And then a couple of years ago, we had a major breakthrough. The major allergen in soybean is a protein called Gly m Bd 30K – also known as P34. It is not possible to remove this with plant-breeding techniques, as the gene is expressed in all strains of soybean, including wild ones. The only route was genetic engineering, but early efforts had limited success – and limited commercial application. But what we discovered was something quite remarkable. If you insert extra copies of the gene that codes P34 into the DNA, this increases the messenger RNA that tells the cells to make the protein P34. This surge of RNA is interpreted by the plant as a viral infection, so it destroys the RNA, and eventually silences the P34 gene. In other words, *adding genes for P34 actually eliminates it.*

Silencing P34 seems to have no adverse effect on the plant. It thrives. But without it, although there are one or two other minor allergens, the soybean is largely hypoallergenic.

When I got involved in the Willowdale research project, a number of studies had been done, with both human serum and animals, which demonstrated the soybean's hypoallergenic properties. However, to develop the bean commercially, NuGrowth, who funded my doctoral research and own the patent on the bean, wanted a more extensive study done with humans – in particular human babies, as they wanted to promote the use of this bean for infant formula. I jumped at the opportunity when they asked me to supervise it – it would give me a break from a few years of huge pressure while working on my doctoral thesis, and I believed it'd be tremendously beneficial to the babies involved.

Now before you draw up your skirts and shriek about testing genetically engineered soy on African babies, let me point out a few things. Firstly, this was, as I said, an elegant transformation. I was not introducing anything foreign to the soybean. I was merely adding more copies of a naturally occurring gene.

Secondly, genetically engineered soy is given to babies all

the time, all over the world. The FDA has declared that genetically engineered food is "substantially equivalent" to other food. Therefore, there is no need to test it for safety, and no need even to label it – legislation that your government has endorsed. People are eating it and giving it to their infants daily without even knowing. Is this ethical? Possibly not. In those days, I didn't concern myself too much with such questions. But ethical or not, it was legal and accepted, and this was the context in which I was operating.

It is important to remember here that we weren't testing the soy for safety because it was genetically engineered. No one has really bothered with that, at least not with long-term safety. There'd only been one study by then, by Dr Arpad Pusztai – a renowned Hungarian scientist, who developed a way of testing the safety of the *process* of genetic engineering – i.e. irrespective of the specific modification that is done. When he published his results indicating that there may indeed be cause for concern in the longer term, he also discovered that years of good standing and a distinguished career were no protection against the march of opportunism. He lost his job and his research was discredited.

I am a cautious beast now. I have learnt that no spoon is really long enough if you want to sup with the devil without burning yourself. But in those days, I was the rising star, a brilliant young scientist, a leader of my pack. My motives were primarily self-serving – I wanted fame and glory like everyone else – but I did want to garner that fame by endowing the world with something beneficial. I dissociated myself from the clunky deformities that NuGrowth released onto the fields of the world – the ones that kill ladybirds and foster superweeds – and I certainly did not set out to enrich NuGrowth. But I foolishly believed that NuGrowth and I could come to an agreement and achieve each of our ends.

What we were testing was whether this soy was indeed hypoallergenic, and the marriage of convenience that I so rashly entered involved a number of parties. There was NuGrowth, who in addition to the motivations I mentioned earlier, also wanted to establish markets for their products in South Africa, and were engaged in an intensive campaign to woo South Africa's somewhat naïve fledgling government. There were the South African politicians, who, as Melissa pointed out, wanted to give the impression that they were taking steps in combating mother-to-child transmission of Aids by supplying formula, rather than through the more obvious and effective administration of AZT and ARV's. There was my university department, eager to build on a very lucrative relationship with NuGrowth. And there was me.

Along the way it was decided that we need not mention to the mothers and the doctors collecting data that the formula was genetically engineered, as this might attract unwelcome attention from the anti-GE lobby. After all, there was no law compelling the labelling of GE foodstuffs, and it was "engineered" only with its own genes. It seemed, as I said before, a minor deception, and I went along with it.

I did not allow myself to dwell too deeply on how much I was deceiving Melissa. There was little point because, as the days passed, it became less and less possible to do anything about it. I was relieved, however, that the end of the road was now in sight. Melissa was no longer handing out the formula, the study was finished, we'd skirted the monsters and now I could lay it all to rest and get on with building a life together. And were it not for some horrible bungling by some half-brained asshole, not to mention a series of arbitrary coincidences, we would indeed have reached the end of that road with her none the wiser and no harm done.

Back in San Francisco, I got on with writing up my data, and missing Melissa with a steady, relentless ache. I worried about her too, and phoned her frequently, clinging to the thread of her voice that dangled in some electronic void over the oceans that separated us.

One night, I asked her where she would choose to go if she could go anywhere in the world.

"Machu Picchu," she replied. "It's so ancient and mystical . . . and the mountains are so spectacular in the photo's I've seen. It's always intrigued me . . ."

That was when I conceived my plan. I would take her there! It'd be a grand surprise, a glorious gesture . . . I'd make all the arrangements and sweep her off before she had time to argue, away from the Willowdale clinic and Aletta Stuurman's grave. I'd fill her vistas with Machu Picchu and me, and I'd win her heart forever.

I also – although I did not tell her this – phoned up realtors in Willowdale and asked them to begin looking out for a farm in the Elandskloof. The idea of the leopard project was taking root in my mind, and my work in Port Elizabeth was ending in December – I needed something more tangible and long term to hold me to the country where Melissa lived.

I got myself through the rest of my trip by planning our Peru adventure down to the last detail, making all the necessary bookings for two days on the Inca trail, a pony trek through the sacred valley, a flight to the rain forest . . . I was enthralled by my own cleverness. So enthralled that I barely registered the chill in her voice during our last phone conversation. I put it down to the lateness of the hour or some hormonal hiccup.

I was confident that when she saw me and was presented with my gift, she would be bowled over with love.

Chapter 23

AS the next few days pass in the somnolent sun-drenched haze of an Elandskloof spring, Sam does everything she can to forget about the misplaced aloe, and to give herself over to the depthless sky that mirrors itself in cascades of early plumbago tumbling down the rocks. The lines her father always quoted come back to her: *Blue, blue, as if the sky let fall a flower from its cerulean wall.* And memories of decking Melissa's hair with the sticky-calyxed blooms, and calling her the sky princess.

But her dreaminess is checked when she makes a disquieting discovery behind the old dressing table in the room she is sharing with Khaya. She finds it by chance, when she knocks her watch as she switches out the light: a book, wedged between the dresser and the wall, thick with dust and spotted with mould.

Women Who Run with the Wolves. She flicks through the pages. Two photographs fall out. One that Sam'd taken of Melissa and Dylan during their first weekend at Cedar Hills. They are sitting on the Rooikrantz beach, Melissa nestled in a cave created by Dylan's encircling arms and legs, both laughing at the camera.

The other is Melissa stroking a leopard cub. Sam turns it over. Written on the back is: *To my favourite wild thing.*

Melissa's book.

She opens the front cover. On the title page is an inscription: *To Wild Woman, from Wolf-Man. May your heart be ever full of wildness, but remember: when wolves mate they mate for life.*

It is the same handwriting as the inscription on the photograph.

Wolf-Man? *Wolf-Man?*

Someone used to call me that . . . a girlfriend, James had said. *She died . . .*

It can't be, surely.

Melissa and *James*? But she was passionate about Dylan . . .

But she is not really surprised. Everything had been pointing to it . . . James's intensity and secretiveness . . . Dylan's antipathy . . . But why has no one told her? Why hasn't James told her; why hasn't Dylan told her . . . well, okay, she doesn't exactly encourage confidences from Dylan, and perhaps he'd been embarrassed. But why didn't Melissa tell her?

Why didn't she tell her?

She thinks of the image she'd carried with her on her travels in the US, the image in that photograph: Melissa encircled by Dylan's arms, Melissa safe, contained, in a bubble of light with her baby and her Prince Charming, freeing Sam to turn her back and go off into her own life. But . . . she wasn't safe at all. She was having an affair with James, who struck Sam as being one of the least safe people she'd ever met. And what had driven her to that point? It must have been some catastrophic disaster in her relationship with Dylan. She was not one to scamper off at the slightest breeze.

She must have been in such turmoil, so disillusioned, so distressed . . . and Sam had not had the faintest bloody idea.

Fuck, Milly. Did you trust me so little? Need me so little? Was I such a crap sister to you that you went through all this without so much as a whisper?

Her ears strain to hear Melissa's reply, but the night is filled only with the cacophony of night-time creatures beating out their ancient rhythms with no interest in her dilemmas.

But maybe I didn't give her the chance to tell me. When she'd spent that weekend with her before going to the US, Melissa had seemed unusually brittle. "I'm just a bit tired," she'd said when Sam asked. And she'd accepted it. Because it suited her . . . because she wanted to be able to go without worrying.

As she puts down the book on the dressing table her eye is caught by a folded photocopy on the floor that must have fallen out of the book. She picks it up and unfolds it. An article, headed "Identification of a Brazil-Nut Allergen in Transgenic Soybeans". She scans it, glossing over the scientific jargon. Key sentences have been highlighted.

Why would Melissa have been reading this? Could Dylan have been right – was James into genetic engineering? What if something in James's research *had* caused Aletta's allergy? And Melissa had found out? And yet, the inscription in the book suggested that Melissa had been romantically involved with James . . .

She turns off the light, but the implications of her discovery have demolished any chance of sleeping. *You should have stayed in Cape Town*, she scolds herself. *Dad always warned you against turning rocks over. You never know what might come scuttling out . . .*

She can't stand lying there any longer. She lurches out of bed, pulls on a track top over her pyjamas, shoves her feet into her trainers and walks through the sleeping house and out into the night.

Oh, the vastness of these Elandskloof nights – so different from the city, where it is a tame thing, diminished by walls and lights. Here it is unbounded, thronging with unseen creatures croaking or whirring or clicking out urgent messages beneath an extravagant canopy of tilting constellations.

She walks down the road towards the gate, imagining how it was for those first humans who lived here, the painters of the mermaids, with no aids to traverse the night and all its terrors – no electric lights, nor fences, nor walls. Nothing but their firelight, their stories, their songs and dances to sweep them into the stars.

The crunch of the gravel reminds her of how the sound of her footsteps had been so shocking to her after Melissa died. She'd felt so insubstantial that any physical manifestation of herself was surprising . . . her shadow, or her reflection, or when people spoke to her instead of walking through her. It'd offended her to the core that she should still have substance when Melissa had none. *Take these fucking hands*, she'd shouted to the heedless sky on the first night after Melissa's death. *Take these hands, and eyes, and ears, and lungs and heart. Take them. Give them to her. Give them to her, because I don't want them any more.*

She reaches the gate, and lies against the smooth white rock that guards her farm, cradling its coolness against her hot cheek. To her left lies Die Slot and Willowdale. To her right is Port Elizabeth – and Grasnek. The fated, terrible, glorious Grasnek.

She is alone in the darkness.

Is she a wave or a particle? A particle, she decides. A little thing dangling in the breeze, like the small caterpillars that hang from the trees at the river.

Oh Milly . . .

Chapter 24
Confession of a Killer

THIS was how I arrived back in South Africa, then: triumphant at the warm reception my research findings had received, gratified by the feedback on my doctoral thesis, and flushed with self-congratulation at my plan to take Melissa to Peru. Oh, glorious me. The janitor's boy is taking a bow, ladies and gentlemen. Autographs will be signed after the show.

I did not for one moment think that she might say no. Why would she? It was only ten days, and she left Khaya for a week at a time every fortnight. And I was sure her clinics could spare her for one small week – she hadn't taken leave the whole year.

I was happily surprised to see her walking up the steps to my office at the university, where I'd stopped to pick up my car. We had no arrangement to meet – when I'd tried to make one on the phone, she'd fobbed me off and told me to call when I got back. I was a little hurt that she was not coming to meet me at the airport, and when I saw her my wounded ego leapt at the notion that she'd decided to surprise me instead.

I wrapped my arms around her and breathed her in, her smell, her feel, her . . . "God, I've missed you," I said.

"I've missed you too," she said, her voice muffled against my chest. But she held herself stiffly, and did not return my embrace. I pulled away to look at her. Her eyes were bleak, and skated away from my gaze.

Something was up, but I lacked the courage to tackle it.

"Come with me to get my stuff, and then we can go get something to eat. I'm ravenous." My voice sounded forced. I felt as if I was being pulled into some elaborate charade, and I had no fucking idea what the rules were.

We walked down the corridor, punctuating the linoleum tiles with words about, I don't know, the flight, the weather, the this and the that. Every one as hollow as the echo of our footsteps. What a very long walk it was, from those steps to my office, as I tried with increasing despair to tack these stilted words into some tapestry that would reconnect us. We reached the office at last, and she sidled in behind me and sank into the beige chair with the wooden arms. I rifled through my drawers, babbling on about my trip. I'd already found my keys, but I was stalling . . . trying to fathom what was going on. Melissa sat staring at the wall, the carpet tiles, the absurdly ugly light fittings, anywhere but my face. I wanted to shake her, to banish her, to tell her to piss off and bring back the woman who'd said goodbye to me at the airport.

And then the realisation came, chilling my heart like a winter frost.

She hadn't come here to see me at all.

She'd come to search my office.

"So what made you come here?" I asked casually.

Her eyes flickered across my face. "I was so wanting to see you. I went to your house, but you weren't there, so I thought I would see if you'd come here first."

Your sister had many talents. Lying was not one of them. She was the worst liar I have ever met.

I came to a decision. "Damn," I said, "the book I wanted isn't here. I'll just go and check if I left it in the lab. Do you want to come?"

She shook her head. "I'll just wait here," she said.

I bet you will, darling, I thought. I smiled at her, and left the room, closing the door softly behind me. My briefcase was on the desk – unlocked.

What was I doing? Testing her? Putting her out of her misery? Confessing to her in my own, terrible way? Or all of the above? I don't know. I just knew with some deep and horribly visceral certainty that I had lost her.

I stood in the corridor feeling all joy drain out of me, its steady drip mocking the absurd hubris with which I'd arrived. Travel together to Machu Picchu? She looked as if she'd sooner sacrifice me to the bloodthirsty Inca.

A pale brown woman bustled past, pushing a cleaning trolley. She was stuffed into a pink overall, bringing to mind those oversized muffins burgeoning out of paper cookie cups. I considered offering to exchange lives. No doubt she had her own dramas and distress, but I found it hard to believe that they were less bearable than my current predicament.

I walked back to my door, and very quietly turned the knob.

I confess to deriving some grim pleasure from the shock I must have given her. She stood before my open briefcase reading a document. I could see her jump from the door, almost hear her heart drop. I hoped with sudden vehemence that it hurt as much as mine did.

I closed the door softly behind me, and walked in slowly, my face frozen into a horrible mockery of a smile.

"Find anything interesting?" I asked calmly.

She stared at me, and then handed me the document – an abstract of my research for a NuGrowth committee. I glanced at it, and laid it on the desk. Melissa stepped away from me. Her eyes were fixed on me now, savage with accusation and desolate with betrayal. The silence hung between us.

"Now what?" I said eventually.

"You lied to me . . ."

"And you came here to spy on me, didn't you?"

She looked away, I think to hide the tears that threatened to spill, but I could see them catch the light. I was watching her from an immense distance now . . . I could feel a coldness settling around my heart.

She turned back, and raised her voice.

"How could you lie to me? How could you fucking lie to me like that? All those things you said . . . Jesus . . ."

Now the tears ran down her cheeks. She batted them angrily with her hand.

"Because you didn't want to know, Melissa. What would you have done if I'd told you? You'd have felt your integrity was compromised. I was protecting you from it."

She walked to the window, and stood staring out. A pigeon was bobbing up and down on the sill. One leg was crippled, the claw missing. I considered swapping lives with the pigeon.

"Tell me," she said, without turning around.

"What?"

"Everything . . . about your research . . . about what you've been giving the babies. I want to know everything."

And so I told her, all that I have told you.

As I warmed up to my story, I found it hard to keep the excitement out of my voice. I mean, it was exciting. I was being showered with accolades at home, with talk of an associate professorship, which was impressive at my age. Everyone I'd discussed it with in recent weeks had regarded me with some enthusiasm – not as if I'd just raped their grandmother.

"Look, Melissa, for heaven's sake, you are totally overreacting here," I said. "These soybeans have a phenomenal potential for infant formula. And with the Aids pandemic, this could be very important in saving lives in Africa."

"Oh please. And I suppose the fact that American women are choosing bottles above breast-feeding has nothing to do with why you got funding for this research?"

I shrugged. "I don't care why I got funding. Babies have benefited, lives have been saved. What else matters?"

Melissa swung round with a glare that would have felled a rhinoceros.

"*Saving* lives? Aletta *died*, James. She's *dead*."

"That had nothing to do with my research. She'd been off that formula for months . . . it was bad luck, for Christ's sake."

"James, she was given formula modified with Brazil-nut protein. We gave that to her. Do you know what it can do, exposing an infant to an allergen like that?"

"Will you stop going on about that? How many times do I have to tell you? The Brazil-nut thing had nothing to do with my project. Besides, we had the milk tested – you saw the results yourself."

"I found the tin she was drinking from when she had that initial allergic reaction – Jasmine left it at my house. I had it tested for its genetic composition."

"You had it *tested*?"

"Yes. I was worried . . . I *had* to make sure. I sent it to a lab in the US. It contains 2S albumin."

The floor tipped up and plunged me into deep black water. I struggled to the surface.

"But that's completely impossible. They never released those soybeans . . ."

"The Brazil-nut soybeans were also developed by NuGrowth, right?"

"Yes, but they were never grown in the field. There is just no way that they could have ended up with our lot . . ."

Or could they? My mind scrambled furiously . . . what if the Brazil-nut protein soybean *had* been grown at the NuGrowth farm in Brazil in anticipation of its release? And it had cross-pollinated, and transferred the genes to our crop? Or some entrepreneur had decided to harvest the Brazil-nut beans for animal feed, and they'd got mixed with ours in the harvesting?

It was a very long shot. But not completely impossible – when plants that can reproduce themselves are grown on a major scale outside laboratory conditions, nothing is completely impossible. There had been that Starlink contamination, after all. Maize crops that were intended for animal feed ending up in human food . . . And if something like that *had* happened, it was quite possible that other babies had been exposed – that Humansdorp baby with the nut allergy . . . we were lucky that only Aletta had died.

I sank weakly into my chair. But then some other part of me moved in to take charge of the situation. There was damage control to be done, and having a Victorian swoon was not going to get me anywhere.

"Melissa, please, look at this rationally. Even if she did drink formula made from those soybeans – and I cannot for the life of me believe it – it's very unlikely that that caused her nut allergy. She was probably born with it, which is why she reacted to that formula in the first place. And even if she hadn't had the formula and had been breast-fed instead, she'd probably be HIV positive dying from AIDS by now anyway."

"Fuck you, James. Don't you see? They *trusted* me. They trusted me to do the right thing, to feed them food that was good, to make them well, and look what I did. I fed them experimental, toxic shit. You know that exposing a young baby to nut protein can bring on an allergy. I killed her. We both did. We killed Aletta."

I rubbed my face with my hands. This was exhausting. I just wanted history to rewind and everything to go away. I wanted to be lying on my bed in the morning sun, making love to her in all the ways I had been thinking about on the aeroplane.

"Melissa, don't do this," I said, wearily. "You're being a drama queen. No one fed anyone toxic shit."

"It was genetically engineered, wasn't it? With viral vectors, and antibiotic markers and all that stuff? You have no idea what the long-term effects of those things are, James – especially for infants. Look at Arpad Pusztai's studies – rats only developed major problems after what would have been *ten years* of human life."

"Yes, but his study was invalidated."

"No, it wasn't – lots of scientists supported him, including the editors of *The Lancet*. It was discredited by people with a vested interest in promoting genetically engineered food."

"Oh, for God's sake, all this is irrelevant, don't you see? If Aletta got the Brazil-nut soy, it was a freak accident. It could have happened even if I wasn't putting GE soy in the formula. And the babies thrived on it, you know they did."

"But you lied, James. You lied to me. You lied to the mothers. You lied to everyone."

"Do you think the mothers have any idea what's in that formula? Most of them can't even read the list of ingredients on the tin. They wouldn't have the faintest idea what it meant if I said it was genetically engineered. A lot of the stuff they eat has genetically engineered soy in it anyway. And, frankly, if they knew it was going to save their infants, they wouldn't care."

"What, so it was okay to fool them because they're ignorant? Is that what you're saying?"

"No, for Christ's sake. Obviously not. I actually thought we should be above board with this thing. I couldn't see desperate mothers hesitating about some vague theoretical threat. But my superiors said no, some anti-biotech alarmist would get hold of the information and cause hysteria. They said this research was too valuable to be jeopardised by PC nanny goats."

"Oh, so now I'm a PC nanny goat?"

Oh, we were angry now. Words were flying to and fro like half-bricks in a race riot.

"Frankly, yes. When you behave like this. It's all black and white to you, isn't it? Of course there are risks in testing. Do you think any life-saving drug has ever been developed without someone taking some risk? Without some doctor somewhere walking on the edge of what is ethically acceptable and what isn't? Do you think any medical advances would have been made if there weren't scientists and doctors prepared to accept the moral responsibility that if something goes wrong with one subject, it is justified by the millions of lives that will be saved?

"The whole notion of 'informed consent' is fallacious, anyway – most of them have no idea of the possible risks they are taking. The onus is on *us* to be ethical. And there were no risks with this research. This stuff is totally safe. The modifications I did on these soybeans were minor – just adding more of a gene that already occurred in the organism. What we were testing wasn't safety – it was seeing whether the risk of allergy was reduced with the hypoallergenic soy. We knew the risk couldn't be increased, so at worst it would be as risky as normal soy. The FDA is not even bothering to regulate GE food for God's sake. I would feed it to my own babies."

"Don't give me that crap, James. If you want to experiment with your own children, that's your choice, but you've got no bloody right to experiment with other people's, and no bloody right to make me an unwitting part of something which sickens me to the core . . ."

She stopped, because her voice had gone tight and squeaky. And suddenly, looking at her, I didn't feel angry any more, I felt only the deepest sorrow. There was our love affair, all mangled on the floor.

"You're not going to let this go, are you?" I said softly.

She shook her head slowly. Forced herself to raise her eyes.

I could see she was shocked by what she saw – my own were brimming with tears.

The big bad wolf was crying.

"I wish you would. What will it achieve? They'll never find out who was responsible for that mix-up. It's not as if this represents an ongoing danger that is a threat to anyone. It was a fuck-up . . . an accident. A horrible, tragic accident, but just that.

"Besides, you'll never get anywhere. NuGrowth has only just got through the bad publicity on this Brazil-nut thing – they're not going to let some two-bit third-world doctor rock their boat. It's a powerful corporation. You'd probably destroy my career, if that's what's important to you. But you won't bring Aletta back. And you won't even touch NuGrowth. They'll tie you up in lawsuits that'll bankrupt you. They'll dig out dirt about your personal history, your marriage, your affair with me . . . They might even threaten you, or Khaya. And I suspect you'll never get a lab or scientist that will testify to those results. I bet you don't have that lab report in your hand, do you?"

She hesitated, then lifted her chin defiantly. "Yes I do," she said (she was lying again), "and I still have the formula. It can be tested again."

"Don't do it, Melissa. I know these people fund my work, and I believe in this technology, but I have no illusions about them. They're big, they're ruthless, and there are millions at stake. You don't stand a chance."

She sank onto the floor, and buried her head in her arms. I walked over, and crouched down beside her. I touched her shoulder, but withdrew my hand when she flinched.

"Melissa, look at me," I said.

She didn't move.

"I love you," I said. "That first day I saw you at the clinic, I thought I never wanted to have another day in my life without you, and nothing that has happened since has made me feel differently. We have something rare . . . don't just cast it aside.

"If you pursue this thing, it'll destroy my career. But what'll destroy me more than anything is losing you. I'm sorry I lied –

I was trying to protect you and maybe that was misguided. But please believe me that I am not lying now."

She was immobile on the floor, as deaf to me as the ugly glass ashtray that I use as a paperweight, which had suddenly, unaccountably, found itself in my hands. I stroked it absently, wondering (I promised to tell the truth) whether smashing it against the wall beside her would make her look at me. And perhaps I considered smashing it on her head. Perhaps I did, in that way you do when you know you won't. I was, after all, a desperate man in a falling castle.

But I didn't. I walked back to the desk, laid the ashtray down as gently as a baby, opened my briefcase, and took out from the bottom the little package I'd prepared for her with her tickets for Peru.

I placed it next to the ashtray. Then I put the ashtray on top of it, lest some ill wind snatch it away. Then I took the ashtray off it again, in case she somehow couldn't find it. Then I put the ashtray back, to draw her attention to it.

"I have two tickets here for a trip to Machu Picchu next week. I planned it as a surprise . . . If you come with me, I promise that afterwards I'll go back to San Francisco and look into this Brazil-nut thing. Someone's sloppiness caused this mess, and I am willing to bust my ass to find out who it was.

"I'll be at the airport at three o'clock on Saturday to catch the connecting flight to Cape Town. I won't contact you before."

She said nothing. I glanced down at her hunched shoulders and buried head. I longed to touch her. God, how I longed to touch her. But she was on the other side of the galaxy.

"Please . . ." I whispered. "Please be there, okay? Just be there."

I walked out into the November sunshine. Doves wheeled in the sky above me; a group of girls strolled past in strappy tops and cut-off jeans, sniggering at some undergraduate joke. A chip packet blew across the path behind them and came to rest in the gutter.

Nowhere was there any sign that my world had just imploded.

Chapter 25

SAM wakes early, her head pounding with questions. There is only one thing for it – she'll have to drive to Skilpadsberg and confront James. This idea is not appealing, but it's either that or asking Dylan. And she's certainly not going to do *that*.

The sun has not yet come up over the mountains when she leaves, and the valley is still shrouded in mist. The grass is silvered by a late frost, each grass head a miniature masterpiece of filigreed ice. A kudu grazes on the verge outside the gate. It raises its head and stares at her as she passes – a mythical beast in the mist, with its great spiralled horns, breathing puffs of steam. It starts away and melts into the grey shadows.

She drives for about thirty minutes along the road winding between Kobus's farm and Cedar Hills, climbing up into the mountains. The large stones and loose gravel are not kind to her Golf, and she regrets not borrowing Dylan's bakkie. As she negotiates the bumps, she considers what she'll say. She composes a fierce lecture, pushing aside questions about the basis for her indignation: is it the affair itself, or the fact that she didn't know about it? Because she can hardly blame him for that.

I just want to know the truth, she tells herself, not sure that she believes it.

She reaches the farmhouse at last and pulls up at the closed chain-link gate, feeling her misgivings crowding in on her, annoyed by the flutter of apprehension in her chest. She considers slinking away, but stiffens her resolve. She *has* to know.

"I'm not scared of you, Mr Wolf-Man," she says aloud as she climbs out of the car. She slams the door behind her, swings open the gate and strides purposefully up the drive.

It is completely deserted. She walks around the house and peers through the windows. The curtains are drawn, but there is no sign of life – no vehicle in the drive, no dogs milling around, no smoke coming out of the chimney. The only sound is a bamboo wind chime, waving in the breeze.

She wanders around the outbuildings. There is a large shed, which smells as if it was once used to shear sheep. She peers through the open doorway – it contains two strongly built enclosures, for leopards perhaps, but neither is occupied. There are also three large cage traps, piled neatly against the wall. The whole place is neat – no rubbish lying around, no sagging fences, no weeds in the pathways. There are three other smaller buildings, all of which are locked.

She walks back to the house. It is an old simple cottage, with a covered porch and small sash windows, perched on the side of a slight rise, and commanding a panoramic view of Elandskloof. *No wonder he likes it here,* she thinks. *He can look down on all the rest of us.* A wooden slatted bench, covered with faded cushions, stands on the stoep on one side of the front door; on the other side is a careful arrangement of driftwood, rocks and succulents in pots. Sam sits on the bench staring at the swaying wind chimes.

What should she do? Wait? It looks as if he'll be gone for some time. A few guinea fowl appear, picking their way through the garden, and peering up at her quizzically. Suddenly she laughs out loud. The sound is strange and a little frightening in the silence, and the guinea fowl retreat with an annoyed chittering. *What a twit I am,* she thinks, *marching along here in high dudgeon with my speech prepared, and then sitting here all dressed up with nowhere to go.* Maybe she should practise it on the guinea fowl.

"Why did you seduce my sister?" she shouts at them. They hold a quick consultation, and decide that despite all appearances to the contrary she poses no threat, and go back to scratching the patchy lawn.

She looks out at the mountains, their slopes golden green in the early-morning light. Behind them tower the purple peaks of the Sneeuberg. A stream of high, pearly white clouds fans out across the sky; a cloud of swallows dives and swoops over the long grass at the end of the garden. She feels her rage drain out of her. She suddenly realises that she is partly relieved at her discovery. If James really had loved Melissa, he surely was not likely to have killed her. It was disconcerting, of course, that Melissa never told her . . . but the thought that he was her lover is a lot more bearable than the possibility that he was her murderer. And this would also explain his odd behaviour, not to mention Dylan's suspicions and hostility.

But why was Melissa reading that article . . . ?

And why had they given money to Stompie Stuurman?

The sun rises over the mountains, stealing fingers of warmth under the roof of the porch. Sam closes her eyes, savouring the rays as her body releases the chill from the early morning. She is tired – really tired – after several nights of poor sleep. *It can't hurt to lie down for a few seconds . . .* She lifts her legs onto the bench and lays her head down on a cushion.

* * *

"Ah! Sleeping Beauty . . . or is it sleeping beast?"

The voice penetrates her dream. She opens her eyes and sits up, feeling stiff and disorientated. James is looking down at her with his annoying, knowing smile.

She jumps up hastily, trying to muster some dignity, which is difficult because her clothes are rumpled, her hair is messed and she suspects that she has sleep creases in her cheek. The sun is higher in the sky – she must have been asleep for nearly an hour.

"To what do I owe this honour?" he asks, and, not waiting for her reply, begins unlocking his front door. "Forgive me, I'm in a bit of a rush. I was checking the trap down at Visgat this morning, and we've finally got our female. You can't believe how hard we've worked to get her – it's been months. She's escaped from three traps and avoided all the others. I just came up quickly to get back-up from our vet. We need to dart and collar her, but I don't want to leave her too long in there because it's traumatic for her. Come in, I've just got to make this call – the radio's not working – sit down, make yourself at home, I won't be a minute . . ."

Sam follows him into the house, completely dazed. She perches on a chair in the small lounge clutching Exhibit A – Melissa's book. The room is sparsely furnished with limewashed wooden armchairs, a wooden couch with blue-and-white striped cushions, and a chunky railway-sleeper coffee table, on which are two large illustrated books – something on big cats, and another on rock art. A few framed black-and-white photographs hang on the walls. She stands up and walks around looking at them, starting when she finds one of Melissa – the same one that was in the book, of her with the leopard cub, but larger. There are no others of people – the rest feature landscapes, wolves or leopards.

She sits down again, shakily. If she'd had doubts before, this seems to be irrefutable evidence.

She can hear James speaking on the phone in the room next door, his voice raised in uncharacteristic excitement as he describes the leopard's capture to the vet. She is totally nonplussed and deeply embarrassed by what is happening – it wasn't meant to be like this at all. She'd meant to come marching in and find him in bed or somewhere equally vulnerable, not to have been discovered napping on his stoep like some homeless creature looking for alms. While her brain is scrambling for a strategy to regain her footing and redeem the situation, James comes back into the room, grinning.

"I can't tell you what this means for us, Sam. It's truly breathtaking. Listen, do you want to come down there with me? It would mean walking for an hour or so, and we'll be there the better part of the day, but I think you'd find it interesting. What do you think?"

What does she think? She wants to weep with frustration. How can he offer her something like this? Anything she says now will sound petty and churlish. It is all going wrong. Frantically she tries to reassemble her dignity and righteous indignation, but all she manages to rouse is some horrid, shrill harridan.

"What is the meaning of this?" she squeaks, holding out the book like an affronted Victorian matron who has found naughty pictures in her husband's bureau.

James looks at her quizzically, and then reaches for the book.

He smiles when he opens it, a smile that is far too tender for Sam's comfort. He reaches out a finger and touches the words he'd written as if he were caressing them.

"So . . ." he says.

"*So?* Is that all you can say?"

He lifts bleak eyes to hers. "What would you like me to say?"

"Were you having an affair with her?"

"That's not the right question."

"What do you mean?"

"The right question is, 'Did you love her?' And the answer to that is easy. Yes."

"*I'll* decide what are the right questions."

He shrugs. "Sam, I just don't have time for this now – I'm sorry – so I'll have to be brief and brutal. Were we involved in a relationship? Yes. Was Melissa with Dylan at the time? No, they had separated. Did she love me? I'd like to think so. Why didn't I tell you? Because she'd made it clear by not telling you herself that she didn't want you to know. And her reasons for that, I'm afraid, only she'd be able to provide. But I think it had to do with not worrying you with her marital problems. She felt that you had looked after her for long enough, you needed to get on with your own life."

"Did Dylan know about it?"

"Of course . . . it's curious that he never mentioned it to you, but no doubt he too had his reasons – perhaps he found it embarrassing."

Sam stares at him, her mind a broiling cauldron of confusion and outrage. How can he stand there looking so . . .

"How could you?" she splutters.

"How could I what?"

What indeed? Sam struggles to nail down the essence of his crime. She can't say, "How could you share a whole secret life with Melissa from which I was completely excluded?" so instead she says, "How could you hit on my sister when she was married with a child and . . . so much younger . . . and so . . . vulnerable?" by which she means: *when I wasn't looking.*

"She was twelve years younger than me – I was hardly cradle-snatching . . . her marriage was functionally over. And I didn't 'hit on her', I fell in love. It happens. And now, Sam, I'm afraid you'll have to excuse me. I have a leopard in distress and I can't leave her any longer, and I am meeting the team there. Actually, it's curious that you should have come here today with that photograph, because that's the leopard we've got in the trap – that cub that Melissa is stroking. I named her after your sister. She was released into this area three-and-a-half years ago. Are you sure you don't want to come along . . .?"

"Yes, thank you."

"Well, in that case . . ." He goes to the door and holds it open.

"Wait . . ." With her heart knocking painfully against her ribs, she pulls out the article which she had folded and stuffed into her pocket. "What about this? Why was she reading about this?"

He takes the paper, and scans the title. He eyes her coolly as he hands it back.

"I haven't the faintest idea."

"It has nothing to do with your research?"

Something hardens in his eyes, but his tone is neutral. "No. The soy we used was neither genetically engineered nor contaminated with Brazil nuts. Now, please, I must ask you to leave."

She slinks out, clutching her book and feeling roundly trounced. There is a humiliating walk down to the gate, with James walking behind her. Then she climbs in her car, slams the door, swings awkwardly around his bakkie which is parked behind her and drives off, ignoring James's ironic salute.

* * *

Well, you really put him in his place, Samantha Campbell, she tells herself as she drives down the road and mentally gives herself a round of slow handclaps. What an idiot.

She lambastes herself all the way down into the valley. But what else could she have done? Tied him up? Singed his toes? Was he lying about the article? About loving Melissa? About any or all of it? Was his hurry really to get back to the leopard, or because he didn't want to entertain her questions? Whatever it was, she is sure that she won't get any more out of him. Charming and open as he can seem, James clearly never reveals anything that he doesn't want you to know. If only Melissa had been more open. But painful as it is, Sam can understand it – she is sure that James was right in saying that Melissa didn't want to worry her. But she also knows that her criticisms had made Melissa so defensive of her relationship with Dylan it would have been deeply humiliating for her to admit that it had broken down.

If Melissa kept her secrets, Sam had only herself to blame.

* * *

She is distracted from these thoughts by the sight of Oumatjie Sass – Chrissie's great-aunt, who used to do their ironing on Tuesdays, and is presently living with her in-laws on Wanhoop.

Oumatjie Sass is ensconced at her post outside her *blougombos* home, perched on an old wooden chair with broken riempies hanging down below the frame. At her knee are several small children, a sprinkling of red-and-black hens, and a couple of skinny black-and-tan dogs. She looks as if she has been there forever, gazing out across the prickly pears, the old tyres, the rusty carcase of a car, the donkey grazing at the road's edge.

What will become of the *oumatjies* if they are forced to move for the reserve? Sam wonders, as she drives on after stopping to exchange greetings. Many have never been further than Patensie or Willowdale. They have never seen the ocean, or a city street, or been to a movie, or ridden in a train. How will they adjust their eyes to the mean, rutted streets of Willowdale township?

Sam sighs. Jannie's vision is compelling, as of course are the ecological arguments driving the Elandskloof wilderness project. But it's galling to think of the *oumatjies* being evicted to accommodate foreign tourists, with their eager grins and leopard-print scarves, assuming without question that they'll be welcomed as they parade around her home ground in game-viewing Landrovers . . . How do you decide what is right in the confusing, shifting reality of Elandskloof, with its sad history and impossible choices?

When she reaches the causeway across the Elands River, she pulls the car over, feeling a sudden urge to dangle her legs in the cool water, to silence the whirling carousel of James and Melissa and Oumatjie Sass and women who run with wolves and don't tell their only sisters about it . . .

She walks along the bank until it is impassable, then rolls up her trousers and wades into the stream. The water is icy, and the stones underneath hurt her feet, but the physical discomfort brings a welcome distraction. She reaches a clump of wild figs growing on the bank, and settles on one of the large knotted roots that anchor them to the earth, feeling the feathery tickle of the redfin minnows sucking her submerged feet for the minerals on her skin. Or perhaps because they worship her, as Chrissie used to say.

They worship us 'cos we're the queens, hey Sam?
Ja, I bet they never kiss Kobus Koekemoer's feet.
Hey, I dare you to kiss Kobus Koekemoer's feet.
No, I've got a better one. I dare you to kiss Oom Kleinhans's feet!
What? Are you mad? Sies! . . .

The sound of splashing comes from down the river as Dylan appears, wading through the water in thigh-high boots, trailing a small net. Khaya is riding on his back. He waves wildly to her.

"Hey, Sammy-potato-head, look what we found . . ."

She looks at them smiling at her across the water, and feels a sudden stab of pity for Dylan. She does not doubt that he never stopped loving Melissa – but it seems as if Melissa may have stopped loving him. And James would be a merciless adversary. She's never invited confidences from Dylan, but she wonders whether he didn't tell her about James partly because he doesn't want to believe it himself. And once Melissa died, it became easier to sustain the fiction that she hadn't left him, hadn't stopped loving him, that she'd been ripped from him by cruel fate and not by her own free will.

It comes to her suddenly, with some shame, that knowing he'd been spurned by Melissa makes him more likeable in her eyes.

Dylan offloads Khaya and sits on a rock next to her.

"Show her, Dad. Show her the kurpy."

Dylan pulls a specimen jar from his bag. She peers into it. At the bottom is a small striped fish.

"It's a Cape kurper. They're model dads, these guys. No going off and leaving spawn. Uh-uh, the male makes a nest. And then entices the female to lay her eggs in it, which he fertilises. He then chases the female off – eats her, actually, if she doesn't go far enough, and guards his eggs furiously until the baby fish are hatched and a few millimetres long."

"Cool!" breathes Khaya.

"Yes, and what's also cool is how the numbers have increased since they stopped farming in this part of the kloof."

"And the scuba spider! Show her the scuba spider!"

Dylan produces another jar, and shows her an unremarkable-looking black spider. "It's a fishing spider from the *Pisauridae* family. It traps bubbles of oxygen to use as tiny scuba tanks when it's under water. That's what I really dig about these creatures . . . that commitment to life, the ways they find to manage things . . . Well, we should get on, buddy."

Sam watches them as they move off, peering into the shallows. Khaya is such a different child here . . . Seldom whiny, or churlish, or intractable. Is it the place, or being with Dylan, or the fact that he has both her and Dylan in one place and actually being nice to each other?

She thinks guiltily of Melissa's book, lying on the floor of her car. Should she tell Dylan? It feels deceitful to hide it from him, but what is the point, after all? It can only bring painful memories, and he'd be embarrassed . . . No, she can't bear trying to discuss it with him. They have come to a fragile harmony, the last thing they need is some overwrought, awkward encounter.

She waves goodbye and walks back through the thick grass, carrying her shoes. Something flicks against her bare foot, like the lash of a whip – she glances down to see an emerald-green boomslang, as pretty as it is deadly, slithering into the undergrowth.

"I guess you were looking out for me there, Milly?" She glances up at the sky. *If only I could have done the same for you . . .*

Chapter 26
Confession of a Killer

I WON'T tell you about the week that followed . . . the sickening jolt that went through me every time the phone rang and it wasn't her, the countless times I dialled her number then killed the call before it rang – once or twice, to my shame, after she'd answered. Just to hear her voice. I'm sure you have little interest in hearing about it, and I certainly have no wish to revisit it. Suffice it to say that when I arrived at the airport a week later, I was already far down a dark road.

I came half an hour early. And sat on one of those horrible moulded-metal seats with my little bag on my knees, watching the ebb and flow of other people's scintillating lives. I had come with little hope, really, but I'd whipped up some frothy little cloud of self-deception. *She'll come round . . . She loves me too much . . . She'll realise she overreacted . . .* Unconvincing to any but the most deluded and desperate, but enough to get me there.

And there was that fairy story I'd been repeating to myself. The fanciful tale that Melissa would see past the malodorous pile of decaying bones that I had become to her, to the flawed but decent man within. That she'd weep for the strayed and misguided wolf, and with her tears restore me in her eyes to something worthy of love.

And so I sat, behind the mask of studied indifference we all assume to conceal our disappointment. As if anyone else gives a damn. The planes landed and took off, the travellers departed and arrived, some to be met with squeals of joy, others to walk briskly through the airport to their cars or taxis with a purposeful air. I hated them all for not being Melissa . . . not one of them was spared – that sweet old lady, that virtuous nun, the babe in arms. Every one was mowed down in a hail of bullets from my eyes.

Four o'clock. As the plane we were supposed to be on swallowed its passengers and took them off to some happier life, I capitulated, and rang her cell. There was no reply. I waited ten minutes, then rang Cedar Hills. The phone rang, and rang. Just as I was about to give up, the receiver was lifted.

"Melissa?"

I could hear her breath catch in her throat.

"Melissa, please . . . I –"

"I'm not coming," she broke in. "I'm sorry, I can't. It's over."

And the line went dead.

"Fuck you, Melissa, come back, don't hang up on me," I yelled into the empty line.

A warty-faced old woman sitting nearby glared at me.

"Yeah, that goes for you too," I snapped. She blinked at me with owlish affront, as I grabbed my bag and stormed out of the building.

As I raced to my car, it struck me with that sudden, terrible clarity that foolish decisions often have that I had to confront her – to drive to Cedar Hills and insist that she tell me face to face that she never wanted to see me again. If she thought she could get away with dismissing me like that . . . like some junior staff member with a hand in the till . . . She *had* to give me a proper explanation. She owed me that, at least.

As I drove, I kept trying her number, but the phone just rang and rang . . . and every unanswered ring drove the madness deeper into my brain. And then, just after I took the Hankey road off the N2, it was answered at last.

But not by Melissa.

"Dylan Murgatroyd speaking."

Dreadlock-boy.

"Hi," I said, reining in my emotions and turning my voice as bland as could be. "Can I speak to Melissa, please?"

There was a brief silence. I could hear his brain ticking over.

"Who is speaking?"

The Easter fucking bunny . . . who do you think, you asshole?

"It's James McIntyre."

There was silence again.

"Melissa's not there, is she?" I said.

"Yes, she is here, but she doesn't want to talk to you."

He sounded as spooked as a kitten that'd just walked into a room full of Rottweilers. Was he lying?

"That's funny," I said wildly, "because I just spotted her walking towards me . . . She's coming with me to Peru. Didn't she mention that to you?"

He laughed, but his laughter had a squeak on the end. Was it supposed to be sinister? I wondered. Or mocking? It sounded terrified.

"Nice try, James. But she's right here, next to me. And she wants nothing more to do with you because you're an evil shit."

Had she told him? No, he was bullshitting me . . . or was he? *Was* she beside him, telling him tales of the big bad wolf? I hated him with a deep and searing passion. I wanted to take his dreadlocks and wrap them round and round his skinny neck.

I laughed too. My laugh didn't squeak.

"Is that so? Well, then I guess she told you that as soon as your divorce comes through we're getting married. I must go, Dylan. She is over by the check-in counter, looking for me. Have a nice life."

I was raving; who knows what I'd say next? Words were just coming out of me in wild stabs. I was trying to kill him with a telephone. I'd say anything to make him feel as crap as I was feeling.

I hung up. I felt like puking. Scrapping like two curs over a bone . . . the humiliation of it.

Things were starting to get ugly now. I was racing down a very black tunnel, and I had no fucking idea how to get out of it. Losing Melissa had stripped away my hard-earned niceties – the hours spent learning about fine wines, or trying to decipher poetry. The dull brutality of my early years was welling up inside me. And that carefully constructed artifice, Dr James McIntyre (MSc. PhD.), was being swallowed piece by piece by good ol' Jimmy, branded by his dear old pop's butt end at the age of seven.

I drove as fast as I could down a road that seemed set never to end. What a long, long drive it is when you're a desperate man. The driving did not calm me – in fact, each bend seemed to feed my outrage. Gone back to Dylan? That sappy boy? I couldn't believe it.

It was just before dusk as I came to Grasnek pass. But it was still light enough for me to make out the VW crawling up the opposite slope. Dylan's van – I recognised that hippy wave thing on the side.

Dylan's van. Was he driving alone? Or was she in there with him? Happily skipping off to a life without me?

This is where it gets very dark . . . where intentions and consequences, regrets and recriminations knit themselves into an impenetrable cloak. I pulled my car over. I waited . . . it could only have been a few minutes – it would not have taken long for the van to reach me. But in retrospect it seemed an eternity . . . sometimes it seems as if I am still sitting there now. I have tried a thousand times to reconstruct my thoughts. I remember dark imaginings . . . frustration . . . fury . . . some kind of roaring in my ears. Despair? Yes, a good dose of despair. Jealousy, possibly. Self-hatred, yes, certainly, truckloads of the stuff, but turned inside out to reflect Dylan's face instead of mine. Did I know what I was doing? Did I have a plan? Was my intention to waylay him? Wave him down for a pleasant chat? Throw myself beneath his wheels?

Or swerve my car into the road as he came around the blind corner?

Did I wait, and wait, until it seemed impossible that he could still be coming, and then swing into the road to drive on, to find out what happened? And turn in just as he came around the bend?

Or did I deliberately swerve my car into the road as he came around the blind corner?

I am not lying when I tell you that I am not entirely sure. On one day, one explanation seems right. On another, I'm convinced it is the other. You probably think this is cowardly bullshit. I would, if I were you. But in these desperate moments something else moves in, and your conscious mind only occupies them fleetingly. They are staccato. There are lapses of time, of awareness. One moment, you're sitting in your car on the side of the road. The next, your car is in the road, and an oncoming van is swerving to avoid you, and tipping over a cliff. How do you get from one moment to the next? Does your desperate longing for absolution impute a fictitious innocence? Or does your guilt impute an absent intention?

I don't deny that my intentions are significant, and I'm sure they are to you too. I know that whatever they were, they did not involve Melissa – at least, not the Melissa I'd loved. But perhaps they *did* involve the Melissa who'd hung up the phone, the Melissa who'd stolen the woman I loved, because I'd packed the suitcase of myself so fucking carefully for her, and she'd kicked it in my face; because without her good regard I was worth no more than one of the professors' turds that my father so despised. But if they did involve her it was so fleeting, so momentary.

It was one of those dark rages that I am sure we all experience, including you, Samantha, that flash across our brains like a thunderbolt, possessing us with violent urges that we had no idea we harboured. That mostly rampage through our minds with no harm done, except perhaps a door slammed, a plate smashed against the wall, a misfired bullet embedded in the wall . . .

Or a car left in the wrong place.

In the end, my intentions are immaterial. Whatever they were, the consequence is always the same.

Chapter 27

THE day of the meeting and celebration dawns at last. Sam feels a certain dread as she lies in bed, but is this caused by the day ahead? Or by the fact that there'll be no reason to stay here after today? Her blanketed existence in Hout Bay suddenly strikes her as so . . . *stifling*. What if, like Hanky, she has grown too big to stuff herself back there? As for Khaya . . . she can't bear to imagine what he'll feel about returning.

And the questions around Melissa. They are *there* now, that is the thing. How can she walk away without knowing the full story? Yet how will she ever discover it, when it is floating somewhere between her dead sister, a man skilled at lying and a man she has never been able to be honest with?

But there is no time to brood on these questions now – she has a celebration to attend. She climbs reluctantly out of bed, and prepares herself to meet the day.

* * *

A few hours later she is sitting in the NG Sendingkerk church hall – a grand name for the dilapidated mud-brick and corrugated-iron shed squatting amongst the dandelions and blackjacks on Neels Koekemoer's farm.

"Our valley is dying," Jannie is telling the gathering. "When the seed trade was good, you could get by. But since Safari Seeds took over the market, things have been going down. Each year you try something new, but it fails. You are too far from the towns to compete with other farmers; your yields are too small. The last great floods washed away much of your fertile soil. Dying farms means losing jobs.

"This is our only chance. A chance to create a beautiful

sanctuary for our animal, plant and historical treasures, and to create hundreds of jobs, here and in Willowdale. Some of you may have to move, but you would have had to anyway. This way, at least, you have a future . . ."

Karel Boshoff from Rust en Vrede mines a hairy ear with his finger, then carefully examines the fruits of this endeavour before wiping them on his khaki pants.

Oumatjie Sass smoothes the fabric of her dress over the skinny peaks of her knees.

"Perhaps Meneer Jannie is right," she sighs. "But the houses in Willowdale are so small. Here I can see God's glory in the kloof every morning, even when my legs are too tired to walk. What could I see there?"

Chrissie demands of Jannie how he can guarantee that the government will deliver on their promises to provide work in the wilderness reserve when they have failed to deliver on almost everything else.

The DG for the provincial Department of Environment, a Mr Leonard Qoza, stiffly informs Chrissie that the ANC in the Eastern Cape – and the Department of Environment in particular – has an excellent record of delivery, and she shouldn't believe everything she reads in white-owned newspapers.

James saunters in late and lifts an eyebrow at Sam – she doesn't know whether this is a simple greeting, an acknowledgement of complicity or a reminder of her humiliating last encounter, but she chooses to ignore it.

A spider lowers itself painstakingly from the rafters above Neels Koekemoer, then scurries back up again when Neels stands to take the floor.

Neels demonstrates his remarkable talents as an orator as he insists that he is just as committed to the environment as the next one, but everyone who lives in the kloof is his brother, be their skins brown or white, and he for one will not let the government ride roughshod over their rights.

"Some brother," Dylan hisses in her ear. "He pays his workers twenty rand a day."

Kobus asks Neels acidly how he thinks quad-biking trails and canned hunting will improve the environmental health of Elandskloof.

A gecko crawls along a beam, then falls onto the shiny bald dome of Leonard Qoza's head. He starts, and brushes it off frantically, glancing around to make sure no one has witnessed this momentary lapse of dignity. The gecko lands, wriggling, on the dusty floor, losing its tail in the process. Sam is relieved to see it scuttle off – shorter, but otherwise unscathed – as Stompie Stuurman rises to explain how Tant Aletta grew her onions and assure all present that they are lost lambs in the eyes of Jesus.

Just when the meeting seems to have succumbed to the heat and Stompie's monologue, and dozed off altogether, the crunch of tyres on the gravel outside announces the arrival of the Minister of Environmental Affairs. Jannie hastens to assist him out of his dusty black Mercedes 4X4, along with his driver, a bodyguard and an expression of some regret.

But before he has a chance to speak, a commotion at the door heralds the arrival of a white woman in an orange two-piece trailed by a tattered assortment of farm labourers singing a loud, tuneless version of "We shall not be moved".

Beside her, Dylan puts his head in his hands and groans.

"Who is she?" asks Sam.

"Marianna Swanepoel. Once a staunch member of the local Nationalist Party. Now a champion of the dispossessed."

Marianna Swanepoel? She remembers Marianna Swanepoel. They'd been classmates briefly at Willowdale Primary, until Daphne whipped Sam off to an English boarding school before she had a chance to adopt Afrikaans habits. In those days, Marianna was a skinny little girl with long thin mousy plaits that she'd been fond of chewing. How on earth had she converted those soggy rats' tails into that towering golden beehive?

Marianna bobs up to the front and loudly alerts the minister to the donkey scandal. People living on Wanhoop were told to keep their donkeys chained up, she insists. And the donkeys' feet got soft, so they can't pull the carts. And how must an old lady like Oumatjie Sass go to worship the Lord on Sunday with no donkey cart?

"We did not fight for freedom," bellows Marianna, "to have the descendents of the first nation of our land treated in this arrogant manner."

"It's all crap," Dylan mutters. "Jannie just told them to keep the donkeys in camps so that they don't get killed by leopards. We even built the bloody camps for them. I'm sure Neels put her up to this. Oumatjie Sass never goes to church on a donkey cart anyway, because of her piles."

And so the minister is forced to address the donkey issue, and the whole meeting careers wildly off-course, its original objective lost in the clamour of point-scoring that follows.

And then something happens. Something mildly surprising to many of the gathering, but positively staggering to Sam. Her dead father gives her a hefty nudge in the ribs, and she finds herself standing up.

"Many of you knew my father," she says. Her voice squeaks alarmingly, and she wonders how she'll manage to squeeze out any more words past the lump of terror in her throat. The familiar faces stare at her expectantly. Her knees feel dangerously close to buckling. What the fuck is she doing?

"He delivered many of you into this world. And many of you knew my sister. Campbells have been in the kloof for five generations, and you all know my father was deeply concerned about the welfare of the land and its people.

"I have thought long and hard about what he would say today . . ." she pauses. Where are these words coming from? She hasn't thought about it at all. What *would* he say? The audience around her shifts patiently. She flickers a glance in James's direction. He is watching her with a small smile, as if she is playing out to some private joke.

"I have thought long and hard about what he would say today," her voice firms up, strengthened by a spurt of irritation at his supercilious smirk, "and I believe that he would've chosen the only future that can sustain us all in the long term. My father would have supported the reserve, and he would have endorsed the decision that I have reached – to take a conservancy on Cedar Hills . . . That is our only future, and I think we should all turn our attention to making it work."

She sits down, aghast. Dylan's face looks like it might be split in half by his grin. She nods at him. *There you are, Dylan boy. I did it. I dug up dead old Dad and waved him around like a banner at a community meeting. I hope you are satisfied.*

Her interjection does not have any heroic or startling effect. The crowds do not toss their hats in the air and cheer. But it seems to give Jannie the courage to take control of the meeting and nudge it down a more constructive path, and some resolutions are passed that might inch the process forward.

* * *

"So," says Chrissie, afterwards, "you're throwing your lot in with the reserve."

Sam nods nervously. She'd been hoping that everyone would now just leave her alone, but several farmers have come up to her and remarked on her contribution.

"Which way do you think your family will go?"

"I'm advising my parents to support Neels's consortium of private game farms – our land is too small to make it work on its own, but it could work in partnership with other farmers. It's not so easy for us, don't forget. Cedar Hills is just a hobby for you. Many of my family members are destitute – we have to try to make Rooikrantz as viable as possible. I just think that what Neels is proposing offers us more control over how the land is used. And, to be honest, I don't trust the government departments much . . . I mean I'm sorry to say this, because I went to jail for the ANC in my day, but I'm just not convinced that they can deliver on their promises – they don't have a very good record. I think you should reconsider."

Sam feels slightly punch-drunk from this barrage of words, uncertain of what to react to – Cedar Hills a *hobby*? Chrissie went to *jail*? In the end she just says, "I've thought about this a lot. I really do think it's the best option."

Something mulish enters Chrissie's expression. For a moment, it looks as if she might set to, declare war, draw the duelling pistols. Mercifully, she breaks into a smile and punches Sam lightly on her shoulder.

"Ag, never mind all that, Sam. Enough politics, eh? Let's just enjoy the party."

And her smile is sufficiently genuine for Sam to think that maybe one day they'll be able to share a bottle of Merlot and roll the past into some digestible morsel that can be shared by old friends.

* * *

The afternoon's jamboree is declared open with a long prayer by Neels's pet priest, who is at pains to remind everyone of Neels's generosity in donating two sheep for the *spitbraai*. Kobus only donated a few crates of cooldrink. Sam footed the bill for the entertainment, but this is not remarked on. All these offerings, Sam reflects, seem a little paltry against the historical debt they are erasing, but perhaps it is the gestures that count.

"And we pray to *God* our Father to show us the *right* path to follow, and we thank him *for* his blessings," the reverend's voice rises and falls as rhythmically as the scrubby hills beyond the kloof.

"Amen," murmurs the crowd of about three hundred – at least a third of whom are Stuurmans – gathered on the level pasture below Rooikrantz.

Once released from this prayer and Reggie Stuurman's rather expansive address, people devote themselves to the serious business of celebration. Long lines form to heap their paper plates with putu, braaied lamb, breyani, rice, beetroot and coleslaw; children run shrieking in between the adults, happily discarding the spit and polish their mothers had pressed on them in honour of the occasion; men slap each other on the shoulders and tell loud jokes, erupting in hearty guffaws whenever a punch line is delivered and as often in anticipation of it.

Entertainment is provided by a band called The Glamour

Boys from Humansdorp. Glamour is evident in their mauve blazers and pink ties, but none can claim more than the most distant connection to boyhood. Still, they beat out old favourites with generous enthusiasm, and no one seems to find them wanting.

The sacrificial sheep are soon stripped to the bone, offering empty ribcages to the afternoon sky. Beer and wine and brandy and cokes flow as effusively as the Elands River in flood. Marianna Swanepoel sits on a wasp – an unhappy experience for both parties – and is tended to by Sister Mariah. Stompie Stuurman whirls a somewhat dazed-looking Chrissie in a furious one-armed langarm. The gathering forms a circle, into which Sam is dragged to endure a few excruciating seconds of dancing with an equally mortified Kobus, egged on by wolf whistles and handclapping from all sides.

"It's lekker, though, isn't it?" Kobus says, after they have mercifully escaped and are recovering with two cans of beer. "To have these people back here again?"

He looks at her slightly anxiously, as if he thinks she might remind him of the names he used to call the Stuurman children. But she is remembering, suddenly, how he kissed her once in the cowshed. Either declaring a truce in their customary war of throwing cowpats at each other, or as an expression of conquest – she was never sure which. But as they'd stood in the hay-sweet air, having their fingers sucked by the newborn calves, he'd leant over, and pressed his lips against hers. She recalls the brief, shocking sensation of his cool lips prising hers apart, as he transferred something small, slippery and hard from his mouth to hers – before running out abruptly. She spat it out onto the concrete floor, and stood staring at his offering: a shiny brown watermelon pip.

She smiles at the memory. "Yes, it's really lekker."

Kobus looks out over the amiable crowd and sighs. "*Ja, wat.* Life is a funny old thing, hey?"

Sam follows his eyes. Sister Mariah and other Stuurman matrons are singing hymns, under the leadership of a devoutly passionate if tuneless Stompie. The malevolent Meisie is snoring stentoriously under the coral tree, failing to stir even when a small dog wanders over and licks her face. Chrissie is dancing with Jannie to the strains of "New York, New York". Khaya is running around with Kobus's kids and a knot of Stuurman children, harassing indignant guinea fowl. Lekker, indeed.

But the broken-down house on the rise above them is a stark reminder of the lost lives represented here.

It is enough, she thinks, suddenly exhausted. She's done it. She's got herself to Elandskloof. She's heard the speeches, she's laid herself on the line. She's drunk the wine and eaten the food. She's danced the dance, she's hugged a hundred Stuurmans, she's felt everything from contentment, to amusement, to doubt, to sadness in one day, and for a woman who's been in a dark box for three years it is all somewhat overwhelming.

She makes her farewells, and walks up the path leading to Cedar Hills. She pauses at the top of the hill to look back at the scene.

"Well, Dad. Well, Mum," she says. "There they are. Stuurmans back at Rooikrantz. What do you think of that?"

The ghosts of her parents rattle and sigh in the dry grass; a flock of hoopoes cackles mockingly in the trees. She wishes with a sudden ferocity that they could have been here to see this. Then she turns away to follow the path home.

Chapter 28
Confession of a Killer

I MUST'VE climbed out of my car, because I remember watching it all unfold from the edge of the road. The white van flew off the road, taking to the air and then plummeting down the cliff like a dying swan. Both front doors swung open and flapped like wings in its downward flight. And then a figure fell out, a tumble of legs and arms, a crumpled bundle in the dying sun.

The van came to land at last. I stood there, paralysed with horror, with some part of me already whining at the gates of the hell I had unleashed.

This was not what I meant.

Then I came back to life and half slid, half fell down the slope.

The figure was lying about halfway between the car and the road. As I drew near, my blood drummed louder and louder until it was screaming in my ears. It was wrong. That was hair, not dreadlocks. The proportions. It wasn't Dylan.

It wasn't Dylan.

I ran the last few feet as the ground levelled slightly, and fell to my knees beside her . . . taking in the white face, the closed eyes, the way her head lolled to one side. For a split second, I thought she was uninjured, and felt some mad surge of hope.

"Melissa," I shouted stupidly, "are you all right? Please say you're all right."

But then I saw the blood seeping out of her head onto the rock below. I felt her skull as gently as I could. The bone grated and slid sickeningly beneath my fingers, warm and slick with blood . . . there were multiple fractures to the skull.

And I knew.

I laid my fingers lightly on her throat – that tender, sensual throat. A small thready pulse fluttered beneath the skin. And then she half opened her eyes, and spoke. Dear God. With her head like that.

"Khaya . . . ?"

"I'll fetch him for you," I said. "I'll be back now, okay?"

I kissed her cheek and scrambled down the slope to the kombi. I expected to find Dylan, but there was no sign of him. Only Khaya, apparently uninjured, screaming in his baby seat in the back.

I carried him back to her. When I laid him against her, he took a strand of her hair in his hand and wrapped it around his finger. The screaming faded to a quiet whimpering.

And then she said, "Don't go."

What was I to do? Cellphones didn't work there. If I were to get help, I would have to leave her. I needed both hands to get up the slope – I couldn't carry her up it unless she was able to hold on to on my back, and even that would be almost impossible. And from the way she was lying, I thought she might have spinal injuries as well. Moving her would kill her anyway, and would put her through agony first. It would be hours before I could get proper medical attention. I was certain she could not live more than an hour with that injury.

No . . . it would do her no good to go for help. She'd just die alone while I was gone. And Khaya was okay for now – shocked, but he'd been well protected in the baby seat. He didn't have a scratch on him.

I made a decision: I'd stay with her until she died, then take Khaya and drive back to Patensie for assistance. I returned to the van and found a blanket, water, a torch. By the time I returned, Khaya had fallen asleep. I tried to arrange Melissa in a kinder position, and covered her and Khaya with the blanket. Melissa did not stir. She didn't seem to be conscious.

I laid myself beside her, cradling her hand, her cool, passive hand, and watched the stars prick out their light against the darkening sky. I sang to her at first – whatever songs I could remember. *If you go away on a summer's day . . . I don't care if the sun don't shine . . . Summertime . . . What a wonderful world . . .* Silly songs, songs about light and sun, far from the bottomless well of shadows I had dropped us into. *I see leaves of green*, I sang. Khaya slept.

It was a beautiful night, clear and still after the earlier rain, a night where it was hard to believe there was evil in the world, never mind one's own soul. If I moved my head so that I could only see the outer part of her face, she looked untouched – like some kind of ethereal spirit asleep on the mountain with her infant son. My *Madonna of the Rocks*.

"Soon you will be better," I told her. "We'll go to Machu Picchu. You'll like that. The mountains rear up like the pointed hats of bishops. There are woolly llamas, and golden light on the slopes, and ancient labyrinths. There is mist and mystery, the whispering ghosts of Inca's – long dead but still guarding their gods . . .

The night passed. It passed in an eternity and in a second as I huddled against her and tried to stem the inexorable ebb of life from her body. I thought about the pitiless dance that her cells were enacting. The ballooning pressure as the blood spread in her brain, pushing it against her skull. The synapses dying, one by one, fluttering and flaring, before going out like candles in the wind. I imagined the conversation going on, in whatever mysterious tongue our cells use to communicate. The swat team rushing in to stem the bleeding, to stimulate circulation . . . the fight or flight . . . some cellular committee making the call that it was all too late. The messages going out: Shut down the breathing. Shut down the circulation. Shut down the heart. Thank you, comrades, and goodnight.

And where was she, our lovely wild spirit, in the midst of this? Was she running into the light? Was she floating above us, like the moon-silvered mackerel clouds that now spanned the sky? Was her life flickering before her eyes? Or was she down in some deep, deep well, beyond all thought and feeling? She had plenty of cause to hate me, but I do not believe that Melissa died with hate in her heart. Her thoughts, if she had them, would have been for Khaya, for you, for Aletta Stuurman, for the untrammelled wilderness of the place where she had lived her last days.

I was desperate to cram the life back into her, to force the world to stop turning, to drive the moon back below the horizon, to unset the sun, to suck everything back to the moment before I saw the van coming up the pass. But I was as impotent as the bats that flitted past us on shadowed wings. I ordered my cells to mimic Melissa's, to frogmarch me out of life. I rubbed her hands, trying to bring the warmth back. They were like ice beneath my fingers.

Once, Khaya woke, and began crying. I picked him up, and walked around, singing some nonsense. I wished he were mine, this living piece of her. This lost boy, with his sweet child's breath. His crying stilled, and he softened against me, lost in sleep. I laid him down beside her. Around us, the mountain creaked and sighed, the night shifts carried out their busy tasks. Nightjars voiced my grief in their eerie wails; crickets sang dirges in the dark. A lone hartebeest wandered near and stopped, snorting, as it tried to take our measure, and then darted off to rejoin its companions on a distant slope. A porcupine shuffled past, unimpressed.

Mostly, I just lay beside her, and held her cold, cold hand, while her body slowly and patiently shut itself down. She died at thirty-seven minutes past two. I never thought she would last so long, but death dances to its own tune.

The whole night I'd listened to her breathe. It seemed as if the mountain was breathing with her. Towards the end were long pauses – fifteen, twenty seconds. I counted them out, holding my breath too. Then the next one would come. Then it didn't. The mountain stopped breathing. And there was nothing, no sound at all.

I kissed her cheek, and whispered goodbye.

"I'm so fucking sorry," I said.

My body was shaking, but I could not give in. No time for that. Tears would be my end – in fact, all feelings. My brain shrivelled, my heart chilled. I was a speck of light in a lake of darkness. Some distant part of me was suggesting that I load Khaya in my car, and drive to Patensie. But I knew I couldn't leave her. Not like that. Alone, on the mountain, in the dark.

Khaya was sleeping deeply now anyway, his hands entangled in her hair. It seemed cruel to pull him away. So I just lay close to him to keep him warm.

Some time later I was startled when something snuffled up against me. I jumped up, thinking it was a wild animal. I shone my torch and found Mimsy, crouched and shivering. She must have been in the van, and run away when it landed.

Just before dawn, I heard the pick-up coming up the pass from the other side. Khaya was still sleeping. I kissed Melissa's brow, cool and lifeless as marble now, and stumbled up the slope.

I debated what to do. Flag it down? But if I stayed, I'd be caught up in the whole thing. I wouldn't be able to get out. And I needed to get out as quickly as I could – I needed to go and find whoever had put Brazil-nut soy in my formula, and nail his balls to a plank.

I made a call. I'd noticed the pink-and-blue tin of formula in the van the night before; now I ran back to the van and got it. She'd no longer need the blanket, and Khaya would soon be discovered – I grabbed it off them too, and scrambled back up the slope.

I pulled an aloe down into the road to make sure that the driver would stop and see the tracks going over. Then I drove my car until I could pull off into the bushes. Some time later, I saw Kobus drive past with Khaya in his pick-up. Then I turned around, and drove back to Port Elizabeth.

Melissa was dead. I had killed her, and my life was ashes in the wind. I would have given anything for a different ending to this story. But it is a bitter irony of the human condition that we write the scripts for our own tragedies – often in the most trivial of choices. And once the script is written, we have no option but to play out the lines.

I wish I could honestly say that I wish I'd never met her; had never blighted her life with my existence. But loving your sister is the only thing I will never regret.

Chapter 29

SHE wakes suddenly in the early hours, startled out of sleep by Melissa's voice, a young Melissa, shouting for help across the years.

She stares at the bed opposite, momentarily bemused, scanning it for the tousled hair and night-fright eyes of her baby sister. But it is Khaya sleeping there, his lips softly parted, the candlewick bedspread twisted around legs in Batman pyjamas. She falls back against the pillows, reluctantly relinquishing that past when Melissa was so accessible that touching her merely involved stepping from one bed to another. How comforting it had been, when she was a morbid adolescent and the world had seemed tilted on some fatal course, to crawl into her sister's bed and hear her breathing.

She lies staring into the darkness, feeling all traces of sleepiness drain away, then climbs out of bed and walks through the slumbering house. The old rooms sigh and creak around her as she prowls through their hidden dreams, lifting and replacing objects, letting her mind drift over memories.

The front door whines softly as she opens it and steps out onto the stoep. The moon is low on the horizon, almost dipping behind the shadowy mountains to the west, but the landscape is still flooded by its cool, opalescent light. An owl hoots in the pepper trees near the driveway.

Sam sinks down on the step and gazes over the familiar landscape . . . etching its contours into her mind as she thinks of their planned departure the day after tomorrow. The flat planes of her life in Cape Town lie before her, grey and lifeless, great leaden weights that suck out her joy. No, that life will no longer do – not for her, not for Khaya.

She recalls a conversation with Jannie and Dylan as they sat around the fire after braaing their supper that evening.

"We should do a book on this area," Jannie had said. "It would really help our project. I'm sure we could get funding for it . . . you should do it, Sam. You can write and you're a bloody good photographer . . . Dylan's showed me some of your work . . ."

They'd babbled on, and she'd half let herself be swept along by their enthusiasm, their vision of this odd household of Dylan, Jannie, Khaya and herself carving out some kind of long-term life together. It seems quite ridiculous now, but the conversation has stirred up eddies in her mind, swirling the contours of her imagination so that suddenly it seems as if her eyrie in Hout Bay and her high-rise cardboard box at Springbok Publishers are not the only places she might put herself.

And Daniel.

The name comes to her suddenly, and she imagines phoning him . . . There was a postcard he'd sent a few months after she'd left, with contact details – Jannie had posted it on from Cedar Hills. *If you ever reconsider*, he'd said. What would he say now? *Jump on a plane right now*, or *Sam who?*

"Silly old cow," she scolds herself. *As if.* But still . . . other people do such things, don't they? Go out and look for love and life?

You go, girl, Melissa whispers, and Sam smiles.

"Well, Milly," she whispers back, "we'll see."

Her mind drifts to the evening she'd decided to come back to Cedar Hills, the shelf coming down, Melissa's ashes still lying under her bed in her suitcase, guarded by the two Indian princesses and their white elephants. She hadn't been able to bring herself to discuss with Dylan what to do with them. Perhaps she should give them to him to look after . . . ? The idea shocks her a little, but she'll do that, a good gesture. *So there, Maddie.* And something to come back for.

But she has to return to Cape Town on Monday, even if not forever, which leaves only one more day here, and she suddenly knows exactly what she wants to do with it. She sits for a while longer with the hooting owl, watching the moon go down, until a thin band of light heralds the dawn.

* * *

Forty-five minutes later she has thrust her feet into boots, her limbs into light cotton pants, a T-shirt and polar-fleece top; fortified herself with tea and a rusk; packed a knapsack with nuts, dried fruit, an energy bar and some bottled water, and is trudging up the path towards Mermaid's Pool. A jade stain seeps across the sky as the landscape shifts from the blue-greys of night to the pink-greys of dawn, and the stars are gradually eclipsed by the sun's greedy light. Only Venus lingers, but then the band of orange over the eastern horizon brightens as the sun pulls itself out of the mountains to gild the land.

Sam walks on, grateful for the cool of the dawn breeze. The sky is cloudless, and she knows they are in for one of Elandskloof's scorching early-summer days. She lets her mind drift, thinking of not very much, soothed by the rhythm of her steps, the scents and sounds of the world around her, enjoying the solitude, the present, the disinterested company of the early birds.

* * *

It is still early when she reaches the pool, although heat is pouring into every crevice of the landscape. She'd hoped to catch a glimpse of the otter, but although she can see its spoor, it seems to have already left. However, as she rests against a rock, she is rewarded by a young, solitary steenbok. He stands on a small sandy beach on the far side of the pool and bends awkwardly to drink, his ears twitching beside two half-grown horns. His reflection rises to greet him as he dips his head, sending ripples out on the satin skin of the water. The swallows swoop around his head and he leaps back skittishly, his muzzle dripping, then turns away and runs nimbly up the path through the scrubby bush behind.

Her eyes hug the memory of his outline on the empty bank, then scan the path that he took up the opposite slope. That must be the path she'd climbed with James. It is hard to see from this side, but she has not come this far for nothing – she is determined to see those paintings once more. She takes a gulp of water, pulls off her top and packs it away with her things, but decides to leave her bag there in case it gets in her way on the climb. She wedges it under a large rock, and picks her way across the rocks and bridge traversing the lower end of the pool.

The path is steep, but easy enough to follow to the top of the cliff. She scrambles up, scratching her arms on the scrubby bushes as she fumbles for handholds. It takes her a while to find the ledge leading off the top of the cliff, but after a couple of false starts she locates it, and then at last she is there. She pulls aside the hanging tendrils, and steps inside.

She stands in the cool darkness. Slowly the paintings come into focus as her eyes adjust: the little swimming mermaids, the long serpentine figure drawing them together, the eland dying quietly beyond them. Again she feels tears pricking her eyes. The small San ghosts murmur comfortingly beside her. *This is the place*, she thinks, *for Melissa*. A kindly place, full of gentle spirits to guide her through that good night. It means telling Dylan about the cave, but that's too bad. James can't keep it all to himself forever.

She sits down near the edge, thinking about bringing Melissa's ashes here, remembering suddenly the small San mummy that'd been discovered not far from here when she was about eleven years old. It was curled up in a pit and preserved with *gifbol* leaves – a young girl-child, they'd said, perhaps her own age. She'd felt so sorry for it, lying there hundreds of years after its family had all gone . . .

As she runs her hand through the cool sand, her fingers touch the corner of something hard and angular. Around it, disturbed sand and scratch marks suggest an animal has been digging. She pulls it out, and holds it up towards the light.

A book.

A black hardbacked journal wrapped in two Ziplock plastic bags. She removes the bags and opens it.

The words on the first page punch her in the solar plexus: *Confession of a Killer*. She turns the page and closes her eyes as a wave of dizziness sweeps over her. But she can see the words swimming behind her closed lids.

Dear Samantha . . .

She forces her eyes open, takes a deep breath, and begins to read . . .

CHAPTER 30
Confession of a Killer (postscript)

REGRET. What a small, unassuming word. Lacking the histrionic grandeur of "anguish", "torment", "despair". But how it gnaws away your soul.

I have come to know it well. It has been beside me every waking hour since that night. It is in the air I breathe; the food I eat. It haunts my dreams, it mocks my achievements, it lies in wait at every turn. It stares back at me from the mirror when I get up, it mutters in my ear when I try to sleep.

For some time, I thought I could silence it with righteous rage. As I drove away that morning, I shouted down my demons with grand declarations of how I would vindicate my unspeakable crime; how I would slay giants with slings and bring multinational corporations crashing to their knees. My litigious American soul howled for justice, and I would see justice done. Someone had polluted my beautiful soy; someone had compromised my integrity; someone had made me a thing of loathing in the eyes of the woman I loved. Someone had set in motion the ghastly chain of events that led to her death. And someone would pay.

Someone else was to blame, and by God was I determined for them to take this mantle from my shoulders.

I drove back to Port Elizabeth. I left my car at home, then took a taxi to the airport, and caught the first plane to Johannesburg for a New York flight.

In New York I phoned my professor – Phil Harris. He'd supervised my PhD thesis, and I trusted him implicitly. I told him only that I had reasons for concern about the nature of the formula, and asked him to arrange for it to be tested as soon as I got to San Francisco. I also asked him to make sure that no one else got wind of this – particularly anyone from NuGrowth –

because I had no idea who I could trust. He said he would meet me at the airport and we could go straight to the lab.

Phil was waiting when I came through baggage check. He hustled me out of the airport with pats on the shoulder and murmurs of "This must have been a tremendous worry for you . . . so sorry you had to deal with this . . . don't worry, we'll get to the bottom of this . . ." It was, in retrospect, a poor act that should have alerted me – I'd never known Phil to be effusive. But I was too keyed up to pay proper attention. I was beginning to feel foolish about the whole thing: What if Melissa had somehow got it wrong? Or the lab? Or if the tin I'd found in the car was not the right one?

He told me that he'd arranged with a colleague to test it at a new commercial lab out of town, rather than the lab at the university or any that we normally use. The parking lot was almost empty, the building so new that it was still enshrouded in scaffolding . . . But I was too preoccupied to question it, and followed him meekly with my hold-all containing the formula. We signed in with a bored security guard, then went down a corridor and stopped outside an office door. The door opened on Phil's second knock. As we walked in, my alarm bells went – too late. I was expecting Phil's colleague in a professional scientist's office. But the room contained only a table and two chairs.

I swung around as the door was closed and locked behind us. Three men were standing against the wall: two built like football fullbacks, their biceps straining against their jackets, the third a pudgy, baby-faced guy in a brown suit. He bore down on me with his arm outstretched and a smile that was all teeth and no joy.

"Dr McIntyre," he trilled, "Bobby Hogan, NuGrowth public relations. What an honour to meet you. I am a great admirer of your sterling work!"

NuGrowth . . . I ignored his hand, and turned to Phil. "What are these people doing here?"

"Well, you see," said the honourable Mr Hogan, "we heard about your little problem . . ."

"Excuse me?"

"Your little problem. This unfortunate mix-up of yours with the soy formula."

"Phil, what the hell . . . ?"

Phil stood at the window with his back to me. Clearly his role in this shameful saga was over. He'd delivered the catch and now he simply wasn't there.

I was on my own.

I turned my attention to the three musketeers.

"Excuse me, Mr Hogan," I began.

"Oh, don't stand on ceremony, son! Call me Bobby."

Son . . . the man was about five years older than me, for Christ's sake.

"Excuse me, *Bobby*," I said again. "Why are we even having this conversation? Do you mind telling me how this is any of your business?"

He laughed again. Then he said, "I told you, sport. I'm from NuGrowth. I'm the resources manager for the public relations division."

"Public relations? You regard this as a *public relations* issue?"

"Come, come, Jimmy, I'm sure you'd be the first to see that we can't let this baby go public. We've only just managed to lay this darned Brazil-nut issue to rest – the last thing we need is more ammunition for the greenies. Can you imagine what a meal they would make out of this one? 'Baby dies after eating Frankenstein soy' – and all that baloney. I'm sure you don't want this any more than we do . . . Imagine what it would do to your reputation . . ."

"Public relations?" I said again. "I don't think you understand. This is a major breach of safety protocol – how many other tins are out there with Brazil-nut soy? This is not a matter of public relations . . . People have *died* because of this."

Bobby Hogan arranged his fat little face into a look of surprise.

"*People* have died?" he said. "Which people? We heard about the infant, although I gotta say there doesn't seem much to connect its death to the formula. Did someone else die? Or do you mean that young doctor . . . but she died in a road accident, didn't she?"

I stared at him.

"Naturally, when we heard about the sample that was tested at the lab, we took steps to find out who had sent it, and asked a source on location to monitor her movements. That soybean was supposed to have been withdrawn. We needed to know why there were foodstuffs out there containing it, and who had them. And let's be honest, her death is regrettable, I'm sure, but under the circumstances, not inconven–"

He didn't finish his sentence because at that point my fist smashed right into his apple-pie face. He screamed and collapsed to the floor shouting about his nose, as if I'd damaged something irredeemably precious rather than the unprepossessing lump of gristle that occupied his face. The goons at the door moved in with a punch to the stomach and a knee in the groin to get me doubled up on the floor, followed by a few well-placed kicks to the kidneys. They seemed delighted that I'd provided them with an opportunity to do their job, which was, I'm sure, to remind me of just how much muscle NuGrowth could command.

"Forgive me, son, I hadn't realised this was such a sensitive matter . . . perhaps you had feelings for this young lady?" Bobby leered at me over his bloodied nose.

I would have punched him again, but my arms were being wrenched behind my back. Phil leant against the windowsill watching this with lowered eyelids and an expression of embarrassed distaste, as if he mistakenly found himself in a dog-fighting pit.

Bobby Hogan raised himself, and sat heavily in a chair, with a handkerchief pressed to his nose.

"In any event," he said, "I am quite sure this was an isolated incident, and we just need to contain the whole thing now, before anyone else gets hurt . . ." He let this sentence hang around a while, just so that we were all quite clear as to its implications. "I take it that the sample is in there?" he said, nodding towards my bag.

"No. There wasn't any left. I don't even know where –"

"Quite." Bobby Hogan smiled at me fondly, as if I were a

four year old who'd just said something particularly droll. One of his pet Rottweilers released me, grabbed my bag, rifled through it, and extracted the tin of milk powder.

"I hope you have good lawyers, Mr Hogan," I said, "because you're going to be tied up in a lawsuit that will clean up your life savings, your house, your kids' college fund and that ugly fucking shirt on your back."

He laughed again. "Oh, we have excellent lawyers, James. But I'm sure it won't come to that. I'm sure Professor Harris here would be quite willing to testify that you co-operated with us totally of your own volition, and he's a very credible witness. Of course . . . if things turned nasty, I'd have to sue *you* for unprovoked assault . . .

"Well, gentlemen, I think we're done here. I'm sorry it got a little messy . . . pretty unnecessary, really. We're all on the same page here, Jim. And you can rest assured that if any negligence caused this, the culprits will be penalised appropriately. Now, if you'll excuse us . . ." He turned to go, flanked by Hammer and Tongs. "Oh, and by the way, son, welcome home! It must be a great relief to be back in a civilised country."

They closed the door behind them.

Phil stood by the window, jiggling his keys in his pocket.

"What the hell, Phil?"

Clinkety-clink went Phil's keys. He glanced up at me, and then looked away.

"I quite agree. It was completely uncalled for, a crass display."

I stared at him in disbelief. "Jesus, Phil, that's not what I'm talking about. I'm talking about betrayal. I thought I could trust you."

He glanced at me irritably. "For God's sake James. Do you think our department would last a day without NuGrowth's patronage? You of all people should get it . . . You're not thinking clearly . . . you're overwrought. Take a few days off, then come back and finish writing up your research. You're a fine scientist – one of the best we have. Don't throw it away on cheap sensationalism."

And suddenly this man that I'd held in such high esteem looked like what he was – a grey bureaucrat dancing to the tune of the people who own our knowledge, our ideas, and evidently our souls.

I think I knew then that my career in the department was over. In the weeks that followed, I tried to pursue the matter. I told myself that I wanted the Stuurmans to win a generous settlement; that I wanted the culprits in NuGrowth to be named and shamed. But in all honesty, those things were of small importance to me. What I really wanted was for Melissa to look down from whatever cloud she was sitting on and realise that I was not the unscrupulous shit she'd taken me for.

Whatever I hoped to gain, NuGrowth was one step ahead of me. I learnt some months later that the formula was quietly recalled, and new formula issued. The Stuurmans were offered a few hundred dollars – as a "gesture of goodwill" – if they signed a statement saying that they understood that Aletta's death was unrelated to her participation in the programme. Jasmine had already succumbed to Aids by then. Stompie signed the form with a thumbprint. The amount they were awarded was about a nanosecond of profit for NuGrowth – if we'd established the Brazil-nut protein link, they would have got a million.

I scoured the labs, trying to find out who had tested the milk. I travelled to Brazil to try to pinpoint the source of the mix-up of the two soybeans. But my reputation travelled faster. I was the unclean, the one-man plague, and just the rumour of my arrival was enough to make everyone leave town. Word that I was persisting with my investigation got back to NuGrowth – I was called in by Phil and told to stop it, otherwise the university would be forced to review my position.

I couldn't stop. Not out of any altruistic fervour, to be honest. But because by killing Melissa, I'd evicted myself from my life. I had no choice but to tilt at windmills until I had shattered myself against their stone-clad walls.

It did not take long. Within a few weeks I was called in for a disciplinary hearing – Phil Harris had informed the university authorities that I'd plagiarised aspects of my doctoral thesis, and laid claim to work that was not my own; that I was suffering some kind of breakdown and "losing my perspective".

It was after this hearing that I found Dylan lurking in the corridor outside my office. I didn't recognise him at first – I'd only ever seen photos, and he'd shaved off his dreadlocks. I took him for a student.

"If this is about the graduate programme, you'll have to speak to Professor Harris," I told him. "I'm on my way out of here."

He followed me into my office.

"It's not about the graduate programme," he said.

I recognised the voice. I closed the door and stood looking at him, weary to the bone. He tilted his chin defiantly, but his eyes were begging to be let out of there.

"Were you with her?" he could hardly get the words out. On a different day, I might have felt sorry for him.

"I have no idea what you are talking about," I said.

"That night she died . . . you phoned, you said you were with her. Were you with her in the car? Did you leave her to die?"

I stared at him. "You have travelled halfway across the world to ask me that?"

"Fuck you," he said. "Just answer me."

"Go home," I said, quite gently. "I wasn't there. We both lost her that night, but you still have your son. Go home and mourn with him."

He began weeping. He walked out, a broken thing. I closed the door behind him and began to pack my office.

I went to lawyers to fight my dismissal, but no one in the department would vouch for my good character. Besides, I was out of a job, and no micro-bio institute in the country would touch me – I could hardly afford to fritter my life savings on a lawsuit. I considered publishing the story, but the contracts I had signed when I received the NuGrowth research grant ensured that I would be bankrupted for the rest of my life if I ever publicly said anything that brought them into disrepute.

The stark truth was that I had no proof. I had, as Bobby Hogan had so crassly pointed out, "conveniently" murdered the only witness. The formula that contained the Brazil-nut soybeans had long been consumed – it was only by chance that Melissa had still had a tin. And now that too was lost. I could not have saved NuGrowth's ass more efficiently if that had been my life's ambition.

So there it is, Samantha. The sordid tale of the janitor's boy who thought he could win the heart of the princess and consort with kings. I have only myself to blame, of course. I'd always known these people were ruthless. The CEO of NuGrowth once called any plants that they'd not engineered "weeds to steal the sunshine". Clearly, they're not big on soul. But I'd lulled myself into believing that I'd mastered the smirk of the secret circle so convincingly that I was seen as one of their own. That we'd all sit down like gentlemen over our whisky and cigars, and do the right thing.

I was wrong.

James McIntyre
December 2000

Chapter 31

AS the sun climbs high into the sky, the neatly formed black letters drag Sam relentlessly through a story she's never wanted to hear. James's words fill the cave, flying round her head like a cloud of demented bats. At last the lines run out, blank pages swallow his voice and the cave settles into a deathly stillness broken only by the muffled roar of the waterfall below.

She stares at the empty page. A sudden urge fills her to fling the book away, to send it arching through the air and into the inky depths of Mermaid's Pool, an offering for the water spirits so that they may consume it and obliterate it from her knowledge. But as she raises her arm, she cannot bear to let go these glimpses of Melissa's mysterious other life.

She lets the book fall beside her and lays her head on her knees. What is she supposed to do, to think, to feel? The screaming of the cicadas outside penetrates her ears until their shrill dementia coalesces into a bolt of fury that roars up her spine.

"The *fucking* bastard . . ."

. . . *bastard* . . . *bastard* . . . *bastard* . . . the walls agree. A distant baboon barks in alarm, a flutter of swallows erupts from their nests in the cliffs below, raised like paper scraps by a whirlwind.

Her rage is cyclonic. It is white hot, volcanic, straight from the core of the earth. It makes her feelings towards Dylan seem like a white bunny hopping in the grass. She's heard that anger can cause cancer; she can feel a tumour ballooning somewhere inside as her cells turn on themselves in murderous wrath. Oh, she will unleash the seven plagues on him, turn him into a pillar of salt, burn him in the fires of hell . . .

And then, almost as rapidly as it arrives, it is gone. And the desolation it leaves in its wake is more than she can bear.

She curls up on the ground beside the terrible book, her cheek pressed against the cool sand, and shields her head from the world with her arms. On the rock above her, the painted mermaids swim their ancient tides, the eland bleeds quietly in his corner. Her mind eddies in broken ripples around the shock of James's revelations.

Snatches of conversation race through her head – with James, with Melissa, with Dylan. Things said and unsaid, gestures, expressions. Underlying it all, like a deep purple bruise, is the conviction that she failed her sister in every way possible. She has no clear idea of how she could have protected her . . . What would she have done, even if Melissa had kept her appraised of every detail? Gone to live at Cedar Hills? Barred the door to James? No wonder Melissa never said a word.

But still. She should've found a way. And she hadn't.

She tries to piece together Melissa's last day, a day that she has imagined and re-imagined a thousand times, the scenarios she's constructed now falling down like a house of cards. Dylan told her that Melissa had already left Cedar Hills by the time he'd arrived in the early afternoon, that he hadn't passed her because he'd decided to come on the Willowdale road because of the rain. He said he was bringing her bakkie back as a surprise – they'd swapped vehicles earlier in the week because the bakkie needed repairs in Port Elizabeth. Sam had always suspected that he was lying, that he *had* seen her, that they'd argued and Melissa had driven off angry and upset. That seemed the only explanation for why he'd not gone looking for her when she did not arrive in Port Elizabeth.

But now a different story has unfolded. A story of Dylan answering the phone to James . . . pacing the house, sitting there all night believing that Melissa had left him, had taken Khaya . . . *No wonder he never went looking for her* . . . and he would not have told Sam about James's phone call, about his fears of her leaving him, because that would have meant telling her about Melissa's affair . . . that would have brought it to life, manifested it, ingrained it in their memories of Melissa. Every time he'd looked at Sam, he'd imagine her thinking about Melissa leaving him for

James. She can understand that he might have found it easier to live with her anger and unfair judgement than with her pity.

***

A sound jolts her out of the maelstrom of her thoughts – a twig snapping, then a dry rustle of disturbed vegetation. As she strains her ears she catches the rattle of a small rock bouncing down the cliff, the muffled tread of a foot in soft sand . . . then the rhythmic sigh of breathing.

Something is coming towards her.

Her heart hammers painfully against her throat. Is it the leopard? She shrinks into the darkened space, willing herself into invisibility, hardly daring to breathe.

The light flickering behind her closed eyelids dims as a shadow falls across the cave entrance. She waits, fists clenched, for the leopard's hot breath, the scrape of its claws, the savage rip of its teeth in her neck . . .

But it is not leopard breathing.

It is *man* breathing.

James? Go away, go away, go away, she begs silently.

And then he speaks.

"Catching up on some reading?"

His voice jolts through her, bringing a wave of nausea as she rolls over and sits up, hugging the book and her knees to her chest and pressing her back into the sandstone behind her. He drops down lightly onto a rock and leans his back against the wall on the other side of the cave mouth. His face is partly shadowed by the creepers hanging down over the entrance, but she can see that he is working hard to maintain his customary sang-froid.

His studied nonchalance is belied by a twitching muscle in his cheek.

"I had a funny feeling you'd be coming here, it being your last day and all. It is, isn't it, Samantha, your *last* day . . . ?"

She watches him silently. It feels as if any speech will somehow expose her, pull her unwittingly into his games.

He shrugs. "I never thought you'd find it, though . . . it was pretty well hidden . . ."

Sam's eyes flicker to the pile of disturbed sand. His gaze follow hers.

"Ah . . . Well, it looks like something was curious . . . a porcupine perhaps, or a jackal, or even our friend the leopard. I guess it was foolish to leave it here, especially after I'd brought you here. But this always seemed such a good place for it, guarded by our little mermaids. That's what comes of being sentimental . . . Well, don't be coy – you've read it, I gather . . . so what do you make of it, Samantha? Of my little story?"

"What the fuck do you think I make of it, James?" she says, the words blurting out suddenly without thought or intention. "You start off with this big *mea culpa* and end up with a portrait of some lone, misunderstood crusader . . . Is any of it even true?"

He smiles thinly. "Truth, Samantha . . . you set such store by truth. What is this truth of yours? Our only knowledge of events is housed in memory, and memory is nothing but a story we tell ourselves to enable us to live with the past."

"Really? You can live with this?"

He shrugs. "I suppose, when I wrote it, I was partly striving to write a story that *you* could live with . . ."

The rage grips her by the throat again.

"Fuck you!" she spits, all teeth and claws now, like the trapped leopard that had so fatally ensnared her sister's heart in this man's twisted intentions. "You've *no* idea what my sister meant to me. Living without her is like trying to dance with one leg. She was the only thing I had in the world, my most precious thing – and you stole her. You made her love you, and you betrayed her, and you killed her. And you tell me you wrote a story I can live with . . . ?"

There is a moment of silence as her words ricochet in the airless cavern beyond them. He waits with an expression of pained distaste for the echoes to die away, then continues calmly as if she'd not spoken.

"Of course, when I say 'live', it is a rather meaningless term in your case, isn't it, Samantha? Really, you've just thrown yourself in the coffin right alongside your sister, haven't you? I'm sure there have been many times, when you have walked beside a railway line, or stood on a bridge across a river, or sat near the edge of a cliff such as this one, when you must have been tempted . . . weren't you, Samantha? When it seemed so easy just to take a step and stop it all, the sorrow, the regret . . . just one step and all that misery would be gone . . ."

She feels a coldness creeping up her spine as her eyes dart involuntarily over the edge of the path . . . Jesus, no, he wouldn't . . .

He smiles, and nods almost imperceptibly.

"Ah, what curious beasts we are, Samantha, so small and predictable when you come down to it, so limited in our gestures. How greedily we cling to our next breath, even if it seems to promise only pain. I, for instance, after Melissa died, believed that I was incapable of enduring life. But that dark night did not eclipse my hunger for the feel of the wind on my face, the sight of a flock of doves wheeling in a dawn sky, the swoop of a fish eagle onto a still pond . . . Now here I am in paradise, saving leopards, honouring my debt to Melissa by preserving the creatures that she loved. And to tell the truth, I find myself suddenly quite attached to this new life I have created.

"You see, Samantha, I wrote that at a dark time when I first came back here and confronted the reality of Melissa's death. But once I'd written it, I realised that it would be quite absurd to give it to you . . . So I decided to see it as an exercise in self-preservation, a way of explaining this shocking sequence of events to myself. Or perhaps a way to conclude the man I was striving to be when I fell in love with your sister, to lay him to rest here amongst these speleological mermaids . . . I imagined, over time, the elements would return it to oblivion, just as my own wrongdoing would be absorbed in the greater wheel of life . . ."

Sam has sat through his monologue in numbed silence, but suddenly cannot endure listening to it for another second.

"Bullshit!"

He breaks off, allowing a moment of naked hostility to flicker across his face.

"I'm sorry?"

"You wrote that thing because you couldn't bear my judgement, even though you'd never met me. You wanted me to exonerate or even applaud you – for being so maligned, so misunderstood, so betrayed by your own misguided impulses, your brutalised childhood, your fickle masters and colleagues . . . But you're not exonerated. Perhaps you did seduce Melissa into loving you, with your leopards and your tragic youth, but she saw through you in the end . . . inside you are rotten to the core."

A cool shadow moves across his face and his eyes harden to opaque pebbles. But he stretches his lips into a small smile – or grimace.

"You judge me harshly, Samantha. But we're not so different, you and I. We are both outsiders, unable to find our way into that charmed circle that others seem to occupy so easily. We were both too greedy in our love for Melissa."

His voice slithers into her ears, twisting her thoughts.

"That's absurd. I didn't kill anyone, James."

"But you are wishing me dead now . . ."

It's true. Dead, or somehow obliterated – from her life, from Melissa's life, from her future and her past. The thought of cohabiting the world with him sickens her. Does that make her a vengeful, embittered woman? No – something in her rebels, some inner voice that has always been Melissa's yet is suddenly, surprisingly, her own. *He's wrong. . . . I can love generously; I have shadows – but I also have light.*

James watches her closely, as if tracking this inner struggle, his chin in his hand, his fingers resting lightly beside the semicircular scar beneath his eye. Sam gives him her own small smile.

"Forget it, James. It won't work. I can see right through you."

He shrugs, his face impassive now. "Well, you're entitled to your opinion, and to be honest I'm not that interested in it. But it does bother me that you got your hands on this book . . . I realised, watching your performance at the meeting yesterday, that you are more spirited than I'd given you credit for – and that you, like your sister, may suffer from misguided messianic urges. I worry that you might feel compelled now to avenge your sister's death in some way, which would really be too bad for the both of us . . ."

He stands up and leans over her, with his hand stretched out.

"C'm on, Sam, give it up," he says quietly, conspiratorially, almost. As if conniving with the more reasonable part of her against her vengeful other half. "I'm doing good work here, work that Melissa cared about. You know she wouldn't have wanted you to go on some revenge spree. Nothing you do will bring her back. Just pass it over, and let's go home. I'll find a way to make it up to Khaya . . . open a trust for his education . . . whatever you think . . ."

She sits, crouched in the dust, assessing her situation. He's blocking her way into the cave or back down the path. There is no way out but past him, and while she is tall, he is a lot heavier and stronger.

She is trapped. Sick with defeat, she holds the book out to him.

"Wise move."

But the flash of triumph in his eyes as his fingers close on it make her hand tighten involuntarily around the hard covers. Without any clear intention, she tugs the book towards her, pulling him with it, then jumps to her feet and kicks sand in his face. He falls back, and she surges forward into the gap, thrusting out a hand to push him away as she slips past. Before she can reach the path he recovers his balance, leaps to his feet, grasps her arm with one hand and tries to grab the book with the other. For a moment they are locked in a desperate embrace, teetering on the lip of the cave, his face close to hers, his mouth twisted into a wolf-like snarl. She holds the book away from him, leaning backwards over the cliff . . . then a rock on the edge of the path lurches and gives way. She goes down, dropping the book and grasping frantically at whatever piece of James she can. But he too has lost his balance, and as her fingers clutch at his shirt he is jerked forward with her into the void.

* * *

She is catapulting down the cliff, plummeting alongside the memory of the descents that have ripped through her life . . . her parents falling out of the sky . . . Melissa falling out of the kombi. Her life narrows into a well of terror walled by the sickening whirl of rocks and sky and the insult of an abrasive edge against soft tissue as she scrapes a ledge on the way down. Then a freefall through space that ends with a stinging thump to her back and punches the air from her lungs before she is enveloped into a cold pit of blackness.

She opens her mouth to suck in air then forces it closed as some dim instinct warns her that she is in water. She flails around in the icy darkness, disorientated and terrified, not sure of whether she is going up or down. She kicks furiously as her eardrums sing and her winded chest bursts with the need to breathe.

Her head breaks the surface and she gasps in burning breaths as her lungs struggle to re-inflate. As the oxygen begins to flow through her arteries, she scrabbles to the small sandy beach where she'd seen the buck that morning – the only part of the pool you can climb out of. Dragging herself forwards, she lies half in the pool, hauling noisy, painful rafts of air in and out of her lungs, vomiting and retching out the water she has inhaled.

For an indeterminate time the pool, the surrounding cliffs, the wheeling sky far above her seem to breathe in tandem, performing some mysterious CPR that exhorts her reluctant chest to breathe, and breathe again. She remembers James's description of Melissa's dying breath . . . But this breath is dragging her back into life, forcing her into a realm of pain so that she becomes aware of the searing, throbbing bruise that is her body.

And then she becomes aware of something else . . . someone

calling her. She lifts her eyes and sees him waving from the pool, about two metres from the steep rock walls below the cave.

"Sam, help me . . . I've hurt both my legs . . . I can't swim. Please . . ."

She sits up and stares at him. Is it a trap? His face is deathly pale . . . twisted in frantic agony. She knows he's a good liar, but this performance is extremely convincing.

Oh Christ.

It would be so easy . . . All she needs to do is walk away . . . He'd have to swim at least eight metres to get to a place where he can climb out. If his legs really are broken, he won't make it. And it will be the end of his games, his self-serving bullshit, his weird obsessions . . . He'll pay for Melissa's death. He deserves to die . . .

"Sam, please . . ." His voice is hoarse. "This branch is breaking . . ."

She stares at his grey face, his eyes stretched wide with terror and pain.

"Oh God, please . . ."

Walk away, she tells herself. You don't have to watch. Just walk away . . .

* * *

She'll have to bloody save him. Of course she will. Otherwise that face will brand itself in her brain, keeping her awake at night, adding new horror to her nightmares. Bloody hell. But she is bruised and exhausted, and there is no way she is getting back in that freezing, bottomless water and swimming to him. She looks at the rock wall – there is a small ledge running a couple of feet above the water . . . if she had a rope she could crawl along it and tow him . . .

She spots a stick lying on the bank . . . not quite long enough . . .

She takes off her trousers, ties the feet together to form a loop, and moves towards the ledge . . .

* * *

As she hauls him at last from the water, his body feels like a sack of rocks, weighty and intractable. She flops down on the sand trembling with pain and exhaustion and watches his shoulders shudder as he grapples for air.

He lies half on his stomach, and retches a gush of water and saliva, then lets his head flop back on the sand, grimacing with pain. She tries to remember the advice of the first-aid book she'd bought when she'd become a parent to Khaya. He appears to be breathing . . . well gasping, at any rate . . . so mouth-to-mouth (thank God) seems redundant. Stabilising a spinal injury . . . ? Too late for that anyway . . .

His eyes flicker open and fix on hers.

"Thanks," he mumbles.

"I'm not sure you deserve it."

"Probably not . . . but thanks anyway . . ."

He retches some more. Then asks, "Do you think you could take my boots off?"

She kneels beside him, and begins to unlace his left boot, recoiling as she realises that the water seeping out of the top and between the laces is stained with blood. She loosens the laces, gently pulls his sock down and tries to wiggle his foot free. James screams as Sam finds herself staring at what for a moment she thinks is a white pebble embedded in his leg, and then realises is the bloodied end of his tibia or fibula or whatever it's called, and she turns away to vomit in the sand.

"What's wrong?" he asks sharply.

"I think it's broken," she says vaguely. "Maybe we should leave that boot on . . . it might dislocate the bones if I pull it off."

She takes off the other boot reluctantly. This foot is swollen and bruised, but at least the skin is unbroken and no bones protrude, although the angle of the foot looks suspect.

She sits back on a rock, looking down on him. He is deathly pale, but his breathing seems to have steadied a little. He is shivering, but the sun will warm him.

"I guess you hit a rock going into the pool," she says.

"I guess so . . ." His eyes flicker over her. "Are you fine?"

"Yes . . . just winded . . ."

His lips twitch towards a smile. "So, God does favour the innocent."

Sam looks up at the cave high above them, and remembers the cautionary tale her father always told about Dawie Kleinhans. Who jumped off a cliff into the river at Smitskraal for a dare on his eighteenth birthday, and bled to death from a ruptured bowel. *It all depends on how you hit the water*, her father had said, *but it's bloody stupid to take the chance.*

"I think we were both lucky," she said.

"I didn't mean for you to fall," he said. "I just wanted the . . ."

He drifts off and his head lolls. She wonders if he has lost consciousness.

"James, I must go for help."

He jerks awake, and stares at her a little bemused.

"Sounds like a good plan."

"It'll take a while. It's at least an hour for me to get back, then we still have to get a rescue team to you."

"Well, honey, I ain't going nowhere. If you could just build up the sand under my legs to support them a bit . . . Fuck it, that hurts."

She does her best to make him comfortable by moulding the sand around his legs and body, and erecting a branch over him to shade his face. She remembers that she's left her bag, and goes across the river to get it. She offers him some dried fruit and water, and tucks the polar fleece under his head. It's awkward, performing these intimate acts for him, and she's relieved when she's finished.

She pulls on her wet trousers, shoes and socks, shivering despite the heat. She sits for a moment, suddenly overwhelmed by the morning, feeling like a bundle of tattered feathers, a waterlogged speck of flotsam spewed out by the tide, as chaotic and meaningless as debris deposited by a river in flood.

She glances around the pool as the wave of dizziness recedes, amazed by the serenity of the scene, the water a still mirror of sky beneath the skimming dragonflies, the waterfall singing to itself, no evidence to betray the drama that has unfolded around it. It is time to leave, but as she turns to go, she remembers spotting something when she was crawling along the ledge – a flash of white in the bush near the bottom of the cliff.

She inches back towards the waterfall, smiling as she sees what it is. She scrambles up the rock, reaches into the bush and pulls it out.

"Just getting this," she can't resist saying to him as she comes back past waving the black journal.

He opens his eyes, but doesn't seem to register what is in her hand.

"Thanks," he mumbles.

* * *

She walks down the path on spaghetti legs, but she knows she'll make it home. Just put one foot in front of the other, as her father used to say. She tries not to think about James. He is a black forest of tangled emotion in the back of her mind. She doesn't know what she'll do with his confession, but she is glad to have it. She knows she'll have to find a way of taking in and living with this story, and with the knowledge of him and what he has done – and the confession might be useful in persuading him to do whatever he can to make this easier for her.

And sometime in her lifetime, she supposes, in ten or twenty or fifty years, she'll have to find a way to forgive him – whatever that strange and recondite word means. A survival thing, this forgiveness business. Hardly a startling insight . . . but what does startle her is the sudden realisation that she has some interest in survival.

The rhythm of her footsteps soothes her, and as her clothes begin to dry and her body warms, the whirl of impossible questions evaporates and is gradually replaced by an awareness of something . . . almost a song, or a symphony, that is herself . . . She hears the roar of her breath inflating and collapsing her lungs; she feels the inexorable sucking and spewing of her heart, the steady contraction and relaxation of the muscles in her legs . . . and it comes to her suddenly, its simple meaning spreading across her brain as the morning light spreads across the sky.

She is alive.

She feels the sun's heat on her cheek, the breeze cool against the wet hair on her neck. She feels the sting of grazes on her hands and thighs, a dull throbbing in her head, the bruises on her knees, feet, back, shoulders . . . Beneath her the earth is solid; above her the sky, occupied by a lone circling fish eagle, stretches to infinity. A small blue-headed lizard darts for cover as she passes; a tortoise lumbers across her path on its way to a better place.

She is alive.

She will fold herself around the hollow space of her sister every single day for the rest of her life. But something inside her has shifted. Despite the fact that she really does now have someone to blame, some hard knot of bitter anger has loosened and begun to unravel.

And she is alive.

She walks on down the path through the brooding wilderness of the Elandskloof, taking one steady step and then another towards the child she loves and the young father who no longer needs her forgiveness.

Acknowledgements

THIS book has been a long, meandering journey, greatly aided by a number of people along the way who have generously shared their time and knowledge. Whatever blunders I have made in the text are entirely my own and despite everyone's best efforts to educate me.

It would take another book to thank everyone, but the people I would particularly like to acknowledge are: Therése Boulle, my friend and fellow adventurer, for ploughing through every single word I wrote, taking me on road trips, never flagging in her belief in this endeavour and generally being the chief midwife; Derek Clark, for opening his home to me, answering all my stupid questions, and making available his prodigious knowledge of and insight into the social and natural history of the Baviaanskloof, the behaviour of leopards, local ghost stories and much else; Sr Angelika Laub of the Catholic Bishops Conference, Elfrieda Pschorn-Strauss (then with Biowatch) and Haidee Swanby (then from SAFeAGE) for guiding my exploration into the muddy waters of genetic engineering; Dr David Green and Jenny Tuft for advising me on medical issues; Dr Jim Cambray for enlightening me on the matter of indigenous fish.

I would also like to thank my many readers – in particular Mike Nicol, Annari van der Merwe, Bronwyn Kaplan, Gill Haagensen and Michael Evans, for plodding through hideous early drafts and giving me much needed rigorous and honest advice.

I would like to thank Janita Holtzhausen and the rest of the team at Human & Rousseau for their faith in this book and efforts to make it a better product.

And finally, my long-suffering family – Michael, Joanna and Lara – for their unfailing love and support through moments of despair and distraction.

To all of you and everyone else a huge and heartfelt thank you.

A Note on Genetic Engineering

I AM not a scientist, but I have read widely around the area of genetic engineering, and the issues portrayed in this novel are based on that reading. I have taken some liberties: For example, I have collapsed the time between the work into the Brazil-nut soybean and recent research into hypoallergenicity using the "P34" technique, which only occurred more than a decade later. At the time of going to press, hypoallergenic soy had not been commercially released. As far as I know, no Brazil-nut soy was ever accidentally ingested, although other genetically engineered foods intended for animal feed (such as StarLink corn) have found their way into food stores intended for humans.

Genetic engineering is a complex field, and this complexity has made it easier for the industry promoting it to slip it past public scrutiny. It has also been eclipsed to some degree by the more immediate threat of global warming. While the European community and much of Africa remain steadfastly opposed to the widespread introduction of transgenic crops and foodstuffs, South African authorities have embraced the technology. GE corn and cotton are both grown locally, and many of our local food products containing corn or imported soy (including infant formula) are now genetically engineered.

The story told in this novel is fictional. The real one is much more frightening, with I believe long-term consequences far more damaging than one accidental death. This is not the place to go into it, but the following points have emerged from my reading:

- The benefits of genetic engineering, both in terms of crop yields and food security, are massively exaggerated by the industry.
- The risks are greatly minimised. Evidence of long-term damage to the organs of rats caused by ingesting GE foodstuffs has been concealed by the industry,[1] as has ample evidence of threats to environmental health and food security.

[1] See for example Joël Spiroux de Vendômois, François Roullier, Dominique Cellier, Gilles-Eric Séralin, A Comparison of the Effects of Three GM Corn Varieties on Mammalian Health, Research Paper, *International Journal of Biological Science* 2009; 5:706-726

- No thorough testing has been done to determine the long-term environmental and health consequences of the widespread growth and consumption of genetically engineered crops.

I would strongly urge all readers who have not done so to acquaint themselves with these issues, and defend our right to the choice not to eat transgenic food. The references I consulted are far too numerous to list here, but a good place to start is the websites for SAFeAGE (South African Freeze Alliance on Genetic Engineering) http://www.safeage.org/, and the African Centre for Biosafety http://www.biosafetyafrica.org.za/.